Also by Bonnie Shiloh

The One, the Only, the Amazing...

The Sunset Girl

Love
at the
French Station

Love at the French Station

Bonnie Shiloh

About the author
Bonnie Shiloh was born and raised in a small town in Texas. She left the one stop light hole in the wall for bigger and better things. With a few college degrees and a thirty year career behind her, she has taken up writing. Love at the French Station is her third book. The first book is The One, the Only, the Amazing...which is a sexual tragedy about a man who can please women with his eyes. Her second book, The Sunset Girl, is a crime thriller about a woman who is different than every other woman on the planet. Both of these books use raw language.

Love at the French Station
Copyright © 2021 by Bonnie Shiloh

Published in the United States of America by
O•Zone Press, El Paso, Texas

ISBN-13 978-0-9976760-7-5
ISBN-10 0-9976760-7-8

Published 2021

To friends and lovers....and all those who ever ran
from something in the night.

Chapter 1

Laurie Delacroix was spending a gap year traveling around Europe. At least she was supposed to be. She discovered traveling around Europe in her preferred style, five-star hotels instead of hostels, was extremely expensive. Out of money the first month, Laurie found herself seeking employment to buy an airline ticket back home to New Orleans.

Her financial demise culminated while strolling down La Rambla in Barcelona. With the purchase of a loaf of bread, a block of aged Manchego cheese and a bottle of rioja wine, her purse was empty. Laurie sat on a park bench in the promenade and consumed what she thought was her last meal before the possibility of begging, stealing or prostituting would became a reality.

In thirty minutes, the loaf of bread was torn asunder with the hardest parts of the crust still resting on the wrapping paper. The cheese was down to a tiny sliver and the bottle of wine was drained. Laurie was drunk as a skunk contemplating her next move which included clearing out of the luxurious Le Meridian Hotel.

Laurie arrived in Barcelona, via train, a few days ago and had seen most of the tourist sites, one of which was La Sagrada Familia. Back when she had money, just yesterday, she was in the basilica at sunset and couldn't help marvel at the reflections of the stained-glass windows. One also couldn't help notice the Jesus on the cross hovering above the alter. A dome of lights illuminated the life-sized crucifix, giving the impression that Jesus was parachuting down from the heavens.

Laurie, in her drunken desperation, thought of the parachuting Jesus and began to laugh, spilling the sliver of cheese to the ground. Since it may be her only morsel of sustenance for the near future, she quickly picked it up observing the three, five or ten second rule, depending on how badly one wanted to eat whatever they dropped, and brushed off the dead grass. The mouse-size bite of cheese wrapped in paper, Laurie, with difficulty, began making her way back to the Le Meridian to pack and move to God knows where. Maybe back to the park bench.

Staggering and hit on twice by local sinverguenzas (scoundrels), Laurie unlocked the door with her proximity key card. Thank goodness it wasn't an old-fashioned key and lock because she couldn't see well enough to get the key in the hole. Her shoes flew off her feet and she collapsed, face first on the made-up bed with a rose on the pillow. Although a beautiful, young nineteen-year-old woman, her akimbo auburn hair, a constant swine-like snore and a slow flow of saliva from her open mouth made her a little less attractive.

In five hours, Laurie woke with a sudden urge to rid herself of the consumed bottle of wine. She wasn't sure how it was going to happen but ended up puking a little and then peeing a lot which she thought was as good an outcome as possible considering the circumstances.

Alone at midnight in her room, sick, hungover, broke and with no prospects, good ideas eluded her. She could call home to Daddy, ask for money and endure the wrath of his 'I told you so' lectures because her gap year only lasted twenty-seven days. She could beg although she didn't know how to start. She could try to manipulate men into giving her money which she had never tried before. Sure, she got high school boys to give her rides, buy her hamburgers and pay for small things like tickets to the carnival or a movie, but Laurie didn't know if she could con a guy into paying for air fare back to the United States without having to give up something for it. Whoring herself out was not yet on the agenda. Maybe by tomorrow night with no food or place to stay, her morals would begin to dissipate. Laurie shed her dress and went back to sleep. Her problems would look just as bleak with a good night's sleep.

Chapter 2

When the housekeepers knocked on the door, Laurie was still tangled in the covers. She hollered for them to come back in a little bit. An hour and fifteen minutes later, showered, hair washed, dried and combed, teeth brushed and dressed to kill, Laurie stepped out of the room, rolling her only suitcase and carrying a large Coach tote bag.

Laurie strode right by the front desk paying no heed to the possible late check-out fee. She had no money so it was fruitless to make a courtesy stop. She thought of it as doing them a favor by not creating an opportunity for an argument.

Back at the park bench, now her place of residence, she sat comfortably, legs crossed, looking stunning in her pink size two dress and matching Balenciaga high-heeled shoes. The dress was long-sleeved and flared out from the hips into a little faux pleated shirt that went from low on the hips to about mid-thigh. Sitting on the bench, cross-legged showed a lot of thigh.

Men noticed her lithe form, alone in the park. Most women also noticed as Laurie leaned her head back, long auburn hair falling behind the park bench, her face in the noon-day sun, her alabaster skin radiating in contrast to the pink couture.

It didn't take long before the parade of men formed and came marching her way. Each presenting with the same basic offerings, a drink, a meal or maybe both. All in hopes of leading to the bedroom at the end of the day, or sooner. Laurie earnestly considered their offers, even from the men old enough to be her father, in one case, grandfather. She turned them all down even though hunger was rearing its ugly head. By nightfall, her whole attitude would probably change and a meal or two and shelter for the night may not be a bad exchange for gratuitous sex.

Although sexier than every other girl in her high school, she only had sex with three boys. The first, her boyfriend of two years who graduated a year ahead of her and pretty much forgot about her after entering the college ranks. The second was a suave college freshman named Lorne. He was Laurie's rebound guy. That affair only lasted a month. Then there was Jacob, her prom date. He was the best lover of the bunch or maybe it was the circumstances of the pretty dresses and tuxes or maybe she gained some experience and learned how to enjoy sex instead of endure it.

Three guys! That's her tale in a nutshell. How was she ever going to go to bed with a stranger every night for a plate of paella, a glass of wine and a roof over her head. After two hours of men steadily approaching her, one about every fifteen minutes, Laurie noticed a man across the promenade leaning against a tree, smoking a cigarette. He fit the quintessential description of a European, olive skinned, dark haired, medium build and he looked slick, like street-smart.

The man pitched his cigarette to the ground, snuffed it with his black patent leather shoes and began striding towards her. His black slacks, black belt and dark grey and black paisley shirt seemed to shine in the afternoon sun. On a summer day in New Orleans, without a cloud in the sky, his outfit would have been soaked through with sweat. However, a Barcelona summer day, high of eighty-two degrees

Fahrenheit (28°C) was nothing compared to a Louisiana August. Plus, the humidity in the bayou is several percent higher even though Barcelona is on the coast. This man was cool as a cucumber.

Laurie sat a little straighter when she saw him coming over to confront her with a proposition like the other men. He sat beside her, just on the edge of her comfort zone. He introduced himself as Alejandro Roberto Navarro a life-long Catalonian and he needed a favor.

Chapter 3

This was a new approach, asking for a favor. Laurie was all ears. Alejandro explained he was on the verge of the biggest deal of his life, the deal of the century, worth millions of euros. Laurie heard enough bullshit in her life to tread carefully but her ears perked up when she heard millions of euros. Alejandro continued to explain the deal involved property in Switzerland. He said it was one of those things where he happened upon some inside information which allowed him to take advantage of the situation. The catch was he had to act within the week and he was constantly being followed by his competitors.

Laurie started to call bullshit when Alejandro pointed out a man standing by a lamp post messing with his phone. He pointed out another man in the doorway of a gelato shop, that man was neither going in or coming out. Alejandro said those were the only two he could identify but there were probably more. Laurie started to believe maybe part of what he said was true.

The favor, as Alejandro explained, was he needed to communicate to a man the intentions of the property transfer. But because of industrial espionage, he couldn't communicate with the contact. His phone was tapped, his apartment was bugged and as Laurie could see, he was being followed night and day. All she had to do was deliver a letter to the contact.

Laurie started so speak but Alejandro cut her off, further detailing what he was willing to pay for the favor. Alejandro slid his hand, palm down on the park bench over toward Laurie's bare leg. He turned his palm up exposing two, one-hundred-euro bills. This was just a retainer. She was supposed to go to the hotel around the corner from the market, check in and wait for further instructions and an additional monetary gesture of appreciation. Alejandro would walk with her to the hotel to look like he successfully picked her up. Once in the hotel, she would go to the room and wait several hours and he would eat lunch and walk out the front with a smile on his face as if he had sex with her. Later, in the middle of the night she would get the letter under her door, with additional instructions.

She agreed because she needed a safe place to stay and food. A girl's gotta eat. They walked together discussing mundane things like going topless on the urban beaches, the island of Majorca and the Costa del Sol. At the hotel, she checked in while Alejandro went to the restaurant. The one-night bill was one-hundred fifty-six euros. Forty-four euros left over with which to eat and drink. In the room, shoes kicked off and pink dress hung on a chair, she laid down on the bed and fell asleep almost instantly.

When Laurie awoke two and a half hours later, her head felt thick as a brick and she was famished. A quick trip through the bathroom in her ThirdLove lace bra and panty set and she was ready to dress for the evening. Thinking laundering clothes may become a problem in the near future, she chose to wear the same dress.

It was five o'clock in the evening and a perfect time to grab an early bite before all the real diners hit the restaurants and took two hours to eat. She settled on a café that specialized in the three P's, pasta, paella and pies, opting for a pizza pie thinking it's been twenty-eight hours since her last meal and was hungry enough to eat a whole pie herself. She so wanted a pepperoni pizza, but in Europe, those were generally called an "American" and were hard to find. This café did not offer an "American" so she settled for the champinon y cebolla con pimiento verde (mushroom and onion with green bell pepper) and a glass of rioja.

After paying for the meal, the second glass of wine, the tip and table charge, Laurie had a whole nine euros left. Feeling defeated, but with her tummy completely full, she retreated to the hotel room to watch one of the two English speaking channels on TV. One actually spoke English while the other had English subtitles. In the room she decided to go all in and ordered a glass of wine through room service. The cheapest glass was seven and a half euros plus tip. Her small stash of money was gone.

Laurie had every intent on sipping the glass of rioja savoring its taste over the evening but in less than fifteen minutes, the glass was empty. The day was done, with three glasses of wine and a whole pizza consumed, she went to sleep with a brick in her stomach like a snake that swallowed a rat.

Dreaming dark most of the night, she startled awake to find the sunrise shining through the window. Smoothing the mat of hair out of her face, she noticed a large manilla envelope on the floor near the door. She went to pick it up but quickly detoured to the bathroom to conduct some urgent necessaries. Feeling almost human, she retrieved the packet and sat cross legged in the middle of the queen-sized bed. She threw her hair to one side of her face so she could more closely examine the file. It was a typical brown, 8.5 X 11 manilla envelope with a small metal clasp. No names or addresses were written on the outside. The envelope had some bulk.

She shrugged and undid the clasp, dumping the contents on the bed in front of her. Catching her attention immediately was the stack of euro bills bound by a rubber band. She quickly popped the rubber band off the stack and counted the money. There were seven, one-hundred euro bills and fifteen, twenty-euro bills. Taking a second to get her brain going she realized there was a thousand euros in the packet.

Also included was a single sheet of paper filled with step-by-step instructions and an unsealed envelope with a folded letter inside. The words on the outside of the letter were 'To the Gentleman'. She began to read the instructions:

> 1. There is nothing illegal about what you are going to do for me today. This is the only way I can keep my business deals private. When you deliver this envelope to the Gentleman, he will reward you with an additional €1.000. Before you leave, buy another night's lodging at this hotel.

Laurie was wary but excited, all of a sudden feeling like an international spy.

> 2. Get yourself to Placa d'Espanya as quickly as possible and buy a round trip train ticket on the R5 train to Montserrat.

The intrigue was mounting. A clandestine train journey.

> 3. Upon arrival at the Montserrat station, board the Rack Railway taking you to the center of the Monastery. Go directly to the funicular and travel to the top of the mountain.

This was exciting and sounded like a whole lot of fun.

> 4. At the top of the mountain, you will meet the Gentleman, he'll be wearing black with a large, gaudy, gold, crucifix around his neck. Hand him the letter, he will give you an envelope with €1.000 in it. Do not say a word to him and avoid him after the exchange. He will go down the mountain on the next funicular. You will wait for the funicular to come and go at least two times before you descend from the top of the mountain.

Scary stuff. The Gentleman was described like a priest or a Mafioso, Laurie couldn't tell.

5. When back at the Monastery, wait at least one hour and take the cable car down to the R5 train to return to Placa d'Espanya and your hotel.

6. This is a test run for a bigger, more important delivery later. This is a complicated set of directives and if everything goes well on this trial run, a €5.000 payoff will be next.

7. Another instructional envelope will be delivered to your room this evening.

Laurie was ecstatic. Such stealth and secrecy. Plus, the money was going to get her home. Two-thousand euros might be enough to get all the way back to New Orleans but five-thousand euros more would do the trick in style. Laurie realized this was the first job she ever had. Not once, had she ever worked for a wage. If she knew earning money was going to be this easy, she would have found a job like this sooner.

Chapter 4

Laurie dressed for work with a pair of short, tight, blue jean shorts, white Keds Kickstart shoes and a modest white halter top. It's what all international spy-couriers were wearing these days. She packed the large Coach tote bag with essentials, including the €1.000 and moved out smartly to buy another night at the hotel and catch a cab to Placa d'Espanya. She could have taken the subway trains but she didn't want to take time to figure them out, plus she had some money. She would have Ubered over but had no working phone. She didn't bring a plug converter and in Portugal, she tried to rig up a way to plug her phone into the strange outlets and fried her phone to a crisp with 230 volts nearly escaping electrocution herself.

At the Placa d'Espanya station, she had a terrible time finding the R5 train. She actually had to ask several people for directions. Getting there thirty minutes early, she sat on a bench singing 'Busted flat in Barcelona, waiting on a train' to the tune of Me and Bobby McGee. Once on the train and riding through the city toward Montserrat, curiosity got the better of her and she pulled out the letter to the

Gentleman and read it. The letter was the most boring thing she ever read and she read several pages of War and Peace for high school literature class. The letter spoke of earnest money, best offers, transfer of property, possession of keys, split of shares, proceeds and a Swiss bank in Zurich, blah, blah, blah. She didn't finish reading the second page. The only good thing was peace of mind knowing the transaction wasn't something illegal, just secret. She blundered into a gold mine. Thank God for her long legs and choice of a sexy pink dress and the perfectly placed park bench.

In an hour, the R5 chugged to a stop at the correct Montserrat station. There were two stations and getting off at the right one must have been part of the test. She exited the R5 and climbed aboard the Rack Railway to take her to the Monastery. The scenery was spectacular but Laurie kept her head down, looking into her tote and flipping through her stack of euros.

At the Monastery, she asked for directions to the funicular. She didn't really know what one of those was but soon discovered it was a "train" that went up a mountain at about a fifty-degree incline. It looked treacherous but this was the work of spy-couriers. Riding up the funicular, her excitement mounted. At the top she would encounter the Gentleman, a cohort in the spy ring. Was he another courier, a partner in the deal, the money man or a realtor for the property, a lawyer? Laurie's mind raced at the possibilities. Then she scared herself and hoped to hell he wasn't a thief who would take her thousand euros or worse yet, a hitman. Now she was thinking of all the things that could go wrong.

When the funicular ground to a halt at the top of the mountain, she stepped out on the landing. There was the Gentleman standing no more than ten feet in front of her. He was tall, gaunt, dressed in black with a large gold crucifix hanging around his neck. His hair was greased back and his rat-like face was pockmarked. The Gentleman was everything she imagined. He had an envelope in his right hand. Laurie reached in her bag and grabbed her envelope in her right hand.

They moved toward each other, passed envelopes, right hand to left in a matter of a second and the Gentleman stepped away to enter the funicular for descent and escape to wherever he was next assigned. Laurie sat on a bench and picked at her nails and counted her second one-thousand-euro payment waiting for the next two funiculars to come and go. She had no interest in exploring the mountain trails, holy cave or other religious structures.

When the third funicular ascended, she boarded and left the heights of the mountain behind. Back down at the Monastery still adorned with majestic scenery, she sought out the cable car. It was a short walk away which she covered quickly and then waited for the car to arrive. Once the cable car cleared of ascending passengers, she boarded to be taken to the R5 train station. The views were inspirational and uplifting but Laurie never noticed. She never went into the Monastery, never walked the trails to the overlooks, never noticed the smell of fresh mountain air and never really saw the beautiful serrated mountains for which Montserrat was named. She was happy to be headed back to the city with over €1.800. She had zero euros just yesterday. She loved this job.

Chapter 5

Back at the hotel, food was the top priority. She'd eaten nothing all day. For a girl with this much money, starving was not on the agenda. At the corner café, she ordered a tapas plate (Iberian ham on bread) with a an Eixample Pils beer. Laurie got hit on twice as she ate. It was the curse and blessing of having a five-foot six frame, gorgeously thick, long auburn hair, size two girth, medium sized breasts that looked large on her thin body, shapely legs that went from here to there and a smile that would make Jack the Ripper forget what he was doing. The second man to hit on her bought her meal and beer as a way of apologizing for intruding on her space. It was really a twenty-euro way of trying to buy his way into her tight shorts.

Laurie had to pay the tip and left a two-euro coin and a one euro coin she accumulated on her trip. She did not like carrying around coins. When she returned to the hotel room, there was already a second packet on the floor by the door. Wasting no time, she hopped on the bed, unclasped it and began to read the instructions.

1 Check out of the hotel in the morning.

2 Wear the pink dress you wore when I first met you.

3 Go to Barcelona-Sants Train station and buy a ticket on the 8:00 am train to Paris, board the train.

Paris! She'd never been to Paris. Her gap year plan was to spend at least a week in Paris but after Lisbon, Seville, Madrid and Barcelona, her money was gone. Now she would get to see it.

4 Do not leave the train station!

Crap, so much for seeing Gay Paree.

5 Buy a ticket for the 3:00 pm train to Zurich, Switzerland. Board the train. (You only have one hour between your arrival from Barcelona and the departure to Zurich.) Again, do not leave the train station!

6 A Gentleman will be waiting for you at the Zurich station. Give him the box of keys. The box is under your bed.

She jumped up from her crossed legged position in the middle of the mattress and looked under the bed. There was a small box about the size of a square Kleenex box. It was a little heavy and was covered in purple velvet. The velvet was nearly worn smooth around the edges and the box was locked.

7 Deliver this box to the Gentleman and he will pay you 5000 euros.

8 At that time our business will be concluded.

Laurie was assigned another high paying spy-courier adventure involving international train travel. How so very exciting and profitable.

She flitted around the room in excitement and finally decided to go to a bar and have a drink but she promised herself an early night. Her job called for a 6:00 am wake up. Just a drink and then back to the room. There were many bars and cafes around her hotel near La Ramblas. She walked a mere half-block before finding a suitable establishment.

She took a stool at the bar, crossed her legs and spun around with her arms outstretched on the counter top, daring any prospective suitor to buy her a drink. In less than thirty seconds a man approached and the bartender asked Laurie what she wanted. Laurie responded by saying whatever the handsome man is buying me. The man held up two fingers and said for the bartender to serve Cava's. Laurie spun around to face the bar as the man stood beside her. They were silent until the cocktail was served. After the first drink, the man asked the usual stupid questions like what is a beautiful girl like you doing in this bar. The answer was of course, getting dumb guys to buy her drinks.

After the less than intelligent flirty lines had all been said the man got down to serious questions. What all have you done since you've been in Barcelona? What did you do today? What are you going to do tomorrow? His line of questioning may have been an innocent way of trying to work his social plans into hers to be able to spend more time with her but as a newly assigned spy-courier, the questions sounded intrusive. Halfway through the second Cava, Laurie decided to end the conversation and leave the bar.

He called her a bitch under his breath when she left so abruptly. At the end of the block, she turned back and noticed the man standing in the bar doorway watching where she went. Scared stiff, she walked around three different blocks before returning to her hotel which was only a half a block from the bar. She felt sure the man didn't follow her but locked the hotel room door with both the security chain and the dead bolt.

She watched a little TV, prepared her pink outfit and went to bed still wearing her shorts and halter top. She didn't want someone to break in during the night and catch her in panties and bra. It was probably an irrational fear but one she had, just the same.

Chapter 6

The clock on the night stand blared an unruly electronic sonic blast at 6:00 am. Five seconds later, the phone rang with the wake-up call that was mildly more gentle than the clock alarm. With no time to waste, Laurie prepared for her train travel. Within an hour, almost record time, she checked out of the hotel and caught a cab to the station. Once there she found the ticket counter and purchased a second-class ticket to Paris.

Her suitcase was stored at a space in the rear of the car for over-sized luggage. She carried her tote bag containing her many euros, the instruction letter and the velvet box of keys. After last night's encounter with the young man in the bar, she put on her spy-courier face and looked at everyone as if they were the enemy. At this heightened mental status, the six-hour long trip to Paris would be unbearable. Laurie sought out the dining car and ordered a light breakfast with a mimosa. Make that two mimosas.

After breakfast, Laurie returned to her seat and stared out the window. Usually she would have spent the next six hours playing on her phone with Twitter, Facebook, TikTok and a host of others. Now she sat and wondered how she could squeeze in her next mani-pedi. The beautiful scenery raced by but Laurie didn't pay it much attention.

At 10:00 am, Laurie got up to find a restroom, dreading what a public train restroom might look and smell like. Once relieved, she washed her hands in gel four different times before heading back to the café car for brunch. She wasn't really hungry but without a phone, what's a girl to do. She disliked carrying her giant tote with her but there was no way she was leaving a potential seven grand on the seat. After eating a pastry and having a coffee, she returned to her seat, once again bored to tears.

In five and a half hours, even Laurie, as unobservant as she was noticed the outskirts of the great City of Lights. Paris! If only her phone was working, she would have live streamed the final moments of the train ride to her friends and followers. She was sure they would be interested.

After flying cross country on the high-speed railway, the approach to the Paris station seemed to be in slow motion. When they arrived, Laurie wrangled her suitcase out the back of the car and marched toward the ticket office. She paid for the ticket with her precious euros. The trip to Zurich would take three hours. By 6:00 pm today, she would be €5.000 richer and that much closer to home.

Laurie found a porter and paid him a fee to make sure her suitcase was loaded on to the 3:00 pm train to Zurich. She was now free to walk around the station asking a few employees about the location of the Eiffel Tower. Come to find out, the tower was only five kilometers away. Laurie didn't know kilometers but if it was anything like miles then it was only five miles away. She went out to grab a cab and at least drive by the tower. Not having a working phone, she couldn't take pictures but could certainly say she saw it. There was forty-five minutes before the departure to Zurich. Just enough time to get it done.

In the taxi, she could see on the dashboard clock, forty-one minutes were remaining before all aboard. The driver cautiously pulled into the Paris traffic. He made his way out of the station only to find himself trapped in a horrible traffic jam. Cars and busses were askew in every direction. There had been a pedestrian accident a half a kilometer ahead and emergency vehicles were in the process of arriving.

The taxi sat motionless for twenty minutes, four kilometers away from the Eiffel tower and one kilometer away from the station entrance. Finally, Laurie surrendered and asked to be driven back to the station. The driver said he would like to oblige but he couldn't get turned around. They were stuck. Laurie paid him what was on the meter, basically paying him for nothing, maybe less than nothing because she was more inconvenienced now than she was before she got in the taxi. She had twenty minutes to make the train and she was one kilometer away.

Laurie had no idea what a kilometer was but she started walking back to the station. A kilometer is about .6 miles, a little more than half a mile. A normal walking pace could get her back in twelve minutes. With her pink high heels, she made it to the front of the station in fifteen minutes counting the stop she had to make because a police municipale stopped her from crossing a street at the wrong place.

With maybe five minutes left before the train departed, she scurried through the station. She stared at the big board wasting precious time trying to find the train to Zurich. She looked on her paper ticket and the train was scheduled to leave on track eleven. She ran to the track terminals only to find the tracks began with the number one. She once again ran toward track eleven a hundred yards away. The train wasn't there! It was a quarter mile down the track and moving with ever greater speed off to Switzerland. Unknown to her, the taxi dashboard clock was four minutes slow.

Chapter 7

Laurie was sick. How could she be so stupid as to miss the train. Follow the instructions, don't leave the station. Trying not to panic, Laurie ran back to the ticket office forgetting how badly her feet hurt. There were lines at every window but the massive ticket machines lined up on the wall had no customers and were beckoning her.

She ran to the nearest machine, stopping in her tracks to stare at it like all tourist did. The thing looked complicated but if she took her time, all would become clear, at least that was the hope. Laurie reached out and touched the metal behemoth hoping to gain some knowledge by transference. It didn't work, but the gesture did manage to alert a local entrepreneur there was a damsel in distress. A beautiful damsel to boot.

The man approached Laurie and asked in very broken English if he could help buy a ticket. Laurie was flustered and readily agreed to receive assistance. When Laurie said she wanted to go to Zurich, the man clicked his tongue and apologized stating the train just left on track eleven. The next train to Zurich was scheduled to leave in six hours. That train would make her nine hours late.

Something else going east, then. Anything, she told him. Something that will take me all the way and leaves immediately. The man punched a few buttons on the machine and told her to insert twenty euros. As Laurie reached into her tote to get a bill, she noticed the man looking in her purse. She turned sideways to dig out the money. The big machine gobbled up the bill, rolled out a paper ticket and a two-euro coin as change.

She asked the guy if this train would go all the way. He assured her it would, all the way to the end of the line he emphasized, heading east. Adding credence to his desire to deliver customer satisfaction, he said the train left in five minutes on track four. Laurie handed him the two-euro coin and ran to the terminal cursing her high heels and aching feet all the way.

Quickly after being seated in a reasonably comfortable second-class seat, the train pulled away from the station. She was fairly proud of herself for only being an hour late. Exhausted, she laid her head against the window and slept as the clacking of the wheels against the rails sang a lullaby.

Awakening sometime later, not knowing exactly how long later because she had no phone, no watch and there wasn't a clock on the wall in the car. Laurie only knew it was time to eat because she was hungry. Finding the snack car, she ordered a sausage in a bun and a beer. The meal cost ten euros, more than half as much as the travel itself.

A conductor came through and punched tickets and she asked how much longer. The answer was an hour and a half. Laurie was feeling pretty pleased with herself. So pleased with herself, she bought another beer. She was bored with no phone, but the time passed quickly. The train started slowing down in a beautiful, deep, luscious valley. From the buildings that started appearing, the town seemed to have a lot of manufacturing and industry. Definitely a working man's town.

The train came to a halt at a modest station. The passengers in the car filed out leaving Laurie alone in the car. Something felt wrong. All the passengers were milling around in front of the station being greeted by family or walking off toward the parking lot. The conductor came into the car looking at the seats to determine if anyone left anything behind. Laurie asked what was going on.

The conductor explained this was the end of the line, as far east as the train would go. There was no more track. The train would turn around and go back to Paris in the morning. Laurie wanted to scream. The little hustler at the ticket machines duped her, all for two euros. How stupid could she be. When she gained some composure, she asked if there was any way to get to Zurich from here.

The conductor, who spoke remarkably good English, told her she could rent a car if she had a credit card and driver's license. Laurie used to have a credit card but one missed payment shut that down. She looked at him with her eye brows up begging him to continue.

The conductor explained a bus would go there in the morning and come back in the evening. She continued to stare at him for he had not yet said the right answer. He took off his conductor's hat, wiped his forehead and said there is another train, but you may not like it.

Evidently, five kilometers out of town, there was a small train station not connected to this track. It handled one train, a freight train that went through the valley to all the manufacturing plants, foundries and production industries to pick up their goods and transport them to Switzerland. The freight train had one passenger car attached to the rear of the train. Tickets could be purchased for this car at the tiny station before 5:00 pm. It was now 4:30 pm. The conductor explained everything in the town closed at 5:00 pm except the night life and it closed around 10:00 pm. This was a church going, working man's town. Welcome to Saint Die Des Vosges!

Laurie thanked him over her shoulder as she flew out of the car and ran to the front of the station to find a taxi. She jumped the line and hopped into the back seat as someone else was about to get in.

She handed the driver forty euros with instructions to get her to the freight train station now. The driver took off leaving the curses of the church going, hard-working town's folk behind.

The station was at the end of the road up a steep hill. The taxi slid to a halt in the gravel turn-around in front of the little building with a sign on it that read Saint Die Station. She leaped out, slammed the door behind her and ran to the track side of the building. There was a small portico at the entrance. Once inside, the station manager greeted her and said she was just in time, he was closing for the night.

She bought a ticket to Zurich on the freight train. The station manager walked with her outside the building, locking the door behind him and asked if she wanted a ride back into town because the train didn't come through until 11:00 pm. Laurie really, really didn't want to sit on the station stoop for the next six hours but she learned her lesson in Paris. Don't leave the station. His kind offer was declined. She was alone in what would basically be described as the wilderness. It was the side of a mountain with trees all around and she was five kilometers from town, not knowing how far that was. She put down her tote and sat on the edge of the one step high porch under the portico. Smoothing her dress down around her thighs, she sat in thought. Thoughts of it getting dark and cold soon, thoughts of hunger and thirst, thoughts of what the Gentleman might do to her for being so late. She laid back on the ancient concrete and put the tote under her head as a pillow. She believed even if she fell asleep, surely the sound of a train rolling in less than twenty feet away from her would be enough to wake the dead. She fell asleep.

Chapter 8

Laurie woke in moments, moved to the middle of the porch, took off her shoes, lay on her left side and really went to sleep. The excitement and shear disappointment in herself exhausted her. She stirred once and noticed the sun was going down. She was afraid to be alone in the dark but not enough to keep her from falling asleep again.

Sometime later, she heard a man clear his throat, "Bonjour." She jerked upright, her long legs splaying out in front of her and the pink dress hiked up to expose her panties. She bounded to a standing position nearly passing out from the blood draining from her head, clutching her shoes and tote in front of her like a shield.

"I'm sorry. I only speak English," she said trembling a little from the adrenalin.

"You're American?" he said in clear English.

"Yes." As her eyes focused, she couldn't believe how gorgeous he was.

"So am I. Assuming from the supine position, you're waiting on the train."

"I am. The eleven o' clock."

"Me too," the man said. "I bought a ticket earlier and went into town to see what Saint Die had to offer." He could tell they were sizing each other up. He was looking at her to see if she had a personality commensurate with her beauty. She was looking at him to determine if he was one of the Gentleman's assassins or just the most handsome man in the world who happened to be at this particular obscure freight train station.

"Well?" she asked. "What does Saint Die have to offer?

The man stepped up on the porch. Laurie subconsciously took a step back. The man noticed, staying where he stood not wanting to scare the young lady. "There was a nice cathedral, a toy train museum and a pretty nice bar at the corner of the main roads. I didn't get much past that."

"Sounds charming," she said somewhat facetiously. After putting the assassin thought behind her, she started to take in details. He was either a well preserved thirty-five-year-old or a road worn twenty-five, she couldn't tell in the fading sunlight. He was tall, six foot two maybe, muscular build, a model's five o'clock shadow, black medium length hair which was a little dirty from the road. He had on well-worn hiking boots and black cargo pants. The outfit was rounded out with a grey cotton shirt. He had a charcoal colored large square back pack slung over his shoulder. If he sported a gaudy gold crucifix around his neck, he could have been dressed like another Gentleman.

'Do you know what time it is?" she asked.

He looked at his military style wrist watch. "Exactly six o'clock."

"Five hours," she said under her breath.

The young man threw his back pack down and sat on the edge of the porch. She joined him, sitting four feet away. He looked at her and smiled trying to think of something charming to say but words failed him when she smiled back. They sat in silence for a while until he said, "Let's get it over with. We have five hours to sit here. My name is Joshua Arlington. I grew up in Reno, Nevada and through a series of very sad circumstances, I find myself at this particular location."

"I'm Laurie Delacroix from New Orleans and I too, find myself in this particular location because of a sad set of self-inflicted circumstances. Shall I start first or do you want to?"

"The porch is yours."

She told her story about a gap year turned into a gap month, spending that month in Portugal and Spain. Then came the intriguing chapter about meeting Mr. Alejandro Roberto Navarro on La Rambla in Barcelona and the series of tasks she was asked to perform, omitting the part about any interim payments. She was doing these tasks on speculation of receiving a ticket home at the conclusion. She also told about missing the train, getting duped by the overly helpful bystander and ending up at the end of the line, right here, right now.

Joshua nodded saying, "A very good story and it has another page to turn. You have something exciting to look forward to when you step off the train in Zurich. Joshua told his story…. a full ride football scholarship to University of Nevada. However, the first summer out of high school before he got to college, his high school girlfriend was killed in a car wreck. He didn't handle it very well and lost his scholarship. He worked the summer and saved enough money to get to Europe and run away from his problems. Six months into his gap year, the European Union threw him out because he had visa problems. Once back in the States, he joined the army with a guarantee to Germany. He liked Europe so much he wanted to come back. It was a four-year enlistment and was hoping to spend all his time in Germany, but he ended up only spending two years in Germany, six months in Bahrain and eight months in Afghanistan. "I was a Military Policeman. After I mustered out, I came back to finish my gap year in Europe. I'm here at this isolated train station because this is the cheapest way I found to get to Switzerland."

When they looked up at each other, they seemed much more relaxed but noticed darkness all around them. As they were looking at the sky, the one street lamp near the train track popped on. "There you go," Laurie said.

"At least we won't have to wait in the dark." Joshua said, smiling at her.

Just as he said that, lightning flared in the distance. They looked at each other again. "This could get ugly," Joshua said. "Do you want to call a taxi to take us back to town?"

Laurie responded with she didn't have a phone. Joshua admitted he didn't have one either and offered, "We must be the saddest examples of American tourist ever." The lightening sparked once more but this time, it was closer. Thunder echoed through the valley.

Joshua stood, "That's moving really fast. We better get up under the cover as far as we can." Joshua picked up his back pack and moved it to the door. Laurie followed with her tote. They leaned against the door as far away from the edge of the porch as possible. In this position, they touched shoulders as they sat. Joshua had his legs extended and ankles crossed. Laurie had her knees up, as much of her pleated dress as possible was tucked between her legs and she was holding her pink heels in her hands. She pointed the shoes at Joshua saying, "Not very practical for this kind of travel. I wouldn't have worn this but I was instructed to wear this pink dress to be easily recognizable to the Gentleman."

"You must be brave or desperate or…" Joshua's thoughts trailed off.

"Go ahead and say it, or stupid, right?"

"Well, I don't know what I was going to say but this is really some cloak and dagger stuff and you don't seem to be the kind of girl who gets tangled up in these kinds of things."

Laurie looked at him and bumped his shoulder with hers and said, "You don't seem to be the type of guy who runs from his problems."

Joshua didn't know how to respond so they sat for a long moment in silence until he asked, "What did you say you were delivering to this, ah, Gentleman in Zurich?"

"The first delivery I made was at a Monastery. I had to take two trains and a funicular just to get there. I didn't even know what a funicular was and then I was instructed to ride the cable car back down the mountain and the train back to Barcelona. All so I could give the Gentleman a letter. I read the letter and it sounded like a bunch of legal real estate language. Boring."

Joshua looked at her with inquisitive eyes because she hadn't answered his question.

"Oh, and on the second assignment I was supposed to take two trains, one from Barcelona to Paris and one from Paris to Zurich but that has now turned into three trains, because of my mistake in Paris, I took the train to Saint Die, however my luggage went to Zurich and now we're going from Saint Die to Zurich."

Joshua still stared at her. His face was now glazed over.

"Oh, what was the question, again?"

Joshua blinked twice, "What are you delivering to the Gentleman in Zurich?"

"A box."

"You just took me on an adventure with eight trains, a funicular and a cable car and the answer to my question was …. a box?"

"I'm sorry," Laurie said. "I talk a lot when I get nervous." She reached into her tote and pulled out the old velvet box and handed it to Joshua. "It's supposed to have keys to a very important and valuable piece of property." As soon as the words came out of her mouth, she got this tingly feeling she was making another mistake, a big one. Now she started thinking about Joshua being the Gentleman's assassin again.

Joshua flipped the box around in his hand like a large Rubik's cube and handed it back to her. Laurie's mind was racing.

Joshua asked, "Aren't you afraid?"

Laurie stood up, "Are you going to kill me?"

"No!"

"Rob me?"

"No!"

"Rape me?"

Joshua took a second before he answered that one because he already had a few lurid thoughts of the two of them going at it.

"That's it! You're going to rape me on the porch of the Saint Die train station." She moved to the edge of the porch.

"No! Sit back down. You're just nervous and talking a lot."

As Laurie was contemplating the correct move, a serious lightning flash with resounding thunder clap transpired right behind her. She let out a yelp and flew into Joshua's arms.

As he held her, he said, "I guess a murderer, robber or rapist is better than the big bad lightning and thunder."

"Shut up," she said and the rain came, sheets of it with more lightning and even louder thunder. Laurie was buried in Joshua's chest. His strong arms holding her tightly. She could feel the strength in his arms and wondered what the hell he did do to stay in such good shape, a thousand push-ups a day?

When the rain eased a little, Joshua got up to survey the area. Standing under the portico, he noticed scuppers at the corners of the building through which the roof water was pouring. He went back to his pack and unzipped it. Laurie asked what he was doing and he said he was going to take a shower under the scuppers.

"Are you nuts? It must be fifty something degrees, with the wind blowing and rain. Are you crazy?"

"No, just dirty." Joshua pulled a small hand towel and a plastic bottle of hotel shampoo out of his pack. "I'm going to take my clothes off here, under the portico so my clothes won't get wet." He pulled out a rolled-up pair of jeans and a denim shirt. "I'm going to go wash off, come back and get dressed here, out of the rain. Your job, is to keep your eyes closed."

"You're not really going to take a shower in the freezing water, are you?"

"Yes, and your job starts now. Close your eyes." Joshua began taking off his boots, followed by socks, shirt, pants and underwear. Laurie sat with her knees up and hands over her face, the short dress tucked between her legs making it look like she was wearing a romper.

Being the girl she was, it only took thirty seconds before she peeped between her fingers trying to see what's what. Joshua was already off the porch, naked, as evidenced by the remaining pile of clothes. She crawled forward and looked around the corner. He was washing his hair while standing under the runoff from the roof. He was facing away and all she could see in the lamp light was a super tight ass and muscles rippling. She wanted him to turn so she could get a full-frontal view and size him up both figuratively and literally.

The temperature was in the fifties after the thunderstorm, the wind was still gusting and Laurie was sure if he did turn toward her, there would be evidence of severe shrinkage and would allow for that in her assessment. She was still on her hands and knees, peeking around the corner. Joshua was scrubbing under his arms and then he turned and started scrubbing his genitals. No shrinkage there. As a matter of fact, it looked to be just the opposite. He looked like he was getting excited. He couldn't be that big just naturally hanging down like that, could he?

She was lost in thoughts about the other three boys she'd been with being no bigger than a handful. Joshua could easily be the size of two of her previous conquests rolled into one. She broke her trance and crawled back to his clothes and began rifling through his pants. There was something hard in the righthand front pocket. It was a fierce looking folding knife. It was a tactical knife but she didn't know what it was called. The other front pocket had €7.75 in coins. She felt the back pocket and found his wallet. Flipping it open, she saw a Nevada driver's license with the name Joshua Lewis Arlington born on and a birth date which would make him almost twenty-four years old. At least he wasn't lying about his name and where he was from. The wallet also contained a ticket for their train and a twenty-euro bill.

Finished rinsing, Joshua started to walk back to the porch, his skin rough with goose flesh from the cold. Laurie felt the need to hurry and quickly replaced the wallet and threw his pants into the pile of other clothes. He hollered, "I'm coming around the corner, shut your eyes." It caught her off guard and she scrambled back to her sitting position by the door.

"Almost there. Shut your eyes," he emphasized.

She put her head in her hands, pulled her knees up and tucked in her dress pleats noticing her panties were moist with excitement. "That was cold," he said as he stepped up on the porch. He reached down and grabbed the tiny hand towel and began drying himself. He started with his hair. Laurie knew this because she was peeking through her fingers, her actions masked by the darkness under the portico.

Joshua was mostly silhouetted against the one dim street lamp out by the tracks but what a show. He squatted down to rummage through his pack to find fresh underwear, his manhood sliding across the concrete of the porch. Joshua placed his boxer briefs on top of the back pack, stood up and wiped the porch dirt off the head of his manhood. Laurie was so wet now, she thought maybe she pee'd a little. He stepped into his boxer briefs, slinging his manhood to the side, wrapped around his thigh and put on the rolled-up pair of jeans. "Okay, you can look now."

Laurie removed her hands from her face and gawked at his six foot two, two hundred fifteen-pound muscular frame stan ding before her in a pair of jeans, barefoot and no shirt. He was still toweling off his long wet, black hair. "You should take a shower before the water quits running off the roof." The rain had lessoned to a sprinkle.

"I couldn't stand the cold but I am filthy. I've been rolling around on this concrete for a couple of hours and now you've tracked water up here which will make things worse."

"Sorry," he said as he continued to dress.

"Is this how you have been living? Taking a bath every time it rains?"

"Pretty much. I would stay at five-star hotels but I find them a little…."

"Expensive." She finished his sentence for him.

"I was going to say pretentious, but now that you mention it. They are quite expensive. Are you sure you don't want to rinse off?"

"Maybe I could stand the cold long enough to do my legs and feet."

"Well alright then." He gave her the hand towel. "I'm sorry but it's all I have."

She grabbed it from him and walked across the gravel to the scupper. He watched for a while as she stuck one leg and then the other under the water fall. She was making "ooh ooh" sounds every time she did it.

Joshua went to explore around the building to see if he could find anything useful or interesting. Laurie got back to the porch but Joshua was nowhere to be found. All his stuff was still there so he couldn't have gone too far.

"Joshua!" she called out. There was no reply. She called out again when he came around the corner carrying and empty barrel and set it down near the porch.

"I think it's used for burning trash but it'll work just fine to keep us warm. There's a whole cord of firewood on the other side of the building." Joshua disappeared around the corner once more, leaving Laurie to wonder what made this guy tick.

In a minute, Joshua came back with a giant load of firewood in his arms and began throwing the pieces into the barrel. Laurie stood on the porch drying her legs and very cold feet but feeling remarkably refreshed. Joshua brushed past her and got a cigarette lighter from his pack. He reached in his pocket and pulled out the knife, flicked it open in one swift move and began cutting slivers off one of the pieces of wood. Laurie was impressed and thought this guy may actually know how to use a knife. When he had a handful of kindling, he lit it with the cigarette lighter and expertly placed it in the barrel. Within minutes, the barrel was ablaze with a warm and friendly fire.

"I didn't know I was going to run into Daniel Boone in Saint Die," Laurie said as she moved closer to the barrel.

Joshua didn't respond to her remark but said, "The trick is to use dry wood. I had to dig down to the bottom of the pile to find these logs." He moved to the porch and stood next to her. They were standing so close, they were almost touching. Still barefooted, she stuck her foot out toward the fire and spun her ankle in a circle. "Feels good, doesn't it?" he said.

Laurie got to thinking. Five-star hotels might be overrated. Here she was, sleeping on concrete, taking showers in the rain and warming herself by a barrel fire and she wasn't miserable. As a matter of fact, she felt content, relaxed, perhaps even happy. Just maybe, it was who she was with that made all the difference. Right in the middle of that thought, Joshua put his arm around her and rubbed her shoulder.

"Are you still cold?"

"No, not at all."

He didn't take his arm away and that was perfectly alright with her.

Chapter 9

The rain stopped and stars popped out. The fire burned down and Joshua went to get more wood. When he came back, Laurie looked at Joshua and said, "Now, if we had something to eat."

"Ah," is all he said as he went to get his pack. He came back with foil wrapped fougasse with sun dried tomatoes and olives. He opened the foil and showed her the bread. Then he closed it back up, placed it between two small pieces of wood and held it over the fire, rotating the foil package after minute or two.

Removing and opening the foil packet, the smell of warm bread wafted to their noses. Laurie said, "Mmm." Joshua broke off a piece and held it up to Laurie's lips. She grabbed his hand to steady it because she wanted to touch him. Seductively taking a bite and shutting her eyes as if it were a kiss Joshua inhaled, wishing he could supplant the bread with his lips. She bit and chewed saying, "Mmm," again.

Joshua turned away and took a bite trying not to show quite so much interest in her. He walked to his back pack and pulled out a metal bottle of water, offering her a drink. Laurie took the bottle and turned it up exposing her long sensuous neck. Joshua turned away again. He looked up at the sky and stars saying, "I wonder what time it is."

Laurie didn't know and didn't care. For the first time in her life, she felt like she was really living. The bread was good, the water was cool and thirst quenching, the fire warm and inviting, the night sky romantic and the guy was hotter than a firecracker. All she could see in her mind was his huge manhood swinging back and forth like a slinky as he dried himself off under the portico.

Joshua answered himself, "I bet it's every bit of eighty-thirty."

"Two and a half hours left," Laurie said while taking another bite of bread.

The fougasse was shaped similar to a New York pretzel and only had about eight good bites in it. When they were half way finished, Joshua wrapped up the remainder of the bread and said, "We better save this for the trip. I'm a hundred percent sure there won't be dining car on this train. He returned the bread to the back pack. Laurie followed him into the darkness under the portico.

When Joshua raised up from the pack, Laurie said, "It would sure be nice if we could lie down comfortably."

Josh went into the pack again and came out with a rolled-up neoprene pad. Laurie laughed, "I feel like I'm with a boy scout."

"Unfortunately, this is only eighteen inches wide. It's only big enough for one of us." Joshua rolled it out with one end up against the door. They looked at each other in the dark.

Laurie spoke first. "I guess you're going to have to lay on top of me." She went completely prone on the mat. Her short pink dress hiked up to her crotch. Laurie spread her legs ever so slightly. Joshua stood almost between her legs looking at the beautiful creature. He reached down with his rough hand and hooked a finger through her panties right at the most sensitive part of her body. She twitched and let out an audible sign of surprise and pleasure. He pulled her panties down her legs with just his finger hooked through the crotch. She put her legs together and raised her feet. Just like that, in one slick motion, her panties were off. He threw the them to the floor.

She could see, even in the darkened portico, he was extremely excited. She waited, not patiently, but waited for him to make his move. She was centered on the mat with her legs parted just enough to give permission for him to take her. He undid his belt, unfastened his jeans and slid everything down to his knees exposing the most massive organ she'd ever seen.

She was five foot six, not a tiny woman, and blessed with a full-grown woman's equipment. She felt sure she could take every one of his many inches. He rubbed himself a little making it bob up and down in the shadows. She was about to experience life at its very best, even better than best. He started to lie on top of her when they heard a vehicle cruise up to the gravel turn around on the other side of the building.

Joshua jerked his pants up like he'd been caught masturbating by his mom. Laurie also jumped up and slipped her panties on, backwards! Great! They heard voices of several people coming around the corner. Joshua quickly rolled up the mat and threw it in his pack. Five very young twenty-something college kids strolled around the corner. There were three girls and two guys. Both guys had an open bottle of wine. All had overnight bags or small back packs.

The group was a little startled to see someone else at the station. The students were French who attended the local Institut Universitaire de Technologie. Joshua made introductions the best he could with his broken French. Laurie just observed the discourse, smiled and nodded at what she thought was the appropriate time. Laurie also noticed two girls and two guys were paired but the single girl was showing a great interest in Joshua.

Joshua threw a few logs on the fire and they stood in a circle around the barrel. Laurie stood on one side of Joshua and Juliette, the single French student, stood on the other side. Laurie hated that bitch from the instant she laid eyes on her.

Every time Joshua picked up on something noteworthy in the conversation, he would translate it to Laurie. As best Joshua could tell, the students were headed for a place called Binz und Kunz, an urban outdoor bar in Zurich to get their party on. Joshua was thinking their party was going fairly strong at the moment. They consumed two bottles of wine before the two bottles they were working on now.

Juliette spoke with Joshua at length and Laurie was getting mad because he didn't translate immediately and he looked like he was enjoying the exchange. When the conversation ended, Laurie asked what was said. Joshua explained Juliette was asking if they were a couple and Joshua told her they just met a few hours ago here at the Saint Die station.

Joshua asked the group if they had always been friends or if they met at the university. The two couples met during their freshman year. They were going to start their sophomore year when they got back from Zurich. Juliette was new to the group and met them at the bar in Saint Die. Joshua translated to Laurie and Laurie didn't like it one bit.

At 10:30 pm, another vehicle could be heard on the gravel pulling up in front of the train station. Everyone around the barrel went silent and turned to see who was going to come around the corner. They heard car doors slam. In a minute, two men in their late thirties or early forties, came around the side of the building, wearing typical European garb and carrying small overnight bags. The students called out a cordial greeting but were disappointed the newcomers weren't more young twenty-somethings ready to party.

With the arrival of the older men, the conversation died down to someone asking every five minutes when the train would get here. A little before the hour, they heard a train whistle cut through the night air which jolted them into an excited state of milling around. The young guys went to get suitcases out of their vehicle. Everyone stood on the porch, each having a piece of luggage except for Laurie. She only had her tote.

Juliette came to Laurie and said something in French which Laurie didn't understand. Laurie looked at Joshua for help. "Juliette says you travel light for a girl."

"Tell her I lost my luggage. No, wait. Don't tell her anything."

Joshua said something to Juliette in French.

Laurie looked at him wanting to know what he said.

"I told her you had everything you needed in the purse."

"Okay, that's alright."

Joshua scrunched his face and said, "What? Do you think you are going to give away too much information?"

"No," Laurie said. "I just don't like her."

"Why, because she's single and pretty…and hitting on me?"

Laurie stormed off to the tracks, looking down them to see if she could see the train coming.

"What's her problem?" Juliette asked in plain English.

"So, you speak English and kept it hidden."

"I also speak German and Italian, but I didn't tell you that either."

"Speaking French, German and Italian makes you a prime candidate for being a Swiss citizen since those are the primary languages of Switzerland. Are you Swiss?"

Juliette bowed her head a little, "Guilty."

"So, you're going home on this train?"

"Correct," she said.

"And why are you going to Switzerland?" Juliette asked.

Joshua gave a crooked smile and said, "Because I've never been there. Excuse me, I'm going to check on Laurie." Joshua left Juliette on the porch and walked out to the tracks with his back pack over his shoulder.

"You know standing out here and looking down the track won't make the train get here any faster." Joshua stood close enough for his chest to touch her arm and back. As soon as he said that, the train light burst through the trees about a mile down the track. "Or, maybe it will."

"You're sitting with me, right?" Joshua asked her.

"Sure," she said noncommittedly.

Chapter 10

The train came to a noisy halt with the last car parked in front of the station. There was no conductor or anybody to give instructions or take tickets. The small group filed on to the car lugging their carry-ons. The car was filled with tabletop seating. One row facing forward and one row facing backward with a table in between. Seven tables on each side. The two older men took seats at the front of the car, both sat facing the rear on opposite sides of the car. Joshua thought that was quite unusual, as if they purposely sat with a view of all the passengers instead of the scenery. The two college couples each took seats on either side of the car facing forward by the biggest window in the middle. Juliette sat on the left, two rows behind the college kids facing forward. Joshua and Laurie took the last seat on the right, facing forward. A door at the back of the car led out to a small porch with an iron railing at the very rear of the train. Steps led down to the track from the porch and served as the back entrance to the train car.

As soon as they sat down, Joshua grabbed a big handful of Laurie's bare thigh and lifted her leg up over his. Laurie was starting feel better about this now. Juliette turned to look over her shoulder at Laurie who glared back. Joshua started to have that old familiar feeling, like he did in the Military Police when something was about to go wrong. This whole night felt off. Laurie was a secret bagman trying to carry keys, of all things, to Zurich, Switzerland, Juliette was a Swiss citizen masquerading as a French student, and there were these two experienced men sitting so they could view the rest of the car. Exactly what Joshua was doing by sitting in the last seat in the back.

This train is not the way normal people got to Switzerland. This train was for college kids who wanted to drink on the way, losers like him, or desperate people like Laurie. The European men were not losers or ones who wanted to party on the way and Juliette was no loser either. Juliette was confident and aloof.

About an hour into the trip, Laurie asked Joshua if he thought this train would pull into the same station as the passenger trains from Paris. Joshua didn't think it would. "The freight train yard and the passenger terminal may be close together or dozens of miles apart but I think they will not be the same. We'll probably need to walk to wherever we're going. I assume you'll want to go the train station and see if you can find your luggage?"

Laurie realized she hadn't thought through her plan for arrival in Zurich. "Yeah, I should try to find my luggage first. And then …. how will I find the Gentleman?" She looked at Joshua for the answers.

"You were supposed to meet at the station, right? Go there and hang out, especially at the time you would have arrived. That's what I would do. If the Gentleman," he used air quotes, "doesn't show up in a couple of days, I'd chalk it up to experience and go on with my life."

"But how will I get home without a plane ticket?" Joshua waited for her to answer her own question. "I guess I could get a job."

"I think that's what you'll need to do." Joshua smiled to himself knowing this girl never worked a day in her life. He didn't dwell long on her work ethic because he had his hand on her thigh, inches away from her sweet spot. With his fingers, he lifted her dress pleats, easily seeing her pink panties. He leaned over close to her ear and whispered, "Your underwear is on backwards."

"Oh my God," she said. "I was so startled by those people coming around the building while we were half naked, I just threw them on. This can easily be remedied." She scooted around on the bench seat a little and pulled them off, tossing them in her tote. "Better?" Joshua smiled and put his arm around her.

Laurie reached in her tote and pulled out the velvet box. Joshua grabbed her hand and pushed it down to her lap. "What are you doing?" she asked.

"I don't really know what's in that box. Why are they willing to trust a total stranger with it and promise you air fare home and send you on a trial run to the Monastery. Doesn't it sound a little too fishy to you?"

"Yeah," she responded, "but I was one day away from desperate."

"I think they know and that's why they picked you."

"So, you don't think keys are in this box and you think this whole thing is a scam?"

"Why would keys be in there for a real estate deal. Property goes to the title holder not the guy who controls the keys. I was a military policeman long enough to see some scams and this has bullshit written all over it."

Laurie was still flipping the box around in her hand underneath the table. "Do you think we can open it?"

Joshua took the box and studied the lock and hinges. "I think I'd break it if I tried to open it."

Laurie sat up straight and said, "Let's take it to a lock smith in Zurich and get him to open it. "

"I think with this box, a jeweler may be a better bet."

"Okay, we go to the passenger train station and get my suitcase, hang around for the Gentleman a little while, then we go find a jeweler and get him to open the box. Agreed?"

"Sounds like an adventure. I've got to warn you, I don't have any money. I'll be sleeping under the stars tomorrow night. You're more than welcome to join me but I know it's not a very attractive offer."

"I don't have any money either," Laurie lied. "Remember they picked me because I was desperate. By now, I should have handed off the box and gotten a ticket home."

"Okay, under the stars it will be. Me and you kid."

Laurie felt excited. Sleeping on the ground in some urban park was not her style but with Joshua, she had this feeling everything was going to be alright. At exactly midnight, the train car lights went out momentarily and two dim lights in the center of the car came on. Night lights. "I guess it's time to go to sleep," Joshua said sarcastically. He looked around the car and noticed the two older men were still sitting upright, looking right at Joshua. The college couple on the left were each playing on their phones, the student couple on the right were piled up on each other trying to sleep. Juliette was lying down on the bench seat with her legs stretched across the aisle and her feet on the other seat.

Laurie leaned her head on Joshua's shoulder and closed her eyes. It was an exhausting day. Joshua wanted to close his eyes too but didn't dare. Something was off and he wasn't about to let his guard down. The hours clickety-clacked away.

Laurie sat up and rubbed her eyes and asked what time it was. "Two in the morning," Joshua responded.

"Oh Lord, I've got to pee." Laurie looked around. "Where do you go?"

"I'm afraid there is no bathroom on this car," Joshua said as he looked around too. He stood up and went to the front of the car but there was no hidden rest room. He asked the two older men, "Ou sont les toilettes?"

One of them responded, "No toilettes."

Joshua informed Laurie she had to hold it. "You're a big help," she said. Joshua didn't tell her but he had to go too. He stood up by the door on the back of the car and pushed it open, stepping out into the very chilly night air. He thought, oh well, pulled out his member and pee'd off the back of the train going forty-five kilometers per hour. He felt like a little boy.

He stepped back in the car and sat by Laurie. She asked, "What's out there?"

"Well, if you go back about a half a mile on the tracks, you'll find my urine."

"Did you pee off the train?" Joshua smiled at her.

"I want to do that."

"I'm not sure if that's possible."

"Why?" she asked.

"It's a train going thirty miles an hour down the tracks, plus I could pee through the rails." He thought for a minute, "Maybe you could lean back on the steps and hang on to the handrails."

"I want to do that. I've really got to go."

"Do you want me to come with you?"

Laurie thought for a moment, "Oddly enough, I do."

They both got up and went out to the back landing. The train was only going about twenty-eight miles per hour but for someone who was facing the prospect of hanging their ass off the steps, the train looked like it was flying.

There were three steps and Laurie went down two of them, turned around and clutched the handrails. "Here goes nothing." Laurie backed down the last step, squatted and relieved herself with immense satisfaction. Her short pink pleats blowing up in the wind.

She stood up, strolled up the stairs and stood in front of Joshua. "Atta girl," was all he said.

She fell into his arms and buried her face in his chest, "I'm so embarrassed."

"Everybody's got to pee sometime," he said squeezing her tightly.

"Yeah, but usually they've been married ten years before they start squatting in front of each other."

"We should get back inside, it's cold." Joshua backed up a step and peered through the glass window on the back door. Everything in the car seemed just like it was when they exited. "I don't want to be away from your bag very long."

Laurie looked in the window too. "Nobody's moved. It'll be alright. I didn't think a little cold bothered you."

"Well, it's not really cold, like freezing or anything. It's that fifty-five degrees with a twenty mile an hour wind in the middle of the night is kind of cold."

"I've seen you take a shower in rain water in these same conditions. You're not cold. You just want to get in there and protect the box. No one knows we have it."

Joshua looked through the window again. "Maybe I'm being paranoid but I have this uneasy feeling about it."

Laurie walked to the other side of the porch, put her hands on the rail and watched the rocks and vegetation rush by. The train was passing through a narrow canyon and if she leaned way out, she could touch the bushes and trees lining the track.

Joshua came up behind her and wrapped his arms around her, his hands inches away from her breasts. She stood, swayback, with her lower body pushed against his. She could feel him ever so slightly start to grind is hips into her. His member began to swell. She leaned a little further over and reciprocated the grinding. In a minute, he was fully erect and bursting to get out. Laurie thought, how can guys with big ones ever wear tight jeans? It must be painful. Poor baby.

Laurie was deciding if she was going to stay where she was, bent over the rail, and let him take her from behind or if she was going to turn around and figure out how to do it face-to-face on the back of a moving train. She wasn't sure what to do but she was aching to get him inside her.

In the middle of her indecision, the door knob turned startling the couple into stiff standing positions. Joshua stood at the rail facing out because his pants were filled with rather obvious excitement. Laurie turned toward the door. The two college aged males stepped on to the porch. One of them said in French, "We need to urinate. You can stay out here or go inside. We don't care, it's going to happen."

Joshua looked at Laurie, "They're going to take a leak. We should go inside."

All Laurie could think about was coitus interruptus before the coitus even began, again! And, it was interruptus by the same people who did it before. She couldn't wait to be shed of this group.

Joshua opened the door and told her to go in, disappointed about the timing but he didn't want her to be away from the box for very long. He didn't trust anyone on the train. Laurie was frustrated and didn't know what to think about all this cloak and dagger stuff, except the fact she wanted to uncloak Joshua and have her way with his dagger.

Chapter 11

After a few bumpy stops at other obscure stations, at six in the morning, the train began its long slow stop at the Zurich freight yard. The scene was not a welcoming one. The yard was filled with derelict train cars, cranes and front-end loaders. Box trucks and eighteen wheelers were parked in columns, waiting to be filled with products and parts to be taken to wholesalers and assembly plants.

The passengers filed out the front door carrying their bags only to be met by a railyard worker dressed in grimy overalls. He asked everyone to show a ticket, which they did. The worker led them through the working railyard to an office building and bid them a good day. There were two taxis parked out front, to which the two college couples made a beeline. They piled in one taxi and took off. The last taxi was waiting for someone to get in but nobody did. Joshua and Laurie didn't know where the passenger train station was located so they didn't know if they were going to walk or take a very expensive taxi. The older men looked around like they were lost, obviously stalling and Juliette suggested they share the cab into town. What a conundrum.

Joshua grabbed Laurie's arm and led her back into the office, leaving the other three standing on the curb of the circle drive with the taxi driving pleading for a fare. Joshua ask the first railyard employee he found about the passenger station. The answer they got was disappointing. It was way too far away for Laurie to walk in her senseless pink heels.

Joshua looked at Laurie and said, "Let's walk straight out front, jump in the taxi and take off. Don't speak to anyone. If they really wanted a taxi, they'd get in that one. They're waiting on us to see where we go."

"It's this stupid box I've got isn't it?"

"I'd be willing to bet. That box contains something very valuable or could lead to something valuable and I think the two guys and Juliette are after it."

Laurie looked worried, "How would they even know I had it?"

"Trust me. People with money and means can find out anything. Here's my concern, the older guys are different, don't you agree? Out of place, right?"

Laurie shook her head affirmative, "Yeah, I guess so."

"Does Juliette seem kosher to you?"

"I don't like the bitch if that's what you mean?"

Joshua continued, ignoring her remark, "Juliette is a Swiss citizen, speaks at least four languages, seems more mature than she was acting and is traveling alone. I don't think I like the bitch either."

"Good!" Laurie said emphatically.

Joshua grabbed Laurie's hand and said, "Let's go get in the taxi. Don't say anything until we've driven away." They walked out the door and jumped in the back seat with their belongings in their laps. Juliette tried to follow but Joshua shut the door in her face as she was asking to share the cab. Both men ran to the curb and watched the vehicle drive off.

Joshua and Laurie looked out the back window and saw the three of them standing on the asphalt watching them drive away. "They are after the box, aren't they?" Laurie said confirming their thoughts.

"I'm afraid so," was Joshua's reply. When the taxi was at the edge of the rail yard, Joshua told the driver to go to the passenger train station or as far as twenty-seven euros would take them because that's all the money he had. Joshua reached into his pack and pulled out the remainder of the fougasse and they shared it, cold, hard and a lot less satisfying than what it was last night. But it kept their stomachs from rumbling.

Laurie looked at Joshua, "You know what would be nice?" She didn't give him time to answer. "A cup of coffee, with lots of cream and sugar."

"Coffee would be nice, but after we pick up your suitcase. If it's there, we need to take inventory of all our assets and see what we're working with."

"You mean see how broke we are?"

"Yep. After I pay for this cab, I'll have about zero euros left. I've been without money before but I have a hunch, this is a first for you."

Laurie laughed a little and said, "I've been through so many firsts in the last week I'm getting used to it. I think I put a couple of extra twenties in my suitcase." She made up a lie. "So, if they're holding it at the station, we'll have some money to eat on."

Joshua didn't respond. He was lost in deep concentration. The taxi meter was rolling up on twenty-five euros and Joshua asked how much further. The driver responded with "Right around the corner." Two turns later, the cab pulled up in front of the station. Joshua paid the man and they went to find where unclaimed baggage was kept.

After a long walk, they found the office and Laurie's bag was there. She showed some identification and the uniformed security guard released the suitcase. Joshua rolled it to a bench in the station and Laurie started going through her stuff. After flipping through a few layers of clothes she told Joshua someone had been in the suitcase.

"How can you tell?"

"A girl can tell when someone has touched her things."

Joshua let it go. "Is the money still there?"

Laurie got down on her knees, putting her body between Joshua and the suitcase. She reached in her tote, grabbed a few twenties and pretended like she retrieved them from the suitcase. "They're still here." She turned around holding three twenty-euro bills.

"Good, we'll need all we can get. You hang on to them until we need them."

"I don't have any pockets." She handed them to Joshua. "You keep them."

"You trust me with your last sixty euros?"

Laurie didn't look up from rearranging the things in the suitcase, "Yes."

When Laurie finished, she sat back down on the bench beside Joshua. She was holding some yellow panties, a travel size tube of toothpaste and a folding tooth brush in her hand. "I'm still not wearing anything under this dress, you know. I'm going to go to the restroom and put these on and brush my teeth. You going to be here?"

"Right here." Joshua watched her walk away, leaving her suitcase and tote bag behind. He was thinking how did this girl ever make it through life trusting total strangers.

Joshua watched her stroll back from the restroom. She was smiling and ran her tongue across her teeth saying "I feel better," as she sat down.

Joshua stood, "I'm going to brush my teeth too. You'll be here?"

"Right here," she laughed as she watched him in his tight jeans saunter away.

Chapter 12

After they cleaned up the best they could in a train station toilet and Laurie changed out of her filthy pink dress and heels, they made a plan. The first thing on the list was to find the big board and see when the next train from Paris arrived. The train was due in about three hours. They would wait to see if the Gentleman would meet this train thinking Laurie may have missed the train last night and took the next available one. If he showed up, Laurie would keep her end of the bargain and exchange the box for a ticket home or enough money to get home. Joshua didn't know she was really supposed to receive five-thousand euros.

If the Gentleman didn' t show up, they would go find a jeweler who could pick the lock and see what the hell was in the box. In the meantime, Laurie wanted a cup of coffee. Joshua talked her into sharing a cup to save money. Joshua sat at a table with his back pack and Laurie's tote. Laurie queued up in the coffee line. Joshua watched her shifting from foot to foot, bored without a phone. He thought she really looked cute in her Khaki shorts, sleeveless button-up shirt and Keds. Compared to all the other people dressed in their dark European attire, she looked as American as they come.

Joshua surveyed the station, searching for trouble, not really knowing what trouble would look like. He glanced up at Laurie who was looking at him. She smiled and turned her back. He thought that's what trouble looks like.

Laurie came to the table with a large cup of American coffee and a small, paper cup filled with powdered creamers and sugar. She dumped the fixin's out on the table top. "Let's see if I can do this without making a mess." She poured coffee from the big cup to the little cup with surprisingly few drops spilled. She mixed three creamers and four sugars into the big cup, stirred with a little wooden stick and took a drink. "Mmm," she moaned with her eyes shut.

Joshua took his baby cup and sipped the black coffee. "Thanks," he said. Joshua started the conversation by asking if she really wanted to find the Gentleman or if she would be just as happy if she never saw him again. Laurie sat considering the question, sipping her milkshake coffee. "I think it boils down to I need to find him. How am I going to get home if I don't?"

"I'll get you home if we don't find him. I promise." They drank without talking, enjoying the luxury of a cup of coffee. When Joshua drained the last drop from the cup he said, "Let's take inventory."

"Inventory?"

"Yeah, let's list everything we own that's valuable. I've got this knife, cost over a hundred bucks in the States. It's probably worth five euros here. I have a small pair of binoculars worth about the same. I have a good pair of running shoes that, once again, I could hock for about five euros over here. If we truly got desperate, I could sell this back pack but then I'd be without a home." He laughed, "I'm worth about fifteen euros plus some change in my pocket."

"What about that watch?"

Joshua looked at his wrist. "My Dad gave me that. It's by far the most expensive thing I own and it has the most sentimental value. I'll sell it or trade it but I'll be starving, naked and in a great deal of pain before I do."

"Okay, we're keeping the watch, got it." Laurie started her list, "Well, let's see. I've got what's left of the sixty euros I had stashed in the suitcase."

Joshua interrupted, "How much did the coffee cost?"

"A little over six euros."

"Six euros! For a cup of coffee? That's ten percent of your total cash assets."

"Obviously, you haven't bought a venti cup of American half-caf in a train station recently."

"That's true, but watch and learn." Joshua walked off in the direction from which they originally came. In five minutes, he returned carrying two small cups of coffee in recyclable paper cups. Setting them on the table, he reached in his pocket and threw down several packets of sugar and four little creamers. "By the way, they're both half-caf. One was fully caffeinated and one was decaf, I mixed them together. Total cost, zero."

"Where did you get them?"

"I guess you didn't notice the coffee maker in the unclaimed baggage office." She shook her head, no. "Well, I did. Since we were recent customers of the office, I felt entitled to a couple of cups of joe."

"Thanks for the hobo 101 lesson. But back to our inventory, I have about a thousand dollars' worth of jewelry, a couple of rings and two necklaces. Nothing very expensive. I have this tote bag that cost three-hundred dollars, this suitcase I paid two-hundred dollars for, my new iPhone that is fried, and some expensive clothes and some regular clothes."

"You're rich in hobo 101 terms."

She laughed a little, finding this broke and on the lamb routine exciting. Of course, she had approximately sixteen-hundred euros in her tote Joshua knew nothing about and she was expecting to get five-thousand more.

Joshua looked at his non-negotiable watch and said they ought to move over to the terminal to see if they could locate the Gentleman. Laurie got a shot of adrenaline in her stomach when Joshua said that because the Gentleman was creepy scary. Joshua drained his second miniature cup of coffee and they walked toward the terminal. Laurie was busy gawking at people in the station, oblivious to anything that might benefit their survival. Joshua's military police radar was operating. Nothing felt right about this whole situation other than the fact that he was inexplicably drawn to Laurie.

At the terminal, they sat on an out of the way bench, with an hour to kill before the train from Paris arrived. "Are you sure you can recognize the Gentleman?" Joshua asked.

"I don't know if it will be the same guy from the Monastery or a different one. The first guy was tall and thin, wearing all black with a big gold crucifix around his neck. It looked more gangster than religious. Plus, I was supposed to meet him at a very specific place and time. Here, we don't even know if the Gentleman will be here. And I was supposed to be wearing the pink dress."

Both of them were looking at every person even if they didn't fit the description and there were hundreds of people coming through the terminal. In thirty minutes, Laurie stood up to stretch. She spread her legs, tossed her hair over her shoulder, held it and bent way down almost touching her face to the floor. Her ass, in those skintight shorts, was up in the air at Joshua's eye level. She arched her back and slowly came up in a cheerleader-slash-stripper movement. Joshua tingled while watching out of the corner of his eye. She did it again and he stared full on and felt a major stirring below the waist. She sat down next to him, giving him a little bump. He hadn't touched her since the train and she was wondering what was going on. He got up to excuse himself to the restroom. Really, he wanted to walk-off his predicament. She noticed his big 'predicament' as he got up and smiled because everything was okay.

As Joshua was leaving the restroom, he noticed a guy in black at the big board. He was studying the train timetable. The guy in black turned and Joshua could clearly see a large gold cross. The Gentleman was here! Joshua was about to go warn Laurie when two other men came up on either side of the Gentleman and started escorting him toward the restroom. Joshua didn't know if he should run or hide. Retreating into the restroom, Joshua hid in the last stall and stood on the commode.

Joshua heard the Gentleman protesting, speaking Spanish, as the other guys shoved him into the restroom. There were some thuds, grunts and the obvious sound of a body crumbling to the floor. Joshua stayed perched on the commode, waiting. In less than ten seconds, he heard other voices speaking German, coming from people entering the restroom. They must have seen the body on the floor because they screamed some expletives and made haste from the restroom yelling for the Polizei. Joshua took this opportunity to exit also, stepping over a very dead and bloody Gentleman. He noticed the two murderers at the big board, studying it like nothing happened.

Joshua ran back to Laurie and told her they had to go now! He explained he saw the Gentleman and two guys, not just any guys, but the two guys from the train last night, who pulled the Gentleman into the restroom and killed him!

"Killed him!" she exclaimed as she was gathering up her stuff. Joshua grabbed her suitcase and they ran in the opposite direction of the entrance. There had to be a back exit to a maintenance area or gate to hell or someplace better than the entrance leading into direct confrontation with a pair of murderers.

At the very back of the terminal, they found a gate that led to employee parking lot. They ran around the entire building and caught a cab out front. Breathless, they told the driver to take them to Binz und Kunz, the bar they heard the college kids on the train talk about. It was the only place they knew by name in Zurich.

The taxi driver dropped them off and collected a large chunk of their meager holdings. "At least we're safe for now," Joshua said. "The train from Paris is not supposed to arrive for ten minutes. Those guys will be at the station looking for us for another thirty minutes at least. We've got to figure out what's in that box. People are willing to kill over it. People have killed over it," he corrected himself."

They easily found an empty table at the outdoor bar. It was barely eleven in the morning and the establishment just opened for the lunch crowd, Laurie and Joshua were their first customers. A waitress came out and turned on several televisions, all of which were tuned to sports channels, with soccer being the sport of choice. "Oh good, grown men kicking a ball," was Laurie's take on it.

Soon the waitress came over with menus and told them she would be back in a minute. She spoke French. Joshua advised they should order as little as possible. Just enough to be able to sit at a table. Laurie agreed but she was really hungry. When the waitress returned the couple ordered rosti, a potato fritter dish, two fritters to a plate. They would share. Joshua convinced Laurie to drink tap water, it was free.

"Obviously the Gentleman will not be greeting you and the hopes of getting your ticket home are out the window. We need to find a jeweler and get that box opened." Laurie's stomach rumbled as she agreed with Joshua. When the waitress returned with the rosti, Joshua asked her where the best jeweler in Zurich was located.

The young waitress said, "Nous les avons tous, Tiffany, Cartier, Piaget, Graff, Bulgari, Bucherer…."

Joshua cut her off, "Tres bien merci." The waitress walked away.

Laurie said, "I heard and understood. I didn't really understand but I heard Tiffany and Cartier and that was enough."

"Do you have a preference?"

"Let's go to the closest one," Laurie said with a smile.

"Right out of the hobo 101 manual."

They slowly ate their rosti, trying to savor every bite while pushing back the horrible sinking feeling of being chased by killers. The tables were filling up because the soccer games were starting, signaling beer call although it was only 11:30 am. The waitress came by twice asking if they needed anything else but she was actually trying to shoo them out the door. They paid what Joshua though was an incredible amount of money for a potato fritter and exited the bar area.

Fifty yards down the sidewalk, Joshua asked Laurie to stop and look past his left shoulder on the steps of the building diagonally across the street. "Make it look like you are talking to me, don't stare."

Laurie looked at his face and cut her eyes to the side without angling her head toward the stairs. "Oh, for the love of money! Is that….is that…" She squinted trying to make sure. "That's Juliette! What is she doing here?"

"I'll give you one guess. She's after the box. The question we should be asking…is she with the two men or is there a third party involved. We've got the Gentleman, God rest his soul, and the greasy slick guy in Barcelona, the two guys from the train and now Juliette. Working together or separate?"

"Juliette's separate," Laurie insisted.

"How did you deduct that?" Joshua inquired.

"She's a bitch. Doesn't play well with others."

Joshua shrugged, "Fair enough."

"What are we going to do?" Laurie took a step closer to Joshua. She was trembling.

Joshua pulled her close, embraced her and she folded into the 'I've got you' kind of hug. Instantly, she felt safe again. Maybe not safe but, at least no longer so afraid.

He whispered in her ear, 'We're going to be alright."

"How can you say that?" she pulled away a little.

"Because, if the need arises, I'll take care of those two gorillas and you'll bitch slap Juliette into next Tuesday."

Laurie hugged Joshua this time as she said, "I hope it's Wednesday when I slap her because I want to beat her for a full week."

"That's my girl. You ready?"

"Yeah, what's the plan?"

"Let's just stroll down the street like we don't have a care in the world."

"Okay, why not. We're broke, homeless in a foreign country, killers are chasing us and we have a mysterious box. Not a care in the world." They started walking.

"Juliette will probably stay a block behind us. Two blocks up I see a taxi stand. We'll stroll right up to one and drive off."

"Where to?"

"Same plan, the nearest major jewelry store."

"Where's that?" Laurie asked.

"Hell, I don't know."

"You're such a guy. Ask somebody!"

Joshua asked a complete stranger and got an answer, "Cartier's."

"You happy?" he said playfully to Laurie.

She smiled as they continued their fake stroll which was more like a controlled panic.

As they approached the taxi stand, Joshua told her to face him and act like they were conversing. "Check behind me. Do you see Juliette?"

"She's back by the clothing store we passed pretending to window shop."

"That's a hundred yards back. Unless she's Usain Bolt's sister, it'll take her thirty seconds to get here. We should be out of sight if we time the traffic right. The first taxi has the trunk open. When you say go, run to the taxi, throw your suitcase in and jump in the back seat on the left side of the cab. I'll jump in the right side. Look over my shoulder and when the traffic has cleared, say go and we'll move."

Laurie stared down the street for a few seconds. "Go!"

The plan worked well. As Joshua was shutting the taxi door, he glanced back and saw Juliette running toward them. Taxi driver took off at Joshua's instruction which were, "Turn right at the next block, turn left and then turn left again."

The driver did what he was instructed. After a mile of winding around, Joshua told the driver to take them to Cartier jewelers which he did for a hefty fare. Running from killers was proving to be expensive

Chapter 13

Laurie and Joshua stood outside Cartier Jewelers. Joshua said, "This is a little rich for my blood."

Laurie patted him on his chest, noticing his massive muscles. "Just think of these things as rocks stuck to metal. Rocks and metal, that's all jewelry is, right?"

"Rocks and metal," he repeated.

They walked in looking like tourists with the suitcase and back pack. A guy in a suit came over to them. His suit cost more than Joshua made in a month in the army. "How may I help you?" He was giving them a once over to determine if they were serious customers. He deduced, they were not, therefore not worthy of his time.

"Is there a jeweler in the house?" Joshua asked lightheartedly.

"I am Reinhardt von Zimmermann, the head sales at Cartier. What are you interested in today?" Reinhardt spoke perfect English.

"I am Joshua Lewis Arlington and this young lady is Ms. Laurie Delacroix."

"Laurie Angeline Delacroix," Laurie added.

Joshua turned to her and said, "Nice to meet you," completely ignoring the head of sales.

"The pleasure is all mine."

Reinhardt cleared his throat. "I'm a busy man. Please don't waste my time."

Joshua looked around and there was nobody in the store. "Can we see a jeweler?"

"Why?" was the staccato return from Reinhardt.

"We have something unusual we'd like to show him. Get an opinion, ya know?"

"We have one craftsman in the back right now and he's busy."

Laurie stepped forward and gently rubbed Reinhardt's tie, "Come on, maybe he can see us for a minute." She was trying to manipulate him but Joshua saw early on, Reinhardt was a little light on his feet.

Reinhardt pushed her hand away and said, "Oh please, honey, you're on the wrong team. Now if big boy here would ask me nicely, I may consider your request."

Laurie turned to Joshua and opened her eyes wide, "Your turn." She smiled.

"Go ahead," said Reinhardt. "Ask me nicely."

Joshua shuffled a little bit and said, "May we please see the jeweler?"

"Oh, that was nice, but you have to come over here and say it."

Joshua was done playing games and started to step forward for reasons Reinhardt would not enjoy. Laurie launched herself between them, "Now, now boys, play nice." She was pushing on Joshua's chest to hold him back.

An old crackly voice came from the back, "Reinhardt, who is it?"

"Nothing to worry about Karl. Just some peasants."

Joshua and Laurie looked at each other and repeated simultaneously, "peasants?" and they laughed.

In a few seconds, and old man with a multi-lens contraption wrapped around his head came from the back room. "Hello young couple. What would you like me to look at?" His English was good but highly accented with German.

Joshua did the talking. "Well sir, we have this antique locked box we'd like you to look at and maybe open if at all possible."

"Come on back and let's have a look. I love a mystery."

Joshua, Laurie and Karl went back into the workshop leaving Reinhardt alone in the store.

The old man grunted as he sat behind a cluttered work bench with a giant magnifying glass on a retractable arm. "Let me see this mystery box. It will be the most fun I've had today and I haven't even seen it yet. My days are quite boring."

Laurie pulled the box out of the tote and set it on the table in front of him. He stared at it without saying a word. Laurie and Joshua stared at it with him. After a full minute, Joshua said, "Herr Karl, are you alright?"

Karl's concentration was on the box and not on his command of English. "I am best than alright. Where did you get this?"

Laurie said, "It's a long story."

"I would love to hear it."

Joshua chimed in, "The less you know the better."

"A second mystery! My day is getting better." Karl finally reached out and gingerly picked up the box and rotated it around in his hands. He gently brushed the worn velvet covering with his soft palms.

Laurie couldn't hold in her excitement any longer, "What is it?"

"Oh, my dear, this is a treasure."

Joshua and Laurie exchanged glances and held hands. "My children, this is fantastic. You see the keyhole?" he put his finger next to it. "The lock is made for a skeleton key. A special, four tooth key. The rarest of all locks." Joshua and Laurie squeezed hands. "There are two keys."

Laurie interrupted, "But there is only one keyhole."

"Correct, child." Karl set the box on the work bench. "The two keys interlock like this." He scissored his fingers together. "Sliding together, they make one four-prong key. Do you have the key?" Laurie told him they didn't have it. "Then we do it the old fashion way." Joshua wrapped his arm around Laurie and held her close.

"What do you think is in the box?" Laurie had to ask.

Karl thought for a moment. "Something very valuable," then he paused. "Or nothing at all."

Laurie looked at Joshua and made a sad face for a second.

"Did you know…" Karl's voice trailed off as he thought. "This box is very unique. I've never seen one, only read about them. A two key, cross locked box covered in purple velvet is special. Made for royalty, maybe around the turn of the twentieth century. The box by itself is worth nearly two-thousand euros."

Laurie almost squealed.

"Children, it will take me hours to figure out a way into this magnificent specimen. If you wish to wait…", he pointed to one old wooden chair in the corner. "If you don't desire to wait, I promise if can get the box unlocked, I will not open it until you are present."

Laurie was giddy with excitement. Joshua was still grounded. "Herr Karl. We can't pay you for your trouble."

"The pleasure of working on this beautiful box is priceless. I should be paying you."

Joshua laughed, "I'm glad you feel that way, because we really have no money."

"Ah yes," Karl said. "But you have love. I can see it." He touched his multi-lens contraption when he said it. "And…you have this box." He held it up and examined it. "I feel the box is magic, like love."

Joshua and Laurie looked at each other like this guy was crazy but then again, as their stare deepened, maybe not so crazy. Joshua cleared his throat and said, "Alright Herr Karl, we're going to get some lunch and let you do your work. What time do you want us back?"

"Come back in three hours. By then, the box will be open or it will not. A four-tooth skeleton key lock is a challenge. If I am successful, we'll look at the contents together." Joshua put his hand on the old man's shoulder and gave a squeeze. Laurie kissed him on the cheek. He giggled a little.

The couple left with the back pack and suitcase in tow and walked through the sales part of the store, completely ignoring Reinhardt. Joshua surveyed the city street looking for any threat. There were several to worry about, the two guys from the train, Juliette, a possible guy from Barcelona and now maybe Reinhardt was going to be a problem. Reinhardt did not directly threaten them, but Joshua thought Reinhardt was a smarmy little bastard.

As they were standing in the doorway, the tram came by and stopped a block away. Joshua suggested they hop the tram, ride ten or twelve blocks down the track and find a place to have lunch. Laurie agreed. They bought day passes which were so expensive, Joshua severely rolled his eyes and said something in French she felt sure was a curse word.

On the tram, Joshua asked, "How much money do you have left? We should be broker than broke."

"Oh, I found another two twenties in my tote," Laurie was still lying.

"I feel like a bum. You've been paying for everything."

"Don't worry, if it wasn't for you, I would have been caught several times over."

"Look!" Joshua pointed. "How about that deli?"

They stood and jumped off the tram at the next stop, two blocks from the deli. Walking side by side, Joshua was pulling the suitcase and carrying the pack. Laurie said, "I'm starving. All this intrigue makes me horny."

"Horny!"

"I meant to say 'hungry'. It makes me 'hungry'!"

"For what it's worth, it makes me hungry-horny too." Both were laughing as they entered the deli.

They ordered a basic charcuterie board, sat in a window table, ate and drank wine like there was not a care in the world. Burgeoning love overshadowed the adversity. Although, Joshua did scan the streets every time he could tear his eyes away from hers.

"You know we have to quit spending money. Or we should find a pawn shop and sell our assets. I'm sure you're on your last few euros and I was broke after the first taxi fare." Joshua looked up at her for confirmation.

He continued, "I can't keep bumming off you. And you know." He looked her in the eyes as she popped a grape in her mouth. "This will be a night under the stars. Neither one of us have enough money for a hotel."

"Unless we hock our stuff, right?" She now looked at him for confirmation.

"We could probably sell enough for a night or two in a hotel if we were good negotiators."

"Then that's what we do. Your job is to find me a place where I can sell my stuff."

"What about my stuff?" Joshua added.

"You hang on to yours until we need it. You'll be the safety net, a parachute, the oasis in the desert."

"I get it. Enough of the metaphors."

Joshua asked the counter worker where they could pawn some items. He directed them a few blocks to the north. A place called Noah's.

Lunch finished and wine glasses empty, they headed north to find Noah's. In three blocks they found the store. It was unmistakable with a large black and yellow hand painted sign. Laurie bent down over her suitcase and took out a few things. One of them was a little pouch containing her jewelry.

She gave Joshua some instructions. "You stay here. I'm going to go in alone. If the clerk is a man, I'll do business with him and be right out. If it's a woman, I'll come out and you go in."

"Are you going to flirt with the guy?"

"Of course." She smiled at Joshua, turned and went into the store. It looked more like a second hand or antique store rather than a pawn shop. Joshua waited with great anticipation. He felt like a doofus on the corner with his rugged pack and frilly suitcase.

In five minutes, Laurie came out smiling from ear to ear.

"Well?" he asked.

She held up a wad of bills. "Four-hundred euros!"

Joshua was astounded. "All I can say is the clerk must have been a man. A very lonely man."

She tried to hand him the money but he pulled his hands back. "That's yours."

"Here take a hundred." She tried to hand him five twenties. "Just in case I need your help to buy me out of trouble."

Joshua slowly took the money and said, "Just for emergencies," and stuffed the money in his pocket.

Little did Joshua know, Laurie didn't sell anything. As soon as she was in the store, she hid her valuables in a tote pocket and peeled off four-hundred euros from her secret stash of money she received from the Gentleman, God rest his soul. She felt bad about hiding the money and didn't really know why she was doing it, but there you have it, she was lying to Joshua.

Chapter 14

Laurie grabbed her suitcase handle from Joshua and said, "Let's go check into a hotel. I saw one back on the main street."

"Maybe we shouldn't get a hotel on the main street. It's expensive and obvious. How about that one." Joshua pointed to a hotel called The Habitat half way down the block. It was a walk up next to a meat market.

Laurie crinkled her nose up at it. "It's perfect," she said as sarcastically as possible.

Joshua was excited. They haven't slept more than an uncomfortable hour or two in the last couple of days. The thought of sleep, in a bed, next to Laurie….

Joshua dragged Laurie along and checked in, paid cash for one night and were in the sparsely appointed room, evaluating their choice.

Joshua said, "Not bad, right? Clean, quiet, dark. Perfect for a good night's sleep."

"It doesn't even have a television," Laurie complained.

Joshua dropped his pack to the floor and stood in front of her. "Are you really going to watch TV?"

"I guess not." She wrapped her arms around his neck and kissed him more deeply than she'd ever kissed anyone. Their full body press stirred something in Joshua both emotionally and physically.

Laurie pulled away. "Wait. Before you get all worked up." They both looked down at the big bulge in his pants. "Sorry," she said. "But before we do anything, let's go back to see the old man."

Joshua stood with his hands on his hips as if he were in pain. He looked up at the ceiling, back down again and blew out a large breath. "Okay. But we have to go right now or…well, we got to go now."

They stepped out, locked the door leaving the pack and suitcase inside. Joshua quickly retraced their steps back to the tram stop, standing around the corner, out of view from the crowded boulevard. Seeing the tram approaching, they stepped out and boarded using their day passes.

They wrapped up in each other on the seat, still feeling the effects of the passionate wet kiss. Reluctantly, they hopped off the tram a long block from Cartier's. As soon as they exited the tram, Joshua grabbed Laurie's arm and yanked her into the doorway of a high-end clothing store.

"What are you doing?" Laurie protested.

"Look down the block in front of Cartier's."

Laurie squinted in that direction. "Oh hell no. That's that bitch!"

Juliette was standing outside the Cartier's, looking up and down the street.

Laurie latched on to Joshua's arm, "She followed us, didn't she?"

Joshua thought for a while. "I'm not sure. I think she may be doing the same thing we did."

Laurie looked inquisitive. "What did we do?"

"We went looking for the nearest jeweler. I think she knows what's in the box and I'm willing to bet it's jewels of some kind."

"The kind fit for royalty?"

"Exactly that kind. The kind worth killing for. The kind worth following someone half way across Europe and sending young women on secret missions." They watched as Juliette got in an Uber and sped off in the opposite direction.

"We've got to get down there and see if Karl is okay." Joshua took Laurie's hand and half way pulled her down the street.

"What if she took the box?" Laurie asked as they were now jogging.

"Then they have it. I wouldn't have a clue how to get it back."

They burst through the front door nearly scaring Reinhardt to death. "Oh, it's you," Reinhardt said in a disappointed manner. Karl came out from the back. "There's the lovers."

Laurie walked over to Karl, hugged him and said, "Thank God."

Joshua wasted no time and asked, "What did that woman want?"

Karl took the multi-lens head band off and rubbed his face. "She wanted to know if any young people have been in the store trying to sell something unusual."

"What did you tell them?" Laurie asked.

"The same thing I tell everyone else with inquiries about Cartier customers…our client transactions are confidential."

Reinhardt chimed in, "I would have told her about you. I think you are doing something illegal."

Laurie and Joshua laughed.

"Why are you laughing," queried Reinhardt.

Laurie answered, "We don't know what we're doing. I was asked to take the box to a man in the hopes of getting plane fare home. The man was murdered."

Reinhardt blanched white.

"And at least three people are chasing us. Juliette, the girl who just came in here, is one of them. We lost the other guys, the murderers, at the train station. At least I hope we did. For all I know, they could be right outside the door."

Reinhardt put his hand to his throat and looked out the window, "Oh my God. What are we going to do?"

The old man spoke up, "I know what to do." All eyes turned to Karl. "We look into the mysterious box."

Joshua exclaimed, "You got it open!"

"Yes, son, I did." He turned to go back to the workshop.

All three followed closely behind. Laurie was about to bust out of her skin with anticipation. Joshua took it all in stride. It wasn't his box. Reinhardt was giddy with excitement through transference. He had no idea what was going on.

They all entered the workshop, standing abreast, gawking at the old purple velvet box on the work table under the bright lamplight.

"Who wants to open it?" asked Karl

"Me, I do, I do," Reinhardt couldn't control himself.

"I think Karl should have the honors. What do you think Laurie?" Joshua asked, looking Laurie in the eyes.

"Perfect. Karl, would you please open the box?" Laurie touched the old man on his shoulder.

Karl quivered a little, like a cold chill or strong emotion ran through him. "It would be my honor, children."

In unison, they inched forward to the work table. Karl strapped on his lens contraption and methodically took a seat. He was moving slowly and deliberately, like someone attempting to defuse a bomb. His bent fingers grasp the box, and with little fanfare or warning, he opened the lid of the box and set it down on the table to observe.

Each of them was craning their necks to see into the box better. "What is it?" asked Reinhardt.

"I think it may be a miracle," replied the old man.

Laurie and Joshua looked on in silence.

The old craftsman, turned the box over and emptied the contents into his hand. He made a sound like one would make upon hearing sad news. The utterance was Karl's way of showing excitement.

He set the object on the table directly under the lamp. It sparkled and glistened. The old man put his hands in his lap, tears welling in his eyes.

"It's beautiful. But what is it?" asked Laurie.

Joshua answered, "I think it's a Faberge egg!"

"Not just an egg, my boy," Karl said. "It's one of the lost imperial eggs. There were fifty-two imperial eggs. Six are lost. Now one is found!"

"It's beautiful," Laurie said again.

"What's it worth, what's it worth?" Reinhardt was acting four years old, but he couldn't help it.

"Worth?" Karl said to no one in particular. "What price is such beauty? What price do you put on history?" He went on to explain, "Peter Carl Faberge made eggs for the Imperial Russian family. By the way, I was named Karl after Mr. Faberge. My father was also a jeweler and idolized the House of Faberge. My apologies, I digress. He made as many as sixty-nine eggs, fifty-two were imperial eggs. This one is the Alexander the Third Commemorative made in 1909. It's been lost for over a hundred years. Now it is found."

Laurie and Joshua held hands and gave each other a squeeze.

"What's it worth? What's it worth?" Reinhardt was a broken record.

"Faberge eggs have sold from time to time at varying prices. This one was given to Nicholas the Second, who gave it to his mother, the dowager. Inside the egg should be a gold bust of Alexander. The things inside the eggs are called the surprise."

Karl reached up and gently manipulated the egg. It opened, revealing a tiny gold bust of the monarch. "This may be the first time this egg has been opened in over a hundred years." Karl took a handkerchief from his pocket and wiped his eyes. Laurie once again, put her hand on his shoulder.

"What's it worth? What's it worth?" Reinhardt was nearly in a panic.

"Ah, yes. The value of such a rare thing." Karl was still emotional.

Reinhardt bounced on his toes.

Karl thought carefully before making the appraisal. "An egg came to market recently and sold for nearly twenty-million euros." Reinhardt was about to faint. "This egg…" He paused to catch his breath. "This egg should fetch thirty-million euros."

Chapter 15

After staring dumbfoundedly at the egg for several minutes, Laurie broke the silence, "What do we do now?"

Karl replied, "I can't get past the now."

Joshua said, "Who owns this? Is it stolen?"

"The world just lost this treasure," Karl spoke. "One day, there was an Imperial Russia. The next, there was not. Some eggs were sold after the revolution to help finance the country. Some were looted, others, like this one, were lost."

Joshua looked at Laurie, "Should we go to Barcelona and try to find the guy who first made contact with you?"

"Bad idea," Karl was shaking his head.

"Why?" asked Laurie.

"These are not good people. If the egg was missing or stolen, there would be international headlines in the news. I think the egg was recently found and whoever has possession is the owner. And right now, that's you, my child." Karl looked at Laurie.

"Me! I was just supposed to carry it from Barcelona to Zurich. I didn't even do that very well."

"Never-the-less, you have possession at this moment. I suggest you take the egg, leave the country and go far from here as fast as possible. I would go swiftly, my child."

Laurie looked at Joshua for confirmation. "I think he's right. We need to go. Juliette is out there close somewhere. Those other two guys, the murderers, who knows, they may be walking in the front door right now."

"Oh my God," Reinhardt spontaneously exclaimed.

Karl put the egg back in its box. "Do you want me to lock it or leave it unlocked?"

Laurie said, "Lock it."

Karl shut the box and they all heard a snap. The box was secure, requiring an expert jeweler or special four-prong key to open it. Karl handed the box to Laurie. Laurie threw it in her tote.

"Run, children." Karl said as Laurie kissed him on the cheek again.

Joshua took Laurie's arm and rushed her to the front door. Karl and Reinhardt stood behind the counter waiting for the couple to exit. Laurie was teary eyed, "I'll pay you when I can."

"You already have my child," Karl replied. "This has been the best day since my schön Gelda's passing. I should be thanking you."

Laurie blew the old man a kiss and asked Joshua, "Are we going to the hotel?"

Joshua shushed her until they were outside the store and walking toward the tram stop.

"Why'd you shush me?"

"I didn't want them to hear where we're going. If Juliette, or worse, the two murderers, come back to the store and ask about us, the less Karl and especially Reinhardt know the better. People are willing to kill over this. It's thirty-million unclaimed euros. If Juliette or the murderers get it from us, it won't even be stealing. Nobody owns the egg."

Once back at their meager hotel, the couple tried to formulate a plan. Joshua spoke first, "I think we should make our way to London and put the egg up for auction at Christie's. Once you sell it, the cash will be yours. No one can take it away from you. You can put it in a bank and transfer it around the world where ever you want. If the old man is right about the value, you should clear over twenty million."

Laurie sat on the bed with her shoes off trying to think of a better idea. Joshua all of a sudden decided she looked mighty cute sitting up there barefooted in her short-shorts. "I can't think of anything better. How do we get to London?" she asked.

Joshua wasn't thinking at all, he was too busy fantasizing. "Joshua?"

"Yes?" He snapped out of it.

"How do we get to London?"

"Count your cash and see exactly how much you have. Trains or buses are probably the cheapest way for you to get there. Maybe take a ferry across the channel would be inconspicuous." Joshua was thinking.

"Joshua, you're coming with me, right?"

"You need to get out of this city and out of this country quickly. I don't think you have enough money for both of us to escape."

"I don't want to go alone."

"You don't have a choice."

Laurie sat on the edge of the bed with her hands in her lap. "What if I tell you there is a way for both of us to go. Would you come?"

"If you want me to. Sure."

"Okay, don't be mad. I've been lying to you."

Joshua stood with his hands on his hips, "About what?" At this point Joshua was prepared for any answer.

"Money," she said." I was paid two thousand euros by the Gentleman to do the things I told you about. I've something around fifteen hundred left of it." She looked at Joshua's countenance to see if he was angry. "And I didn't hock my necklaces and rings. I just showed you some of the money I already had." She drew her face up like she was waiting to be slapped.

"Well, I don't like being lied to but I completely understand. Is there anything else I need to know?"

She shook her head from side to side. "Then I have a confession," Joshua countered.

"Oh?"

"Yeah." He reached down to his hiking boot and pulled out a twenty-euro bill and held it up. "I've been holding out with a little emergency money too."

They both laughed and she flew off the bed into his arms. He dropped his last twenty on the floor and embraced her. They kissed like they were being chased by international assassins and this was their last night in Switzerland, a truth more than an analogy. He started inching her towards the bed. Once at the edge, they went down with Joshua on top. Laurie wrapped him up in her incredibly long legs. She felt him spring to life at the crotch. Finally, she thought, he's finally going to take me.

Joshua raised up and started trying to undo the tiny buttons on her blouse. His big fingers mostly fumbled. She slapped his hands away and finished what he started. Joshua grabbed his shirt and pulled it up over his head and it was on the floor in a matter of two seconds.

While he showered under the scupper, naked, at the Saint Die station, she couldn't see the details because of the darkness and panic from the circumstance. Now, in the brightness of the hotel room, two feet away, Joshua looked incredible. How the hell does he stay in shape, she thought. A thousand push-ups a day wasn't enough to sculp what she was looking at.

She tossed her sleeveless blouse to the side of the bed and lay back. She was wearing this see-through mauve colored bra. Joshua couldn't take his eyes off the vision. He reached up to her tight khaki shorts and started to undo them. He had the zipper half way down when there was a knock the door.

Joshua put a finger to his lips indicating to be quiet. She laid quietly, half naked on the bed wanting to scream because of the interruption. The knock on the door continued. Joshua shook his head side-to-side.

"Pizza delivery," came a voice in English from the other side of the door. Joshua still shook his head. The person or persons, knocked again. Neither Joshua or Laurie moved. After a long silence, the door knob turned and the door rattled in the frame.

Joshua reached in his pocket and removed the tactical folding knife. He slowly opened it so the blade lock wouldn't make a clicking sound. In fifteen more seconds, footsteps moved on down the hall. Joshua lay down by Laurie on the bed and whispered in her ear. "I think they were just trying to see if we were in here. Obviously, they know we've checked into this hotel and this particular room. Now, all they have to do is wait, and catch us coming or going. They'll be there in the lobby, a café across the street, standing at a bus stop, somewhere. But they are definitely out there."

Laurie drew her knees up and wrapped her arms around them, "Okay, what do we do?"

Joshua didn't know how they would do it, but he said, "Sneak out of here."

Chapter 16

Joshua asked Laurie, "How would you feel about leaving your suitcase behind?"

"Why?" she asked as she was putting her blouse back on.

"I think we ought to leave the suitcase and backpack in the room, put some clothes around like the place has been lived in, leave a clue or two to throw them off and then we find a way out of here without being seen."

"With just the clothes on our backs?"

"Yes, and a few other essentials we can easily carry. We can travel faster without our luggage. If they bust in here, which they will, it's only a matter of time, then they'll find our fake clues. Maybe they'll think we're coming back to the room. Hopefully that will buy us some time while we're heading to the French coast. What do you think?"

"I think we're both nuts."

Laurie opened her suitcase, hung up a few clothes, put some more on the dresser and set up her toiletries as if she were going to use them.

Joshua threw some underwear on the floor and hung socks on the back of the chair. Laurie looked at him with her hands on her hips. Joshua saw her staring at him and said, "Looks real, right?"

Joshua asked her to change into something a little less American. Khaki short-shorts and a sleeveless white blouse made it hard to blend in. She complied and emerged from the bathroom wearing dark grey skinny jeans, a maroon blouse, a black sweater and black flats. Put a beret on her head and she would have been a poster girl for a metropolitan French setting. Perfect.

"Here's my plan," said Josh. "We load everything we can into your gigantic purse."

"It's a tote."

"Whatever. We go out the door, turn right, away from the elevators and main stairs. Then it's up the service stairs at the end of the hall to the roof. This whole block is made up of four-story buildings. If we can access the roof, run down a few buildings and exit through another business."

Laurie had a blank look on her face. "Really? That's the plan?"

"Feel free to come up with a better one."

"Before we go." She reached into the tote and pulled out the money, handing Joshua a one-hundred-euro bill and five twenties. "In case we get separated or you need something and we're apart."

Joshua said, "You keep giving me money, I feel cheap," but he took it with a nod of his head and a smile. Laurie pitched a couple of more essentials into her tote and looked up at him as an indication she was ready. Joshua went to the door and quietly opened it. Laurie was right on his back. Joshua looked out and saw nothing in the hall. He held the door open for Laurie, "Go, go." Laurie took off toward the exit stairs. Joshua closed the door, making sure it locked and joined Laurie in the escape.

They went through the exit door and headed up the stairs. No problems so far. Joshua hoped they could get on the roof or this plan would fail before it even started. At the top of the stairs, the door leading to the roof had a push bar to open it. There was a warning written in French, German and Italian. Joshua suspected the door was alarmed and told Laurie so. They stopped to inspect it. Joshua could see two wires running out of the top of the door into the door jamb. He pulled out his knife and tried to slice through the wires but the knife didn't cut through. Instead it pulled both wires out of the door. They hung loosely in the air without triggering the alarm. Joshua pushed the door open and they were on the roof. Laurie was beginning to think the plan might work but with all the misfortunes surrounding her as of late, she deferred her enthusiasm.

Moving down the roof tops was easy. The hardest part was negotiating a three-foot-high wall separating the individual businesses below. At the last building, they decided to try the roof access door but it was locked from the inside. Joshua looked over the back of the building to the alley and discovered an old rusty exterior metal fire escape. "Here!" he called out. "We can go down here."

Laurie looked at the thing with disgust but scaled the wall on to the top metal landing. Joshua followed. They easily descended to the last landing but from there they had to extend a ladder down to get to the ground. Joshua beat on the ladder for a full two minutes before the rust and atrophy surrendered and the ladder slid into position. They climbed down into the alley.

Joshua saw a door across the alley labeled Parfum Internationale. He pulled on the handle and the door opened. They ste pped into a ritzy perfume shop, "bonjoured" a few sales clerks and walked right out the front door to the street on the next block over. Joshua said to Laurie, "Let's find a tram and jump on it no matter where it goes. We'll hop off someplace safe and make a better, long term plan."

"Okay," she said as she was practically running to keep up with him.

Three blocks away at a right angle to the road on which their hotel was located, they came to a tram stop, and the tram was in sight. They ran to catch it using their day passes. Joshua studied a map of the route posted at the front of the car. All he could tell was this tram took them away from the city center. Exactly what they needed right now. Laurie sat beside him, breathing hard from exertion and excitement. Her hand on his thigh.

The tram came to its final stop in a working man's neighborhood. They disembarked and found a coffee shop nearby. Joshua insisted on splitting an American cup. Laurie really wanted to have a half-caf latte but that would have been nine euros for two cups. She acquiesced and Joshua skimmed a little all black off the top into a paper cup before Laurie started doctoring her coffee. Laurie decided a creamed up and super-sugared plain ol' cup of coffee wasn't so bad.

Joshua moved around the shop asking different people about where they were and how was the best way to get to different places. He sat back down at the table with Laurie and offered another suggestion.

"Two blocks over is a bus stop that has a number 47 bus that will take us to the main bus station where we can catch a bus to Paris. It's an all-night trip. I think we're fairly safe because we don't even know where we are so how can anyone else know either. What's your vote?"

Laurie opined, "Just what I'm looking forward to, an all-night bus ride."

"So that's a yes?"

"Of course, it's a yes. I'm with you."

"Finish up, then. Let's go."

Laurie slurped it down then put the cup on the table. Night had fallen and the streets weren't well lighted. Joshua was hoping he was going the right direction. Laurie never doubted him.

In exactly three blocks, Joshua looked to the left and saw the bus stop. They sat on the bench, holding each other in the chilling air. The whole scene reminded Laurie of Saint Die. In twenty minutes, bus 47 came into view. They boarded using their day passes which turned out to be good for all sorts of municipal transportation.

Laurie sat next to Joshua, holding his arm and leaning her head on his shoulder. She was thinking about how long it had been since she had any sleep, or sex for that matter. How many times can one lovelorn couple be interrupted before consummation. She squirmed a little in the seat thinking about it.

At the main bus station, they found a ticket counter and purchased tickets to Paris, with two bus changes along the way. It would be a long and miserable night. Joshua was the only thing making it all worthwhile. This man was a keeper.

Just before 10:00 pm, they boarded a bus heading west. This bus was much more comfortable than the city bus. It had a TV on the back of the seat in front of them, reclining lounge chair seats, an electrical plug, and a USB port available which did neither one of them any good.

Before the bus traveled the first kilometer, Laurie was reclining and asleep. Joshua was almost asleep but he couldn't keep from thinking how much he wanted her. Eventually, mere thoughts of having his way with her were not enough for him to keep from succumbing to sleep also.

They stirred a little at each stop which were quite frequent but they didn't fully arouse. At 11:00 pm, they changed buses at a large station somewhere on the border of France. An hour later they were deep into the French countryside with very few stops.

Chapter 17

Sometime after sun-up, the bus rambled into a giant terminus in Paris. Joshua woke Laurie who, to her horror, was sleeping with her mouth open. Joshua tried not to make it obvious he was looking at her as she cleaned spittle off her chin.

"Okay," Joshua said. "Here's the plan. We go to the train station, hop the first train to Calais. Then from Calais, we snag a ferry to Dover. There should be at least one every hour or so. From Dover we catch another train to London. In London we can get lost in its ten-million people, get a decent place to stay, eat something good, sleep…"

"Yes, sleep," Laurie interrupted.

Joshua continued, "Sleep and find Christie's."

"I like the plan." She noticed he didn't mention anything about having sex which was a high priority. She was hoping sex was a part included in the plan section entitled, 'get a decent place to stay'.

They went to the entrance where all the taxis were queued and within minutes, they were at the train station. "I don't much like train stations anymore," Laurie said under her breath.

"Me either," agreed Joshua. Why that was said, he didn't know because both of them loved the trains.

Forty euros slid through a plexiglass hole at the ticket counter and they were ready for the train to Calais. Sitting on a bench, trying to stay awake the thirty minutes before their train boarded, Laurie wrapped herself around Joshua's arm and laid her head on his shoulder.

Out of the blue, Laurie said, "I've been to Paris twice, this train station twice and I've never seen the Eiffel Tower."

"Well, I can't pretend to know how an auction at Christie's works or how soon they'll hold one but the day after the auction…. you can come back and buy the Eiffel Tower."

Joshua looked down at her and she was smiling, half asleep. In a mumble, she said, "Of all the train stations I've ever been to, I liked Saint Die the best."

"And just how many stations have you been to?"

"Six, but I've been to this one twice."

Joshua felt her head go heavy on his shoulder as she slipped into slumber. His thoughts were of her beautiful body ready for him at Saint Die. Her last thought before she fell asleep was, God, I hope I don't drool on him.

Joshua nudged her awake and they took the tote bag to the train car. She nearly stumbled up the steps to the interior like a sleepy six-year-old instead of a grown woman. Joshua held her arm for support, plus, he liked touching her.

A relative short train journey and a very quick taxi ride brought them to the coast. Numerous ferries traversed the channel daily and their ferry left in an hour. Instead of assuming a position on a bench, they went in search of food. It was 11:00 am and they were trying to decide on breakfast, brunch or lunch when a person caught Joshua's eye. He grabbed Laurie and pulled her aside, "Look at that guy up ahead dressed in black."

Laurie scanned the area, "The one across the street?"

"Yeah."

"What about him?"

Joshua thought for a moment trying to convince himself that he was acting crazy. "He just looks out of place."

Laurie took Joshua's hand, "How could anyone follow us. We took a tram, a bus, a train and now we're getting on a ferry. Our travel was almost random and we haven't stopped for more than an hour and that was just because we needed to wait on the next form of transportation. I refuse to believe we have been followed." Laurie crossed her arms in a pout.

"I know you're tired and hungry…"

"And filthy," she injected.

"I think we should hide until the ferry. Stay off the street, stay out of cafés." Joshua raised his eyebrows, "What do you think?"

"But…." Was all she could muster.

They went back to the ferry wharf and stood with a crowd of tourist waiting to board. The tourists were all part of a Trafalgar Travel tour group for senior students at the University of Virginia. Laurie and Joshua fit right in. The couple yucked it up with the students until it was time to board and then they all went on together. Joshua was ever vigilant for the man in black, of course most of the French were wearing some form of black or dark colors so that particular man would be hard to spot.

Joshua stood on deck scanning the area until the ferry was several hundred yards off shore. He relaxed and went to sit with Laurie who was eating a croissant she purchased at the miniature snack bar. She handed one to Joshua. "Thanks," he said as he saluted her with the bread.

"Any sign of the asshole?"

Joshua blinked, "No, I didn't see any assholes out there."

She laughed a little, "Sorry, I'm tired."

"Me too. But, by tonight, we'll be laying up in a London hotel with a hot shower, clean sheets and full bellies."

Laurie never heard anything much past 'laying up in a hotel'. She had been traveling with this beautiful man for what seemed like forever and he hasn't even made it to first base. Not even first base, she lamented to herself in frustration. That was going to remedied toot sweet, as an American would say.

Laurie finished her croissant, leaned over on Joshua and shut her eyes. Laurie had grown up in Louisiana and spent some time on bass boats in the bayous and shrimp boats in the bay with her Dad, but she had never been on a ship the size of this ferry in a rolling English Channel. In a few minutes she awoke, with her stomach screaming 'the sea is angry today, my friend' and she jumped up to find the head.

She was going to vomit, no way around it. When she got to the bathroom, there was a line of Virginia Cavaliers waiting to purge the excessive amounts of beer and wine consumed their last night in France. Laurie tried to find a trash can but the first one she saw was occupied with two young women casually talking, taking turns holding each other's hair and throwing up.

Laurie exited the cabin and spied a bucket under a firehose locker. Holding the bucket with one hand and her long auburn hair with the other, she purged. Then again. And…once more. When done, she replaced the bucket where she found it, feeling somewhat guilty and embarrassed.

When she got back to their seats, Joshua was gone.

Chapter 18

Laurie didn't panic, although she really wanted to. Taking a few steps back, she stood behind a column scanning the large cabin for Joshua, the man in black, or whoever the hell else could possibly be playing this deadly game. Joshua came out of the men's bathroom looking out of place carrying her tote bag. Laurie ran over to him and smacked him hard on the chest, then hugged him. "Don't scare me like that!"

"Geez, I had to pee."

"You're not allowed anymore."

"To what? Pee?" he asked while still holding her tightly.

"Yes. I thought you left me alone."

Joshua smiled and pressed her into him, "Never."

After hugging it out, they went to their seats to complete the uneventful journey across the channel. Although Laurie was exhausted, she didn't dare sleep, afraid Joshua might vanish again and she couldn't stand the thought. They stayed awake by telling each other what they would do if they had thirty million euros.

Their answers to "What would you do with thirty million euros?" were fairly standard. They'd travel, eat good food, drink fine wine, have nice stuff and basically try to buy their way into being a better person and finding happiness. When they finally got down to it, neither one of them really had a clue about how they would spend thirty million euros.

Over the last few miles of the ferry trip, Joshua and Laurie stood on deck marveling at the cliffs. Laurie had never been to England but Joshua once road the Chunnel Train from Paris to London. The boat docked in Dover and all the people herded off. Many of the passengers, including the Virginia Cavaliers, were headed the same way as Laurie and Joshua, to the train station.

The first two trains going to London were full. The couple sat for nearly three hours before they could board the third train. The scenery was typical British countryside which was gorgeous but lost on the weary travelers. All they wanted was to land somewhere safe, eat real food and sleep, have sex and then sleep again. After eating some calorie laden, non-nutritious train food, Laurie couldn't keep her eyes open any longer.

The seats on this train were arranged such that Laurie could put her head in Joshua's lap. This made for a comfortable pillow for Laurie, but Joshua found it anything but comfortable. Every time she scratched her nose, twisted or otherwise adjusted her position, Joshua had to fight the urge to become aroused. Needless to say, it was a very long hour and a half before they reached London.

On the platform at St Pancras International Station, Joshua was stamping his feet trying to get blood circulating through his lower legs again. Laurie knew what he was doing and said, "Sorry. I would suppose that most of the time a woman's head in your lap would assure a blood flow in a different direction."

Joshua looked at her sideways, "Ha Ha," he said sarcastically.

Once Joshua's legs worked properly, they walked out of the terminal, hand in hand, and stood in the afternoon sun of London.

Although the sun was shining brightly, the temperature was somewhere around sixty-nine degrees with a breeze. Laurie shivered and offered, "Geez, I think it's colder here than it was at Saint Die….in the storm…at night…. wet and naked."

"Welcome to London." Joshua thought for a minute and said, "I have an idea." He grabbed her hand, spun her around and they went back into the train station. He pulled her into a pub called Betjeman Arms. Joshua ordered a pint of Guinness and Laurie ordered one of Stella Artois. Each ordered a plate of fish and chips. While waiting for their food and sipping on cold beer, they decided the very next thing to do was find a hotel and sleep. After a good night's rest, they would go to a moderately priced clothing store and pick out a new set of clothes. They had been wearing their only set of clothes for the last twenty-four hours and they were starting to feel a little rank.

The fish and chips came out as a heaping pile on giant plates. It was more food than any six people could eat but they dove in and did some damage. Joshua was halfway through his second Guinness when Laurie declared she was finished. She had one piece of fish and a handful of chips left. If they had brought out a plate the size of what she had leftover, she would have not been disappointed. Joshua managed to eat most of his.

They leaned back and made predictions they would pop, split open or otherwise burst if they ate one more bite. Joshua stood on weary legs and said, "Let's go find a place to stay." They exited the station, crossed the road, walking blindly hoping to find accommodations. What they found was The Harry Potter Shop at Platform 9. Laurie wanted to go in, Joshua talked her out of it by saying they could go tomorrow after a good night's sleep. A hundred yards further and they found the Great Northern Hotel.

The hotel cost 150 euros which Joshua thought was a good price for the King's Cross area. They could have found a cheaper one but they were dog tired. Not sure how tired a dog really gets but dogs do sleep and average of fourteen hours a day and that's what they needed.

The rooms were perfect in Joshua's eyes, they had a bed and a shower, done. Laurie checked for a hair dryer, a mini fridge, microwave, a coffee pot and high-quality shampoos and conditioners. Check! The room met with Laurie's seal of approval.

Laurie went to shower first. Joshua sat on the bed fighting sleep even though there was a naked woman in the next room, one unlocked door away. Laurie felt it necessary to wash her long hair. She didn't want Joshua burying his face in a mat of dirty hair when he was lying on top of her. Joshua heard the hair dryer going and groaned. Her hair was full and long requiring at least ten minutes to dry. Joshua threw himself on the floor and ripped off ten push-ups in a matter of five seconds. He sat back on the bed with his heart beating faster and more awake. In ten minutes when he still heard the hair dryer, he did ten more quick push-ups. As soon as he sat on the bed, the dryer shut off. Oh, thank goodness, he thought.

She stepped out with a towel wrapped around her, covering her breasts and the other essentials, barely. Her hair was perfect and her legs were long. Joshua swallowed and stood up like royalty just walked in.

"Hurry up now, I'll be waiting out here."

Joshua did as he was told. He took a shower, washed his hair and contemplated shaving off his five-day stubble but there was no razor available. She would have to suffer beard burn everywhere because he was planning on putting his mouth in all the right places. He ran the hair dryer over his black locks for a minute and combed them out with the wide tooth comb Laurie left on the counter. He brushed his teeth with a toothbrush he thinks Laurie put there for him or maybe it was a hotel amenity. He didn't care. After numerous cups of coffee, beer and several meals, he would have used a stick to brush his teeth.

He looked in the mirror and decided it was as good as it was going to get at that moment. He stepped into the bedroom with a towel covering his essentials. He was holding it in place because he was dropping it to the floor in a matter of seconds.

Disappointment crushed him. Laurie was on top of the covers, fast asleep, lying on her stomach with the towel she was wrapped in hanging off the side of the bed. Joshua smiled through the frustration because she was beautiful. He covered her with half the bedspread and slid under the sheets by her side. His last thought before he faded into slumber was how many times can one man possibly get blocked?

Chapter 19

"Housekeeping!" and a knock on the door. Joshua jumped completely out of bed, naked with evidence of morning excitement protruding in front of him. Laurie sat bolt upright not bothering to cover her breasts with the spread. They both were wide-eyed and in a state of panic until Joshua regained his wits.

"Can you come back in a little bit?" he asked.

"Yes." The sound of a rolling cart gave them some relief and even more when the voice called out "Housekeeping," at the next door. Without saying a word, Joshua went into the bathroom, stayed a few minutes, flushed the commode and came out fully dressed.

Laurie's eyes showed disappointment. "What are you doing?" she asked somewhat surprised.

"It's already 9:20. Check out is at 11:00. You still have to get dressed, we need to eat, we have to buy some new clothes, find the auction house, broker a deal, find another place to stay and make a long-term plan…"

Before he went on any longer, Laurie stopped him. "Okay, I get it." She got up completely naked and strolled past him to the bathroom.

Joshua had some really, dirty, bad-boy thoughts. He shook his head to snap himself out of it.

In a record twenty-five minutes, she was prepared for the day. Although the clothes were the same ones she wore the day before, she looked stunning. It's amazing what a meal, a bath, a beer and a good night's sleep will do for some people.

Laurie picked up her tote and they were ready. The first item on the agenda was breakfast. The hotel provided a free breakfast and they decided to try that. It was late in the morning and the only thing available was a plate of drop scones drizzled with honey. Joshua facetiously said, "Well I guess we'll have to settle for these."

They ate as many of them as they could possibly eat. Carbed and sugared up to the max, they set off to compete their mission. First stop, at Laurie's insistence, was the Harry Potter Shop at Platform 9¾.

"This is not part of the plan," was all Joshua could muster. When she looked at him forlornly with those big brown eyes and long auburn hair flowing down the side of her face, he caved in rather quickly.

She went through the shop hurriedly, at Joshua's urging, and bought Hermione's wand in a box for fifty euros. She tossed it in her tote looking pleased with herself. "It's for my little sister."

Joshua realized, he knew very little about Laurie, basics, but no details. He supposed no one really knew anyone else until they spent some time with each other. Afterall, they had only been traveling together a few days but it seemed like weeks.

There was a giant, massive library down the block and Joshua thought it was a good place to get some information. "That's how they used to do it, right? Go to the library and do some research. Wow, this building is big."

It was the National Library with literally millions of books, magazines and articles. They went in and were a little overwhelmed, but one of the numerous desk clerks helped them with what they needed which was information on Christie's Auction House. The clerk was a fountain of information. He gave them the times Christie's was open, the location and which buses and undergrounds to take to get them there.

They popped up out of the tube at the Green Park station across the street from the Ritz London Hotel. Joshua knew they were getting close because everything started looking like money. They walked about five blocks to an area of high-end shops. Laurie settled into a Gucci for Women and purchased new pair of pants and a blouse. Euros flew out of her hand when she paid for them.

They walked another half a dozen blocks or so and came across Turnbull and Asser, a clothing store for men. This store specialized in shirts and Joshua bought one shirt off a hidden rack in the back that was marked as seconds. Even though the shirt was flawed, Joshua still paid thirty-eight euros. The Turnbull and Asser name tag had been removed to keep a sub-par shirt from being associated with their enterprise. Joshua thought it looked like a shirt, he needed a shirt and it was the cheapest one in the store. He didn't buy anything else.

Laurie looked beautiful in her new Gucci threads and Joshua could rock a tow sack. Their new apparel was fine for the task and their dirty clothes were stuffed in the tote. They continued their march to Christie's, only a few more blocks.

They turned the corner and there it was, a grey stone building with a red flag flying at the entrance. At the very bottom of the flag, the word 'CHRISTIES' was printed in white. Joshua thought the flag had a dumb design. At the front entrance to the renowned auction house, Laurie looked at her reflection in a window and applied some lipstick. They went in not knowing what to expect. Laurie was snuggly attached to Joshua's arm.

In less than three seconds a man approached who was impeccably dressed and reminded them of Reinhardt from Zurich. That time seemed like such a long while ago even though it had barely been a couple of days.

The man introduced himself as Edmond.

"Well Edmond," cooed Laurie. "We want an audience with the person in charge of all of this."

Edmond laughed a quick chortle and said, "That is impossible."

Joshua stepped forward and drew up his most imposing stance, "And why not?"

"That person, is not here today."

Laurie chimed in, "What person is in today?"

"Ms. Vanderweerdt is here but it will be impossible to see her too."

Joshua stood in Edmond's social space and said, "Why not?"

Edmond took a step backwards, "She's busy."

Joshua stepped forward, having this awkward sensation he was dancing with Edmond. "How do you know? Maybe I'll go see for myself." Joshua strode off in a direction in which he thought some offices might be found. He got about six steps when a security guard approached him. Joshua wasn't really going to cause a major scene in the most renowned auction house in the world but he wanted to give them a little excitement in their stuffy, highbrow lives.

The security guard was armed with a night stick and a small spray can of mace. Joshua was sure he wouldn't use the mace. Joshua couldn't imagine what Ms. Vanderweerdt might think if a lowly security guard stunk up the joint by spraying mace all over hell and gone.

Joshua was three inches taller and twenty solid pounds heavier than the guard. After spending four years in the Military Police, Joshua knew how to handle himself in a fight. This guard looked very British with puffy red cheeks, white skin and stiff upper lip. Joshua figured the only action this guard had ever seen was the continual fight against Edmond's disdain.

"Edmond, is there a problem?" came from an attractive blond woman, early forties, dressed impeccably, as she stepped around the corner.

"No, Ms. Vanderweerdt, these people are just leaving," said Edmond.

The elegant lady looked over the intruders twice before she decided Joshua and Laurie were the finest looking couple she had ever seen and she knew fine things. "What do you want?" she asked them.

Laurie looked at the striking woman and said, "Just a moment of your time."

"Alastair, come with us." Ms. Vanderweerdt waved her hand at the couple and the four of them went to a conference room, leaving Edmond standing in the middle of the foyer. "Alastair, you can wait outside the door," she instructed the security guard. They took seats at the conference table.

"Now, what's so important that you have to disrupt our afternoon?"

Laurie began talking. "I'm Laurie and this is Joshua."

"I'm Sarah," said Ms. Vanderweerdt.

Joshua began thinking maybe this lady was human compared to Edmond.

Laurie continued, "I'll leave out the sordid details but we have come into possession of one of the finest pieces of art in the world and we'd like to have it auctioned off at the earliest opportunity."

Sarah wasn't sure if they were crazy or not but continued with hopes it was true. Christie's hadn't had a true showpiece item to auction in a long time and maybe she stumbled on to something. "What do you have?" Sarah asked.

Laurie looked at Joshua, "Without telling you anything about it, I'd like for you to look it over and give me your opinion without any input from us."

"A mystery, I love a good mystery." Sarah rubbed her hands together. Joshua wasn't sure if she was teasing them or not.

"Funny, you're the second person who said that," added Laurie. "Karl, from Cartier's in Zurich said the same thing."

"Karl?" blurted out Sarah. "You now Karl?"

"We don't really know him, know him," she used air quotes, "but we met him a few days ago and he said we had something special."

Now Sarah was really excited because Karl was one of their appraisers for antique jewelry. The auction house used Karl because he was a master jeweler and was so old that he many times had firsthand knowledge of the item they wanted appraised.

"Where is this piece?" asked Sarah.

"It's in my tote," responded Laurie.

"Can I see it?"

"Yes and no," Laurie said, "It's in an antique box that takes a four-prong skeleton key to open. The key is actually two parts that fit together to make the four-prong key, with each set of teeth being unique. And we don't have either key. It takes a master jeweler or a lock smith to open it."

"Or a hammer," Joshua added, but neither of the ladies found his remark to be humorous.

"Do you want to see the box?" Laurie asked.

"Absolutely." Sarah was animated.

Laurie reached in her tote and set Hermione's wand box on the table.

Sarah looked at it thinking the whole routine was a ruse.

Laurie saw her reaction, "Oh no, not that. I bought that at the Harry Potter Shop for my little sister."

Sarah's face showed instant relief.

Laurie pulled out a wad of dirty clothes and put them in Joshua's lap. Joshua flushed red. Then Laurie set the purple velvet box with a four-prong lock on the table.

Sarah's eyes widened. Sarah had never seen a box like that before. Just the box was worth her time with the couple. Her mind ran wild with what might be inside. Sarah reached in a drawer under the conference table and pulled out a set of white cloth gloves and put them on. Joshua and Laurie looked at each other.

Joshua said, "I guess carrying this around in a bag f ull of dirty clothes probably wasn't the smartest thing to do." His statement fell on deaf ears.

"Can I pick it up?" Sarah asked. Laurie just made a gesture.

Sarah cradled the box in her fingers, turning it over and over, inspecting every inch.

"Alastair!" Sarah hollered. The security guard stuck his head in the door. "Go get Gustav, now."

The security guard ran off down the hall, the soles of his highly polished leather shoes slapping against the floor.

Sarah placed the box on the table and drew in a great breath. "This, is exciting."

Chapter 20

While they were waiting for Gustav, Sarah asked why a couple of Americans would come to Christie's in London instead of New York. Laurie told her they just met in Saint Die, France a couple of days ago, at the train station, in the rain. Laurie and Joshua looked into each other's eyes. Sarah took a deep breath because she was a sucker for love.

In a few minutes, footsteps rang out down the hall. Alastair opened the door for Gustav who entered in a huff not liking the fact he had been summoned. "Well?" he said.

Sarah spoke smoothly, "Gustav, this is Laurie and Joshua. They brought us a special item locked in a box for which we have no key. I hope you can open the box for us."

Gustav took out a handkerchief and wiped his sweaty forehead. He was not accustomed to being dragged down two floors at a fast walk. Gustav harrumphed and approached the desk. He was a middle-aged man with dark receding hair and a thin moustache. He was overweight from hours of sitting behind a jeweler's bench while eating biscuits and drinking tea with cream and sugar.

Sarah reached in the desk and pulled out another set of white cloth gloves. Gustav gave Sarah a look as he put them on. Joshua didn't understand the man's attitude. The jeweler seemed like this simple request was way beneath him.

Gustav picked up the box and examined the lock. Laurie started to explain, "It's a four-prong lock…"

Gustav cut her off, "I see what it is little Miss. I am the expert here."

Laurie and Joshua looked at each other. Joshua raised his eyebrows and mouthed the word 'expert' while pointing at the man and Laurie smiled. Joshua looked at Sarah and she was smiling too.

After a long period of time, Gustav finally declared, "I can open it." All three of the others leaned forward in their chairs. "I will need to make a mold of the key slot and fabricate a key for each section. Then I'll solder the four parts together to make the key and we'll have it open in no time."

Sarah asked, "How long is no time?"

Gustav didn't answer not wanting to set himself up to fail.

"Gustav," Sarah said in a sterner, supervisor-subordinate tone. "How long will it take you to open the box?"

"If I forego all of my other duties and solely work on this, I can open it in three days."

Laurie quickly injected, "Karl had it open in less than three hours."

Gustav made a spitting gesture and cursed Karl.

"I guess they know each other," Laurie said.

Sarah told Laurie that Gustav used to be an assistant under Karl but the relationship didn't work out.

"I can see why," said Joshua. "This is ridiculous," he continued. "We could fly to Zurich, get Karl to open the box, again, spend the night, fly back and still have it open quicker than Gustav can do it. Laurie, what do you say we fly to New York and auction it there?"

Sarah held up her hands saying, "Please wait, let's not be hasty. Alastair!" The security guard stuck his head in the door. "Go get everyone from Gustav's shop and bring them here."

"Ms. Vanderweerdt, that's a dozen people."

"I didn't say to count them. I said bring them here."

"Right away." The security guard was off and running, having more action today than in his entire career.

Gustav set the box on the table and removed his gloves. An obvious sign he was through handling it. In a moment, it sounded like a herd of buffalo coming down the hall. Alastair escorted all the craftsmen into the conference room.

Sarah stood behind the table and addressed the herd. "There is a crisis. We have reason to believe a priceless object is contained in this locked box. The lock requires a four-prong key with each prong having a separate set of teeth. I need the box open in less than three hours. Any suggestions?"

The herd moved toward the table. Laurie and Joshua got out of the way for fear of being trampled. The herd mumbled, cajoled and proselytized but no one came up with an answer. Eventually a younger craftswoman said, "I think I can get it open if I can take it back to the shop." She pushed her glasses back up her nose as she said it. The herd was stunned as were Joshua and Laurie.

Sarah was skeptical but said, "Alright Wilhelmina, take the box and see what you can do. The rest of you go back to work. You too Gustav." The young craftswoman gloved up and took the box with her.

Joshua looked at Laurie and asked if she was okay being out of sight of the box. Laurie shrugged, "They're professionals."

Sarah asked them if they wanted to wait or come back in a few hours. The couple chose to wait. Sarah ordered some bangers and mash and a pint each of stout to be delivered from the local pub. Sarah was turning out to be human afterall.

Thirty minutes after they finished their meal, Alastair came puffing into the room stating Wilhelmina got the box open. Wilhelmina entered the office cradling the box. She walked around the table and gingerly laid it down in front of Sarah.

Wilhelmina started to walk out. "Did you look inside?" Sarah asked.

"No, Ms. Vanderweerdt."

"Do you want to see?"

"Yes, Ms. Vanderweerdt."

"Come then. You too Alastair."

The five of them huddled around the table as Sarah put on gloves, stood up and slowly opened the box. Laurie and Joshua looked at each other waiting in anticipation to see their reaction. Sarah pulled the box top back and exposed its contents. Sarah put her hand to her mouth and sat down. Her face turned white.

Wilhelmina asked, "Is that what I think it is?"

Alastair didn't have a clue, "What is it?"

Wilhelmina said, "I think it's a Faberge egg."

Sarah regained her composer, "Not just a Faberge egg, but one of the six missing Imperial Faberge eggs." Sarah stood and gently took the egg out of the box, setting it on its spindly looking silver stand. "This…." Sarah almost went into tears. "This…is the Alexander the Third Commemorative egg." She popped it open to show the 'surprise' in the middle, a solid gold bust of the Czar. "Oh, my," she expelled. "It's not the prettiest of the eggs but it may be the most desirable. Collectors are strange that way."

"What's it worth?" asked Alastair, still not knowing anything about what Sarah was talking about

"Worth," Sarah said. "How can you put a price on something this special."

"Somebody will," said Joshua, breaking the spell.

Sarah cleared her throat and said, "Sorry, I was lost in the enormity of this moment."

"How much do you think it's worth?" asked Joshua, leaning forward in the seat.

"If the piece can be verified as authentic, if the market is just right and if the advertising catches the interest of the right collectors and if a crisis doesn't happen between now and the auction…"

"That's a lot of 'ifs'," said Joshua.

"I know. I hate to promise anything to the clients because there are no certainties. But I do believe this piece will easily reach a reserve of twenty million dollars."

Laurie looked puzzled. "What does a 'reserve' mean?"

Sarah gave the explanation. "It simply means you have a starting minimum bid at twenty million. It could go up from there."

Laurie reached over and squeezed Joshua's hand. "Karl said he thought it might go for thirty million euros."

Sarah thought for a second, "It very well could but we deal with and plan for lower end action. If it goes higher, the better for everybody."

Sarah couldn't keep her eyes off the beautiful work on the egg. Laurie couldn't keep her eyes off Joshua and Alastair couldn't keep his eyes off Wilhelmina. Wilhelmina couldn't keep her eyes off Sarah, not because Wilhelmina was a lesbian but because Wilhelmina wanted to be Sarah, a beautiful blonde woman, in an important, high profile job who got to wear fine clothes everyday instead of wearing a magnifying glass headset and sleeve protectors.

Joshua, as usual, broke the trance, "What is the house cut for an auction?"

Without averting her eyes from the egg, Sarah said, "Thirteen and a half percent."

Joshua looked at Laurie, "That's fair. When can we expect it to be auctioned?"

Sarah finally pulled her eyes away from the egg. "It will take at least a week to verify its authenticity. Then several weeks to advertise. To be certain, let's say we can auction it in one month at our Fall Gala."

Laurie's mouth dropped open. She looked at Joshua, "How are we going to survive a month?" They had less than five-hundred euros left. Joshua leaned over and whispered in her ear, "We'll be fine. I'll help you through it."

"Okay Ms. Vanderweerdt, what paperwork do we fill out?" asked Joshua with renewed confidence balancing out Laurie's expectation of living like street urchins for a month.

Sarah looked at Alastair and Wilhelmina and told them they could go and not say anything about what they saw. Sarah placed the egg back into the box and made a series of phone calls that got a whole bunch of people stirred up. Eventually, paperwork was placed in front of Joshua and Laurie to sign sealing the deal to auction the egg with a reserve price of twenty million dollars.

Laurie looked at Joshua and asked if he wanted to sign too. He declined saying it wasn't his egg, the deal was all hers. Laurie pleaded but Joshua stood firm. With all the paperwork and other preparations done, Joshua and Laurie walked out of Christie's as the sun was setting.

Joshua unexpectedly, picked her up and kissed her with a deep wet kiss that nearly made her shoes fall off. When he set her down, she asked, "What was that for?"

"For having the time of my life'" he said and kissed her again.

Chapter 21

They stood on the sidewalk in front of Christie's contemplating the possibility of Laurie being a multi-millionaire in a month. In a moment that thought faded to black and Laurie asked, "Where are we going to stay tonight."

Joshua was quick to respond. "Can you say 'hostel'?" Laurie's nose crinkled up. "It's not that bad." He put his arm around her and they started walking back from the way they came. "Let's go see our friend in the library. I bet he can tell us where the nearest hostel is."

"I don't want to appear ignorant but what is a hostel? I've heard of them before but never imagined staying in one. Is it like Airbnb?"

"Not exactly, but it's cheaper."

"How cheap?" Laurie's face looked uneasy.

"I bet we can find one for thirty pounds." Joshua looked at her for approval.

"Yeah, okay."

They got to the library and the young men working there fell all over themselves trying to help Laurie. After gaining the information they needed, Laurie made a tactical retreat and the couple went in search of the first hostel on the list of three.

The first one they visited had dorm style rooms with three bunk beds per room. There was a common kitchen and bathroom with a small three head gang shower. There was also a tiny lounge area with an old tv and two couches.

"All of this for twenty-five pounds," Joshua said being serious.

Laurie thought he was nuts. She had never seen a hostel before and wanted to look at another one before she made a decision. Joshua was fine with that, it just meant he could walk around London holding her hand for a little longer.

They had to go about eight blocks before they came upon the next hostel. It was set up similarly but with four cot-style beds to each room. The price was thirteen pounds fifty pence each. "The other one's cheaper," Joshua added.

Laurie was not pleased and wanted to see the last hostel on the list. They walked together feeling the chill of the London evening envelope them. Joshua was happy as a clam but he could tell Laurie was apprehensive. "It'll be fine," Joshua encouraged. "Hostels are safe and the ones we've seen have been very clean. The only drawback is they get noisy sometimes. You know, a bunch of gap kids coming in at all hours of the night." Laurie cut a sideways glance at him.

When they got to the hostel, the doors were closed, 'Out of Business'. "Well, shit," Laurie said.

Joshua quickly spoke up, "Which one did you like best? The first or second one?"

Laurie thought for a minute and couldn't make up her mind. "You choose. You obviously have more experience at this."

"I liked the first one."

"Why?"

"It had a washer and dryer in the back room. We can wash our clothes."

"If I put this Gucci outfit in a washer…"

"Look, Laurie, we have got to cut some corners. It's going to get worse before it gets better. Even if we stay in that hostel every night, we can only last fifteen days or so. A hostel is a luxury we won't be able to afford for the entire month before the auction."

Laurie grunted in acquiescence and they went back to the first hostel. They paid in euros which had an unfavorable exchange rate. The night cost them twenty-eight euros. They claimed their beds by throwing dirty clothes on top of the mattresses. They went back out to shop for sheets and a few toiletries. It was going to be an expensive first night.

After shopping and walking around London all day, they both wanted a shower. They fixed their bedding, locked the other things in the locker and went to the shower attired in the minimum necessary to keep from being called nudists. At the shower door Joshua asked her if she wanted go first or did, they want to shower together. There were three shower heads. Laurie took no time in responding. "Together."

They turned on the left and middle shower and hung up their towels while the water was warming up. Laurie stood so close to Joshua she rubbed against him as he turned toward her. They began kissing, a full body press passionate wet kiss. Joshua, being young, virile and in tremendous shape, wasn't finished with the first kiss when he sprang to life, poking Laurie's belly.

She led him to the middle shower and started soaping up his broad chest when they heard a noise from the common area. They quieted and tried to listen over the rush of the shower. The noise from the common area was people, several people, men and women.

The shower door flung open and a stocky but attractive blonde female stuck her head in and said something apologetically in German. A man and another woman felt compelled to look at the couple as well.

Joshua and Laurie began washing themselves as quickly as possible under their respective showers. Within minutes Günter, Ursula and Ingrid joined them in the shower. All completely nude. Joshua's excitement dwindled down to normal which was still an outstanding piece of manhood. Joshua and Laurie were the objects of many sideways glances. Laurie was beautiful and Joshua was the world's human equivalent of a Greek god. Joshua was sure he caught Günter staring at him a couple of times too.

As soon as the soap was out of their hair and off their bodies, Joshua and Laurie vacated the shower room and stood by their beds wrapped in towels. The couple noticed three other beds in the room were now occupied because backpacks were on them. The packs were open and contents strewn about. It was going to be a long night.

Chapter 22

Joshua and Laurie dressed in their underwear, took the remaining clothes and headed to the laundry room. The machines required a couple of British pounds to operate and neither one of them had any pound coins. Change of plan, they dressed in filthy clothes and went out to get supper and coins for the laundry. As they were dressing in the room, all three Germans entered in some state of indecency. Germans didn't seem to be nearly as bothered by nudity as Americans.

Joshua and Laurie exited quickly and were standing in front of the hostel surrounded by the chilly London fog trying to decide which way to go. They knew there was very little the way they came to the hostel so they walked off in the opposite direction. Choosing wisely, they found a pub around the corner on the next block. There was a sandwich style chalkboard out front advertising Shepherd's pie and a pint.

They shared a pie and a pint being sure to pay in denominations that would give them the most amount of coin change. After consuming the rich Shepherd's pie and drinking a half pint of ale, Laurie's eyes started to flutter shut. Joshua's running lights were about to go out also. They went back to the hostel to find their room void of other guests. Joshua figured the young Germans would be out to three or four in the morning.

Joshua told Laurie to take off her clothes and get in bed. He would do the laundry. She tried to protest but Joshua was willful. Laurie stripped down to the bare nothing and slid between their newly purchased sheets. Joshua's mind was going a thousand miles an hour. They were alone and she was already in bed. Sure, it was a narrow bottom bunk bed but where there is a will there is a way. As he was regathering the clothes and plotting his next move, Laurie mumbled something and faded into slumber.

Blocked again! How is this ever going to work out? Joshua went to the laundry, loaded everything into the single washer and got some shower gel to use as detergent. Back at the washer, he put in the gel, took off his underwear, threw it in and started the machine. He sat in the single straight back chair wrapped in a towel.

At 11:30 pm, Joshua had the sets of clothes washed, dried and folded neatly. He carried them back to the room and placed them in their locker. Joshua looked closely at Laurie in the dim light and could see her sleeping soundly, making quiet breathing noises. Joshua climbed the ladder at the end of the bunk beds and slid between his new sheets.

They were both sleeping naked in beds separated by only a few vertical feet. The room was dark and they were all alone. Make a move, he thought. But he didn't. He fell asleep instead and dreamed of having his way with her. Not nearly good enough.

At three-thirty in the morning, the Germans came banging into the room, drunk as skunks. They made a big deal about trying to be quiet but that feat was an impossibility in their condition. They were being so loud trying to be quiet, Joshua heard Laurie giggled a little. Joshua slithered down the side of the bunk bed in his boxer briefs and went to use the bathroom. The German girls were mesmerized by Joshua's form.

The German ladies stripped down to their panties, breasts laid bare and climbed into the bottom bunks. Günter was forced to ascend the ladder to the top bunk. After several attempts at which Laurie thought the guy would break his neck, the man flopped on the top bunk and collapsed on the mattress. He had no sheets.

Joshua returned and both German girls sat up on their elbows to get a better look. Their bare breasts peeking out from underneath the covers. Joshua noticed their display. As he stood by his bunk observing the show, Laurie reached out and pinched him on the butt. "Go to bed."

Joshua jerked away from the pinch and in one bound, jumped up on the top bunk, sitting with his feet hanging off the side. After one last look, he laid down on the new sheets and went to sleep.

Chapter 23

Joshua woke early in the morning. In this case, early was about 8:00 am. He smoothly descended the wooden ladder and went to do his business in the bathroom. Fully dressed he gently shook Laurie awake. "Hey, wake up," he whispered.

She rolled over, her hair covering her face. "What?" she groggily said back.

He shook her again. "Come on wake up. I want to get an early start."

She raised up on her elbow, having a fight with the hair entanglement. "Early start for what?"

"I want to find a job. We're going to need one."

"A job!" Laurie exclaimed. Joshua chalked up her surprise to not being awake yet.

Joshua shushed her so she wouldn't wake their roommates. "Yeah, I think the minimum wage here is eight or nine pounds and hour. If I can get the lowest paying job in London, we can still live like this indefinitely."

"Indefinitely?"

Joshua laughed. Laurie was still half asleep. "Get up," he pulled her up to a sitting position. "Go to the bathroom and do whatever girls do in there, get dressed and let's go." Joshua clapped his hands quietly.

She threw the covers back and exposed her exquisite body. The boy couldn't take it anymore. Laurie smiled at him, knowing he was feasting with his eyes as he bolted out into the common area away from temptation.

Both sporting their two outfits, they went to find breakfast. After walking nearly a mile, Joshua pointed ahead of them, "There's a McDonalds."

Laurie looked at him sideways. "Don't worry, when you're a millionaire you can eat wherever you want. Until then, we split a breakfast."

They went in, Laurie hanging on tightly to Joshua's arm, like she was going into a scary place. They ordered and ate something resembling an American Big Breakfast. It was filling. Finished eating, they walked back to the area where they bought their clothes. Laurie enjoyed the window shopping. Joshua was looking for a help wanted sign.

After an hour of meandering, Joshua saw an authentic looking Asian restaurant. How did he know it was authentic? It had chickens hanging in the window. Also hanging in the window was a help wanted sign, hand written in both English and Chinese.

Joshua went in and offered his services. He was hired on the spot by a crotchety old Chinese man. Joshua's job was dish washer and chicken chopper. He would cut up raw chickens for the dishes, bus the tables and wash dishes. Pay was only seven pounds an hour, less than minimum wage but it paid in cash daily. Perfect, Joshua thought. Gross, is what Laurie thought. Joshua would start tomorrow.

They decided to go back to the hostel and try to take a nap. Maybe their companions would be out looking for something to eat, or in their case drink. As they approached the hostel, they saw several emergency vehicles out front including an array of fire trucks. Smoke was billowing forth from the hostel. The lady from whom they rented the rooms was standing out front in the arms of a policeman. She was crying, wailing more like it. Joshua and Laurie approached with caution. They asked someone in the crowd what happened. The answer was simple and obvious. It was a fire.

Joshua held Laurie close and said to himself more than her, "This can't be a coincidence, can it?" Laurie's stomach churned. She had hoped this part of the adventure was over. Joshua snapped out of his daze and said, "We need to get out of here."

"What about our stuff?" Laurie asked.

"It's gone."

"You mean we're back down to the clothes on our backs and the handful of euros we have in our pockets?"

As Joshua was about to answer, the emergency personnel rolled a body in a bag out of the structure. The couple stared as they rolled two more bodies out.

"I think those might be our German friends."

Laurie had her hand to her mouth, tears were forming in the corners of her eyes.

"What are the chances that Juliette and the murderers are at it again?" asked Joshua.

"How would they know where we were?"

"It had to come from the auction house. A twenty-million-pound Faberge egg hits the auction block, people are going to know. Right? We've got to lay low."

"Lower than we've been laying?" asked Laurie incredulously.

"Yes, we need to be invisible."

Chapter 24

Back at the Chinese chicken restaurant, inappropriately named 'Happy Chicken', they looked around trying to find a magic solution. "I'm afraid to stay in another hostel and we only have enough money for two nights in a decent hotel. I think we are under the stars tonight. At least until we can figure something else out."

"Okay. Where are we going to stay?"

Joshua pointed up.

"On the roof?" Laurie nearly screamed.

"Would you think to look there?" Joshua asked her.

"Of course not, but I'm just a girl from Louisiana. I'm not an international organization of assassins!"

"Good point but, we're sleeping on the roof tonight and maybe for a while."

They walked behind the building down an alley that smelled of chicken grease. They found the back of 'Happy Chicken' and Joshua leaped high in the air grabbing the fire escape ladder. His weight pulled it down to the ground. As he held it, he said, "Ladies first."

She looked at him with daggers in her eyes. Joshua couldn't tell if she was being playful or serious. Laurie climbed the fire escape like a champ. Joshua followed. The roof was cleaner than the alley and had a couple of nooks and crannies that provided an adequate sleeping area. Joshua was pleased. Laurie was not.

"Wait here, I'll be back."

Laurie reached out and grabbed him like he was the last life preserver on the Titanic. "Where are you going?"

"We need a few essentials. A blanket, water, a little food." Joshua looked at her with sympathetic eyes. Laurie felt a quiver run down her spine. Even in the direst of circumstances, Joshua was still the sexiest man alive. "I'll be back shortly."

"Can you buy me a set of warm-ups? I feel a little funny wearing Gucci on the roof of 'Happy Chicken.'"

"Done!" He turned and climbed down the fire escape.

Laurie sat, alone as she had ever been in her life, contemplating how she got to where she was at this very moment and how she was going to get out of it. Her answer was, I'll let Joshua handle that part. She looked over the side of the building down the street searching for Juliette and the murderers. She laughed to herself thinking it sounded like a band, Juliette and the Murderers. All she saw was Joshua quickly walking away from her. "Please let him come back to me," she prayed.

In a little over an hour, Laurie heard the fire escape ladder slide down. She jumped up and went to the side of the building to see Joshua clambering back up with two bags in his hands. She hoped he wouldn't fall because it looked somewhat perilous.

Joshua reached the top, threw the bags over the side and climbed the rest of the way up. As he was in the process of saying "Did you miss me?" Laurie threw her entire body at him and hugged him. "Whoa," was all he could say as she nearly knocked him over. When the hug was done, she raised her head, her big brown eyes aching with desire, auburn hair flying in the wind and they kissed.

This kiss, truly felt like their first kiss. It was soulful. They pulled apart, lost in each other's eyes. "Hey, are you alright?" Joshua asked quietly.

Laurie shook her head up and down, "What did you bring me?"

Joshua picked up one bag and pulled out a grey sweat suit and a pair of wool socks. "Nice, huh?" he said. Laurie thought he was making fun but wasn't sure. He reached in the other large bag and pulled out two wool blankets, like army blankets and a cheap foam pad.

Laurie could see there was still some things in the bag. "What else do you have?"

Joshua showed her two blow-up pillows, a plastic tarp, three bottles of water, two travel toothbrushes and some power bars and snacks.

With all the stuff laid out on the roof top, Joshua stood with his hands on his hips looking proud. Laurie could tell he was wanting some recognition and she gave it to him in the form of a full body hug with her hands on his rock-hard butt. "You are the man." She said poking fun at him.

They set up a little nest in one of the nooks and laid down to try it out. Joshua had his hands behind his head and Laurie was lying on her side facing Joshua. He was about to go to sleep when she asked, "Who do you think Juliette really is? A thief? Gangster? Assassin?"

Joshua thought for minute and said, "I think she's been sent by someone rich, powerful, well connected and motivated. She's chased us across three countries, committed arson and murdered several people." Joshua let the thought linger for a moment and then said, "Maybe it's not Juliette at all. It could be somebody else here in London."

Laurie made a grunting sound and said, "It's that bitch. I feel it in my bones." Joshua didn't disagree.

They took naps and talked all afternoon. When the sun started to set the air turned cold. Laurie and Joshua ate a snack, drank some water and huddled under the blanket. Finished eating, Laurie said, "I've got to pee."

"Me too," replied Joshua. "I'm going to pee over the side in the back of the alley. What are you going to do?"

Laurie's mouth fell open. Joshua said, "You can go over to the next roof top and squat behind the wall, no one will see you. You can climb down the ladder and do it in the alley or you can go into the restaurant and use their toilet. I'll go with you to the restaurant if you want, after all, I am an employee." Joshua smiled. Laurie did not.

"Don't look and don't listen," she instructed him. Carrying her warm ups, Laurie went to the adjoining roof top, stripped, pee'd and changed into her new clothes. Joshua walked to the edge of the building facing the alley and relieved himself. When she returned, she said, "How do I look?" spinning around so Joshua could see all of it plus she didn't want to give him time to say something snarky about her choice of toileting facilities.

They laid back down together and Laurie threw her arm across his broad chest. He put his hand on her arm and said, "Don't let me sleep past ten o'clock if I should be so lucky to sleep that long. My shift starts at ten-thirty." He closed his eyes and faded away. Laurie hugged him closer and wondered when was it going to be their time. They'd been constant companions for several days, including sleeping with each other. Sleeping, in the literal sense, unfortunately.

She watched him toss a little trying to get comfortable. As she looked on, enamored, she decided Joshua was the one. She liked him, he was funny, handsome beyond measure, strong and she knew he would always do the right thing. What a man. She gently ran her fingers through his hair. "I could just eat you up."

Chapter 25

Joshua walked into Happy Chicken at exactly ten-thirty. The old Chinese man instantly started shouting at him, in Chinese. "Can you speak English please?" Joshua pleaded.

"Chop-a-chicken. Chop-a-chicken!" he yelled. The old man tossed Joshua an apron, not a clean one either. "Chop-a-chicken!" he yelled one more time pointing to a counter with a mound of whole plucked chickens stacked at the end.

Joshua had never performed 'Chop-a-chicken' before so he asked, "How do you want me to cut them up?"

The old man yelled, "Quarter, half! Quarter, half!"

Joshua didn't know if the guy wanted a quarter chicken and a half chicken or to cut a quarter chicken in half making it an eighth. 'Chop-a-chicken' may prove to be more difficult than Joshua imagined. He laughed to himself. "Can you show me?"

The old guy grabbed a raw, whole chicken and not so gently smacked it down on the counter. He snatched a giant cleaver from under the counter and Bam! Bam! Bam! The chicken was cut in half and each half into quarters. He threw the cleaver on the counter making a loud clatter and pointed, "Chop-a-chicken!" The old man scraped the chicken quarters into a five-gallon pickle bucket on the floor and walked off screaming "Chop-a-chicken" over his shoulder.

Joshua couldn't help but laugh. He then proceeded to desecrate the dead bodies of no less than forty chickens. Joshua, the counter, the floor and the bucket were a slimy chicken juice mess when he was done. Dying of salmonella poisoning seemed inevitable.

After he finished 'Chop-a-chicken' he had to 'direst!' About the time Joshua finished 'Scrubba-scrubba' on the counter, floor and himself, the lunch crowd started to pile in. They were mostly Chinese men who worked in the area. Joshua bussed tables, washed dishes, mopped the floor and repeated until eleven o'clock that night.

He washed himself the best he could in the sink using the sprayer but nothing would get that chicken-soy smell off him. It was going to be a long month.

He climbed the fire escape ladder carefully carrying two take-out boxes of sesame chicken and broccoli. When he crested the roof top, Laurie was waiting by the edge. "Oh, Thank God," she said and hugged him.

"What's wrong?" he asked.

"Nothing, I was just worried and lonely."

"I'm here now and I brought you something real to eat." He handed her a box.

"You know," she said kind of like a question. "That was the longest I've been away from you since we met. I didn't like it one bit. Not one bit." She dug into her chicken box using the plastic spork instead of chopsticks.

"I didn't like it one bit either," replied Joshua remembering being elbow deep in chicken parts. "I do have this." He reached in his pocket and pulled out eighty-four pounds and gave to her.

Laurie looked excited, "We could live in a hostel every night and have fifty pounds left over to eat with or do anything else we wanted!"

"Just think if you got a job too. We would have more than twice that amount because your job wouldn't be as crappy as mine."

"Joshua," she said. "I have something to confess."

Joshua laughed with his mouth full of sesame chicken, "You've never worked a day in your life, have you?"

"Not one," she replied.

"Would you be willing to work?"

"Of course."

"What would you like to do?"

"Something cleaner and less smelly than what you do."

"Alright, don't get personal." Joshua sniffed himself. "Tomorrow, we'll get up early and look for something for you to do."

Laurie nodded, "Check," she said a little wary of what was coming.

Chapter 26

Joshua moved his bedding ten feet away from Laurie because he smelled so much like soy, ginger and charred chicken. Laurie didn't like him sleeping that far away but she appreciated the courtesy of the move.

When there was enough light in the morning to see, Joshua nudged her awake and told her to get dressed in the cleanest clothes she had. Dressed in her only other street outfit and hair pulled back in a pony, she was ready for whatever if it included a stop at the coffee shop for a cup of her favorite latte and a bathroom break.

After spending twelve pounds in the coffee shop on drinks and a danish, Laurie groomed and brushed her teeth in the bathroom. Gastronomically content and much cleaner, they went looking for Laurie a job.

They walked a different direction than Joshua had walked before and, in a few minutes, they were in a part of town that was filled with immigrants. Most of them were from the Middle East. Joshua and Laurie turned around and headed a different direction. The neighborhood was packed with an abundance of people willing to work for nothing.

A half-hour later they were in a different world filled with many chain stores and struggling Mom and Pop shops. Laurie saw a second-hand store that looked promising, it was called Once Again. Joshua stayed outside as Laurie went in to try to persuade them to give her a job.

The owner was a portly lady, friendly but wary. She asked numerous questions but, in the end, decided Laurie was okay, just a young girl on a gap year who ran out of money. Laurie came out of the store and saw Joshua standing on the corner. His face was poised in anticipation.

"I got a job!"

Joshua hissed the word "Yes" with a fist pump. They hugged it out and Joshua asked, "When do you start?"

Laurie looked at her wrist as if she were wearing a watch, "In two hours."

"Well, that was fast. What are you going to be doing?"

"The lady, Margerie, has a second floor filled with junk or treasures depending on your point of view, and she wants it cleaned out. She said it would take a week maybe. I'm only doing it from noon until four until the second floor is sorted out."

"Four hours a day," Joshua reiterated.

"Yeah, forty pounds a day. Is that good?"

"That's more than I make an hour," confirmed Joshua. "You did good."

They hugged once more but this time Laurie didn't let go. She looked up at him and in slow motion, batted her brown eyes in manner that wasn't obvious but still done deliberately. Joshua responded by bending low and kissing her tenderly. As she pressed harder into his body, the kiss intensified. When she felt his excitement grow, she pulled away and said "Go on now. I've got to go to work."

She walked up the three steps to the shop door, turned and said, "I'll see you at home a little after eleven, right?"

"Can you get the ladder down by yourself?"

"I forgot about that. I don't think I can."

"Just come by Happy Chicken when you get off and I'll pull it down for you."

Chapter 27

Joshua had to jog back to Happy Chicken to make it there by ten-thirty. He went to the back, put on an apron and commenced 'Chop-a-chicken' like a pro. Laurie went into Come Again and talked with Margerie about the business.

Margerie and her husband, "God rest his soul," had been in the antique business for thirty-five years. They were once the owners of a premiere shop always having high-end items. Margerie said it was nothing for them to sell a Victorian era desk for twenty-five thousand pounds. "That would have been just another Tuesday," Margerie grinned from somewhere in the past.

Laurie touched her on the arm, snapping her back to present day and said, "Maybe I'll find one of those treasures upstairs."

Margerie patted her hand and said, "I hope so dear. I haven't had many sales lately. Cleaning out the second floor is the first stage of closing the shop. I'm losing money every month and have been since Arthur passed."

"We'll find something special up there," Laurie said not even knowing what the second floor looked like. "Can I go on up now and get started?"

Margerie looked at a cuckoo clock in the corner and said, "I can only pay you for four hours, so if you start early, you can quit early."

Laurie gave Margerie a little squeeze on the shoulder. When she did, she noticed several pamphlets on the counter. One was from Christie's. Prominently displayed on the front cover was a beautiful picture of the Alexander the Third, Commemorative Faberge Imperial Egg!

"Oh my gosh!" said Laurie and snatched up the pamphlet. "Look at this!"

Margerie said, "I know. Look at the price, twenty million pounds, minimum bid."

Laurie couldn't tear her eyes away from the advertisement.

Margerie continued, "Christie's sends these flyers out to all the antique stores hoping some of our more uppity customers will see it. I just got it moments before you walked in." Margerie held a flyer in her hand too. "Look at that thing. Missing for over a hundred years. It was in the palace, held by the Romanovs themselves." She looked up at Laurie, "You know the story of the Romanovs, right."

Laurie reluctantly admitted to only knowing what she had seen in the cartoon Anastasia about ten years ago. Margerie snorted, "Americans," and proceeded to tell her the not so 'G' rated version of the story.

"Lucky bugger," said Margerie. "Someone probably just found that in an attic or it belonged to grandmother and the instant she died; the kids put it up for sale."

Laurie didn't tell her the real story how there was a chase across the continent that culminated in several dead bodies, Laurie living on the roof of Happy Chicken and taking baths in the sink at the coffee shop and especially not the part where the murderers are still after them.

"Yeah, lucky buggers," repeated Laurie. Laurie trudged up the stairs wondering what work was going to be like. As it turned out, work was fun.

The first thing she did was focus on an old steamer trunk that blocked the path to anything else. Laurie opened the trunk with a grunt because it was frozen shut. The trunk was packed full of papers. She picked up the one on top and it was an advertisement for an opera, Don Giovanni, London, July 19, 1902. The playbill was in perfect condition. The star of the show, Enrico Caruso.

Laurie carried it down to Margerie and said, "I know it's going to be ridiculous to bring everything down for you to look at, especially since this is the first piece of paper I picked up out of thousands that are in the first box I opened. I'll never get the place cleaned out if I keep doing this but maybe we should go through this stuff together instead throwing it out. There may be thousands of pounds worth of antiques up there." She handed the playbill to Margerie.

Margerie looked at it. "It's a hundred and twenty years old. Fine condition. Enrico Caruso, the greatest opera singer of the time. A London venue. I'd say it's worth between five and fifteen pounds depending on the buyer."

"It's the first thing I picked up Margerie. I bet there is truly a thousand of pieces just like it up there. Let me bring it down box by box and let's go through it." Laurie was excited. Not as excited as she was with the egg but still excited. Maybe this was her calling, antiques and second-hand treasures.

Margerie was excited about Laurie being excited. Margerie's kids grew up with no interest what-so-ever in the business and it was nice to see such a young person interested in something besides their cell phone. "Right-o," Margerie said. "Let's have a go at that mess together."

Laurie gave her a hug and went back upstairs to drag the giant trunk down to the work room in the back of the first floor. Margerie helped her guide it down the stairs. As soon as they got it in the back room a customer walked in, the little bell on the door alerting the ladies.

Margerie went to the front and asked, "How can I help you?"

The tall, thin man in casual clothes said, "I'm looking for a metal milk jug."

Margerie took him through the back room to a mini-warehouse. She walked to the very end and pointed. There were six metal milk containers neatly bunched on the floor.

"How much?" the man asked.

"Seventy-five for the big ones and fifty for the little ones."

"I'll take two of the big ones."

The man picked out his containers, carried them to the register and paid in new pound notes.

Laurie observed closely because she was now in the habit of examining every stranger. Margerie returned to the back room and said, "I'm going to start calling you Lucky Laurie. I haven't had a sale that big in over three weeks."

Margerie made tea, brought out biscuits and the ladies started going through each item in the trunk. They put them in three piles, those items suspected of being worth something, those needing additional research and obvious trash. The obvious trash pile was very small.

When they finished, the sun was going down. Margerie turned on the lights. "I haven't been in the shop after dark for three months. I'm usually home by now."

Laurie started to apologize for keeping her too late, but Margerie ended up thanking Laurie for giving her some fun. "We'll do it again tomorrow, yes?" questioned Margerie.

"You bet we will. It's my job." Laurie smiled.

Margerie handed Laurie forty pounds.

Laurie said her good-bye and left to find Joshua at Happy Chicken. When she arrived, Joshua was wearing an apron and carrying a pan of dirty dishes. He smiled at her when she walked in. Laurie felt guilty, Joshua was doing filthy work while she sat around, drank tea, ate biscuits, conversed with a kindly lady and sorted papers all the while making more money per hour than Joshua.

Joshua dumped the dishes in the sink and returned to talk to Laurie. "How was your first day ever working?"

"I feel guilty to say this, but I loved every minute of it."

"Don't feel guilty just because I cut up forty-seven chickens into quarters, washed two-hundred dishes, mopped the floor twice and wiped down every table and chair no less than four times each and you loved your job. Naw, don't feel guilty."

Laurie wasn't sure what to do or say.

Joshua looked at her sideways, "I'm teasing. I'm glad you like your job. You can tell me all about it when I get home. Right now, sit for a minute while I get you a plate of food and then I'll take a break and get the ladder down for you." Joshua went off to get her a to go plate of chicken fried rice to be eaten with a spork. Laurie used the restroom one last time before she went to the penthouse.

"Come on, we've got to go now. I have fifteen minutes." Joshua was carrying her dinner.

Laurie and Joshua went down the alley, he took her in his arms and kissed her passionately. He let her go, jumped up and retrieved the ladder, "Don't wait up," he said as she ascended. "I'll be home a little after eleven."

Laurie waved good bye from the roof while holding her Styrofoam plate of chicken fried rice. She was curious why Joshua called the roof top pallets 'home'. She felt like home was with Joshua, maybe he felt the same way.

At twenty minutes after eleven, although she didn't know what time it was, Joshua came up the ladder holding a small sack. He knelt near Laurie, who was lying under the cover on her pallet. Joshua handed her the sack and said, "I brought you dessert."

Laurie opened to see two round cakes. "They're mooncakes," Joshua said. "Filled with custard. I've already eaten three."

"Pig," she said playfully as she fished one out and devoured it in three bites.

"Who's the pig?" asked Joshua.

"Shut up, I've been wanting something sweet." As soon as she said that, she knew what she really wanted.

Joshua saw the look in her eyes and backed away. "I double stink like ginger, soy, sweat and two-day old chicken grease. I'm sleeping way over there tonight." Laurie showed disappointment. Joshua changed the subject. "Did you get paid today?"

"Oh, yes." She leaned over, exposing her naked torso. Joshua turned his head to avert his gaze. Laurie noticed. She grabbed her money from under her clothes. She handed him one hundred twenty pounds, Joshua's wages from yesterday and hers from today. Joshua took it and put his eighty-four pounds he just earned with it.

"Since both of us have tomorrow morning free, why don't we go find another hostel with a shower and a bed? We have two-hundred pounds. We're rich!" He held up all the notes, fanned them out and shook them in the air.

Laurie raised up on her knees letting the covers fall to the roof surface and she hugged him. "I was hoping you'd say something like that."

All Joshua could think was, she's naked! They kissed and Joshua, becoming excited, decided to move back near Laurie for the night and take care of some long over-due business. Just as the possibility of some savage sex appeared in his brain, she pushed him backwards and said, "Yes, let's please take a shower." She crawled back under the covers.

Joshua was acting stunned but knew he smelled like a three-day old road kill skunk. "What? I put this eau de poulette cologne on just for you." He leaned over in a push-up position and kissed her. I'll be over there," He pointed at his pallet. "Goodnight."

"Goodnight, Joshua. And thanks."

"For what?" he asked as he was brushing his teeth.

"I think I'm having the time of my life."

"Hell of a gap year then, huh?" He spit his rinse over the side of the building.

Chapter 28

They rose with the sun, packing all their things in a make-shift bed-roll Joshua expertly devised. Everything they owned was stuffed in Laurie's trusty tote or the improvised bedroll.

They scurried quickly to the coffee shop because both had to pee to the point it was urgent. Refreshed and coffee'd up, the search for a hostel began. Laurie's demeanor darkened because she remembered the last hostel, the fire, the poor, young, dead Germans.

After asking around, Joshua found a reasonably priced hostel called The Walkabout with quadruple occupancy per room. Joshua paid a little less than thirty pounds and they moved in to room number three. The room had two bunk beds. One set of bunk beds was occupied with neat people. The beds were made with tight hospital corners and there wasn't a single item out of place. Joshua nodded his head toward their roommates' beds and said, "Anybody who is that disciplined surely won't stay out until three in the morning drinking." Laurie agreed.

Joshua and Laurie made their own beds but failed to make them as neatly as their bunkmates. Joshua's was better made than Laurie's but

Joshua had much more experience making beds. He figured Laurie probably never had to make her own bed before.

"I'm taking a shower," announced Joshua.

"Me too," said Laurie. "Right now."

When they went to the shower, they discovered a His and Her shower room. Disappointed, they went to their respective places and cleaned up. Joshua had to turn the shower to as hot as it would get to cut through the chicken grease.

Back in room number three, dressed in clean clothes, Joshua said, "I've got to go. I'm going to be late. Don't fall asleep. I know you're as tired as I am, but you have to be at work in an hour and a half."

Laurie replied, "I think I'll go on in and visit with Margerie a little."

"Good girl," he said. "I've really got to go." They stood in the middle of the room, hands at their sides, facing each other.

"This 'parting is such sweet sorrow' shit is for the birds." Laurie looked him in the eye as she said that.

"Shakespeare knew what he was talking about didn't he," Joshua said as he moved forward to hug and kiss her. She sprang towards him also and they bumped bodies hard as they embraced. Joshua bent her slightly backward and forced a kiss on her. He easily held her up with his strong arms as she started going limp, like putty in his hands.

Joshua's mind was going to the irresponsible place that told him to ditch work for a couple of hours and take care of Laurie. They deserved this he rationalized. As his pants began bulging with anticipation, an older couple entered the room.

"Don't mind us, we just live here too," the lady said. Joshua and Laurie pulled apart swiftly with Joshua standing canted toward the back corner of the room, trying to hide what Laurie's sexiness did to him. "How long have you two been 'in-country'?" the man asked.

Joshua answered, "Only a few days in England, but I've been on the continent for several months."

Laurie answered for herself, "I've only been in Europe a few weeks."

"Did you guys know each other before coming over?" the lady asked.

Joshua and Laurie looked at each other. Joshua spoke, "It doesn't seem like it but we've known each other less than a week."

The older couple looked at each other with raised eyebrows like they knew the score. They envisioned the young couple squirming around on each other every day or maybe even every few hours. Little did they know, Joshua and Laurie had been blocked at every opportunity, including the conversation they were currently having.

"I'm Joshua and this is Laurie."

"I'm Dale and this lovely thing is Daisy." The older couple were in good shape and attractive in a grandparent sort of way.

"We're sorry, but both of us have to go to work," Laurie said tactfully.

"Working your way across Europe. Isn't that sweet Dale?" Daisy grabbed Dale's arm and let the kids pass by them. "See you around," said Daisy as the young couple left the room.

Out on the street, Joshua said, "I don't know about you but that creeped me out."

"They're a sweet older couple. You just felt creeped out because you had to stand in front of them with a raging erection." She laughed, loudly.

"It's your fault," he said, then kissed her a peck on the lips. "I'll be home after eleven. You be careful out there." He ran off down the street trying to make up time.

Laurie slowly walked to Come Again and started sorting through bygones while talking with Margerie.

Chapter 29

When Joshua finished stacking the last chair, he asked the old Chinese guy if he could leave. The old man grunted one syllable and spit out another. Joshua took that for a 'yes'. Throwing the apron on a coat rack in the corner, Joshua went running out the front door of the restaurant. He was hoping to get a close encounter with Laurie.

When he entered room number three of the hostel, Laurie was lying on her bunk bed, the bottom one, and she was fast asleep with a paperback book open on her chest. The juxtaposing bunks were occupied with the older couple. The man was on the lower bunk and the lady had the upper, both people were snoring away.

Joshua showered and climbed the ladder trying hard not to wake Laurie. When he got situated and the springs quit squeaking, Laurie sleepily whispered up to him. "Goodnight."

"Sorry to wake you."

"I tried to stay awake but the real bed was so comfortable…" and she was a sleep again.

Joshua laid with his hands behind his head, contemplating pretty much everything until he became overwhelmed with the comfort of the bunk. He curled up facing the wall and snoozed.

At some time after midnight he heard a moaning sound emanating from the darkness. He listened for a second before he realized what it was. He rolled over to the edge of the bed and looked down at Laurie thinking she was pleasuring herself. Laurie was asleep!

He looked across the room and in the glow of the blue night light, Joshua could see the older lady on the top bunk, legs spread, 'doing herself'. She was looking directly at him!

Joshua didn't know exactly how to act so he said, "Sorry."

"It's okay. I don't mind," the lady replied quickly as she continued doing what she was doing, only faster.

Joshua turned back to the wall and pulled the pillow over his head. The pillow didn't prevent the moaning sounds and short set of gasps from reaching his ears. He thought she was trying to be quiet, but the resonances of her climax reverberated through the room like it was bouncing off canyon walls. To Joshua's surprise, the husband, nor Laurie, ever stirred.

In the early morning, the older couple packed up and left for parts unknown. Joshua and Laurie stayed in bed because they didn't have any place to go until later. Joshua leaned over the top bunk and saw Laurie awake and fighting to get the hair out of her face. "Good morning, sleep well?"

"Like a log," Laurie answered.

"Me too, once I finally got to sleep."

"Something wrong," asked Laurie looking up at him.

"No, not really. It's just when I went to bed last night, about eleven-thirty, the lady in the other bunk masturbated and didn't try very hard to hide it."

Laurie sat up on the edge of the bed, bare feet on the floor. "The old man did the same! About ten-thirty, he started jerking off under the covers. He looked straight at me!"

Joshua jumped down and sat by Laurie, both in their underwear. "The lady and I even had a conversation," Joshua teased.

"What did ya'll say?"

"Nothing really. I just apologized when she caught me looking and she said it was okay."

"Okay for you to look?" asked Laurie.

"I don't know. I turned away. You know…. when I heard the moaning coming from the darkness, I thought it was you, giving yourself some."

"Well I have been known to do that from time to time," she said playfully. "I'm taking a shower and who knows? I may give myself some." she said as she walked off with a towel in her hand, leaving Joshua dumbstruck on the bed. Women were such a mystery to him.

Several hours later, Laurie was sitting at the work table with Margerie going through box number four. The treasures were piling up, easily estimated to be worth in the three-thousand-pound range. That wasn't even counting the 'need additional research' pile of items.

Margerie brought out biscuits and tea and Laurie made a space on the cluttered table. "I'm having so much fun," Laurie said.

Margerie cupped Laurie's face with her hand and said, "It is fun isn't it?" Margerie sat and grabbed a biscuit. "That's why I got into the business to begin with. After several years, with a bigger shop, larger warehouse and a dozen employees, it turned into a real business and wasn't fun anymore."

They ate their treats, drank their tea and Margerie told Laurie about some of the surprising things she sold in her store at one time or another. They were great stories about the epaulets from the uniform of King Leopold II of Belgium, the Victorian table she mentioned earlier and a shotgun once owned by Winston Churchill. Laurie was dying to tell Margerie about her one big treasure, the egg, but Laurie felt there still might be some danger. She'll tell Margerie after it's sold.

Laurie had a contemplative moment thinking the gap year during which she planned to figure out what she wanted to do may have worked out. She was really liking the idea of the antique business, saving a piece of history and all that.

For the next several days, Laurie and Margerie worked side-by-side, going through the boxes from upstairs. After the next box, they would take a break and do some of that additional research and post up a few items online to see if they would get some bids. Laurie agreed to do all the online work because Margerie lost most of her computer skills years ago, if she ever had them in the first place.

Chapter 30

Laurie was upstairs looking for the last box to sort through before their break and Margerie was dragging the empty steamer trunk out of the work room to the display area so she could try to sell it. The little bell on the front door dinged and Margerie left the trunk in the middle of the floor to go help the customer. "How can I help you?"

A woman was standing at the counter looking at the Christie's flyer. "You don't have any of these lying around, do you?" The customer held up the flyer, pointing to the Faberge egg.

Margerie laughed a little hoping the customer was playing around, "No, but we have a lot of interesting things."

"Anything from imperial Russia?" the young lady asked.

Margerie replied, "No, not anymore. I had some things at one time years ago but now all I have that is vaguely Russian, is some military gear left over from when the Soviets were in Afghanistan."

"Do you know anything about this egg?" The young lady pointed to egg on the flyer again.

Margerie responded, "It's the Alexander the Third Commemorative egg. One of the imperial eggs, made around 1909…"

The lady cut her off. "I know all that, I can read it right here on the flyer," she said somewhat rudely. "I want to know who owns this thing."

Margerie decided she didn't like this customer very much. "I don't know any more than what you know."

The young lady pulled a cigarette out of her purse and lit it. Margerie protested but the young lady continued to smoke. "I've been walking around for three days checking every antique shop in London trying to find out anything about the owner of this egg. Then I come into this hell hole of a shop and not only do you know nothing, you treat me brashly." The young lady approached Margerie. "You like that word, brashly?" Then she blew smoke in Margerie's face.

Margerie apologized and asked her how she could be of help.

"That's better," the young lady said. "Now, get on the phone, computer or tune in to your old lady gossip circle and find out who owns the egg."

Margerie quickly replied, "I wouldn't have a clue how to find out. Christie's is a highly respected establishment. They won't give me that information."

"Let me motivate you." The young lady pulled a tiny Beretta pistol from her purse and placed it on the counter. "It's small, I know. All the boys try to tell you size doesn't matter but it does. A single, twenty-five caliber bullet from this gun probably won't kill a fat old lady like yourself. So, I'll have to shoot you several times. Now get on the phone or computer and find out who owns this egg."

Margerie was pissed but what could she do? She went behind the counter and the lady picked up the pistol and said, "Don't do anything stupid." Margerie started to call her colleagues when Laurie walked down the stairs.

"Hey Margerie, I found the next box I want us to go through." Halfway down the stairs, she saw Juliette holding a gun on Margerie.

Juliette's and Laurie's eyes locked. Juliette's lips curled and Laurie jumped down the last three steps and bolted to the back door.

Juliette started to give chase but Margerie grabbed Juliette's arm. Juliette let out a scream of frustration and shot Margerie in the stomach. Margerie collapsed behind the counter. Juliette ran to the back of the store but couldn't immediately see the exit door which was behind a Japanese Shoji screen. Laurie was in the wind, running for her life, again.

Juliette finally found the back door and to no avail, searched the alley behind the shop. Enraged, she went back to the front of the store and looked around for a security camera but didn't see any. Juliette leaned over the counter but Margerie's body wasn't there. The old lady crawled off into one of the many nooks and crannies in the old building. Juliette departed, spinning the 'open' sign on the door to 'closed'. Margerie lay behind an oak armoire, curled in a ball holding her stomach. It hurt fiercely.

Laurie ran into the nearest store and used their phone to call 999, England's version of 911. Within minutes, an ambulance and unfortunately, the police were in front of Come Again and Margerie was being tended to. Laurie never went back because she was too afraid Juliette or her henchmen were lurking about. Laurie made a beeline to Happy Chicken and the safety of Joshua's arms.

Chapter 31

Laurie burst into Happy Chicken. Joshua threw down his mop and ran to her, instantly interpreting the fear on her face. She couldn't say anything because she ran the whole way at her top speed and she was out of breath to the point of collapse. Joshua pulled a chair close and sat her down. He got her a glass of water. She took a miniature sip and placed the glass on the table. Laurie took two deep breaths and told the story, crying into Joshua's shoulder when she got to the part about Juliette shooting Margerie.

Joshua helped her to her feet and they walked outside the restaurant. Joshua spoke, "I don't think anybody in there understood a word you said, which is good, but just in case I think we need to talk out here."

Laurie held on to him like there was no tomorrow, which there very well might not be. After Laurie felt reassured by his strong arms and gentle whispers in her ear that everything was going to be alright, she asked, "What do we do now?"

"You go up top again."

"To the roof?" Laurie grimaced.

"Yes," replied Joshua. "I think it is one of the least likely places anyone would ever look. It's close to my job so I'm only on the street a few minutes each day. Every three or four days we'll go to a hostel or even a cheap hotel and wash our clothes and our nasty selves because I will be covered in giblets at the end of three days."

Laurie managed a little lip curl smile. "Then I better get this out of the way before you start smelling like a trash can." She wrapped herself around him and kissed him so good he felt light headed or maybe that was because she was squeezing him so tightly, never wanting to let him go.

Joshua took her down the alley and retrieved the ladder for her. She climbed, looking back at him several times. When she reached the safety of the roof he said, "I'll go to the hostel after work and get all of our stuff. We'll set up house just like we did before but it will be better."

"Better? I'm all for better, but how?"

Joshua smiled, "You'll see."

She blew him a kiss which was way out of character for her. Joshua didn't know what to do about that. "I guess I was supposed to catch that," he said jokingly.

"Yes, you asshole."

"I'll bring you a real one later."

"I'll be waiting."

Joshua waved, walked off to go back to work but turned around, "Stay away from the edges. I don't want anyone to catch a glimpse of you up there."

Laurie saluted and moved back from side of the building. She sat on the hard roof surface leaning against the outer wall wondering when this was going to end, and how.

Chapter 32

After Joshua's shift ended, he went to a discount store about two miles away which necessitated a bus ride. He bought some rope, a waterproof tarp, a bucket, a back pack, a bunch of non-perishable snacks and four gallons of water. Loading it all into the large backpack which weighed over forty-five pounds, he rode the bus to a stop near the hostel. He went in and gathered up their stuff and wrapped it in a bedroll.

Joshua donned all the gear weighing nearly ninety pounds and walked to the alley behind Happy Chicken. Standing by the ladder he hollered up at Laurie in a loud whisper. She didn't answer. After several attempts at calling out he threw a substantial sized rock up on the roof and hollered again.

Laurie peered over the edge and said, "Scare a girl to death next time."

"Sorry, but I'm going to need your help getting this stuff up." He dropped the two large bundles to the ground, digging through the back pack to find the rope. "I'm going to throw this to you. Then you're going to pull the stuff up, okay? Just stand back." She took a step to the side.

Joshua easily tossed the coil of rope up as he held on to one end. "Got it?"

Laurie answered back, "Got it."

Joshua tied two gallons of water on the end of the rope and Laurie pulled them up, sending the rope back down after she untied them. They repeated this process until every item was up top. Laurie felt a little pride at having accomplished something essential to their survival that would have been a nightmare for her just a month ago.

When Joshua ascended, Laurie hugged him the best she could, hindered by the smell of chicken grease and sweat from lugging nearly a hundred pounds through a mile of city streets. Joshua smelled to high heaven but he sure did work hard for her and she hoped someday soon, she would be able to show her appreciation.

Joshua made their sleeping pallets a proper distance away from each other. He poured a gallon of water into the bucket and draped a washcloth over the edge. "At least we can wash up a little using this." He reached in his back pocket and pulled out the paperback book Laurie was reading in the hostel. "I brought you this. It's going to be a long day of boredom hiding up here tomorrow."

She took the book and ran her hands over the wrinkled cover like it was a precious heirloom. To her, it might as well have been. Laurie didn't know when she started to love him, but at that moment, she knew she did. She almost cried, but held it back.

Joshua asked, "You good?"

She shook her head up and down.

"It's a little after one," he said glancing at his watch. "I need to get to sleep."

They went through their nightly routine of brushing their teeth and peeing in their respective places. Joshua stripped down to his underwear and slipped in between the covers, Laurie watched intently wishing he didn't smell and feel like something the cat threw up. He was beautiful though, in his dark grey boxer briefs with that impressive manhood hanging left, muscles rippling across his chest. Laurie tingled all over and stripped down to her panties, making sure Joshua got a good look before she slipped into the sheets.

Laurie started trying to count the days in her head to determine how many they had left before the auction. The math and madness made it too much for her to figure out so she fell asleep.

In what she thought was no time at all, Joshua shook her foot. "Hey, get up. I've got to go to work in an hour and I want to take you to the coffee shop for whatever sugary drink you want and something to eat."

Laurie fought her hair like she always did in the morning. When it was parted enough for her to see out, she said, "Good morning to you too."

"Sorry, good morning. Now get up." Joshua smiled.

"I can't believe I slept until 9:30."

"The sun never came up. It's awfully grey and the temperature is dropping. I think our luck with the weather has run out."

"What are we going to do?" asked Laurie forever relying on Joshua's survival instincts.

"While I'm working, you pack up the best you can. Leave out the tarp in case you need to get under it. We'll check into a hostel tonight. Pack all the essentials for a one-night stay in the back pack, plus all the dirty clothes you can find. We'll wash them too. Everything else, we'll leave up here. Let's go get a cup and a bite before the rain comes."

Chapter 33

Finished with their coffee and Danish including a quick trip to the loo, Joshua escorted Laurie back to the roof and went to work, expertly proceeding to chop-a-chicken. Laurie began packing the best she could having learned an immense amount in the last few days about what was necessary. By eleven thirty in the morning she was packed, leaning against the roof wall reading her book, wrapped in the tarp for protection from the threatening wind.

At three in the afternoon, Laurie heard the ladder being pulled down knowing it was Joshua but scaring herself just the same. Joshua jumped up over the roof wall and walked toward her carrying a take-out box of Kung Pao chicken. She rushed forward and hugged him; dead chicken smell be damned.

They pulled apart and he handed her the take-out box and a key card. "We're staying at the Cavendish tonight. But only for one night. It's very expensive." She set the Kung Pao down on the roof top and pressed herself into him. God, he smelled bad but was he ever all man. Their lips met first as just a slight brush against each other and then slowly parting. They plunged their tongues into one another, ravenous for something they had to put off for days. Tonight, at the hotel, their time would finally come.

As Laurie began to feel Joshua get excited, they pulled away. Laurie looked disappointed. "We need to unpack the sleeping gear because we won't need it at the hotel," Joshua stated, trying to hide the fact he was extremely aroused. He walked past Laurie to the pack and started removing the bedding. When he got it all unpacked and stowed, he said, "Let's go get you checked in so you can enjoy the room while I'm working." Laurie was beaming.

They climbed down from their hobo loft and walked toward the Cavendish. The hotel was located near Christie's. Laurie ate the Kung Pao as she walked and fed Joshua a bite every block or so. She thought it was cute, feeding him like a baby while he lugged their pack. Joshua just thought it tasted good, too bad it was chicken!

Once at the hotel, Laurie placed the key card in the slot and turned the handle on the door. She swung it open to view a nicely appointed room that looked to her like a room in a palace. There was a queen-sized bed with spotless white sheets, a mini fridge, a microwave, a coffee maker, a closet, an iron, a desk and chair, a TV and best of all, a fully supplied bathroom with hair dryer! Heaven, she thought.

Joshua didn't set foot inside the room for fear of what might immediately occur. "I've got to get back to work. I was only supposed to be off from two to three but I'm going to be late." Joshua handed her a hand full of money. "The room is already paid for. This is everything I have left over except a twenty. Hang on to it for us."

Laurie reluctantly took the money. Joshua cupped her hands in his. "Use it to get away if anything goes wrong."

"Nothing will go wrong," Laurie injected quickly. "You'll be here tonight, right? About eleven thirty?"

"I'll be here. I've got to go. I'm so late. I'll be home sooner than you think."

He pulled away and walked off down the hall. Laurie slowly shut the door and leaned against it thinking of all the things she would do to him in a few hours. But first, a shower. She stripped, turned on the hot water and got all the dirty clothes out of the pack. She threw them in the bottom of the tub and showered right on top of them, washing her hair with copious amounts of shampoo.

After she finished scrubbing herself, she rinsed and rung out the clothes the best she could and hung them over everything she could find. She looked around hoping the new ambiance of the room wouldn't kill the mood. After working in a Chinese restaurant for eleven hours a day, she felt sure Joshua wouldn't want to come home to something that looked like a laundry at night.

She lay on the bed, naked, thinking she may read her book but the specter of sleep overcame her quickly and she turned on her side in slumber.

Joshua was busy at the restaurant that night and had to stay late because the proprietor had seven friends over to play Pai Gow. Joshua was the cook, waiter and bus boy/bottle washer. Of all nights for this to happen! Joshua used the greasy office phone to call the Cavendish. He thought about leaving a message for Laurie because he didn't want to face her wrath, disappointment or both. However, he got the operator to ring the room.

Laurie answered the phone with an excited, "Are you alright?"

"Yes, I'm fine but I can't come home until later. Little did I know that Happy Chicken turns into Happy Casino on Thursday nights. A group of guys are here getting wasted on Baijiu. It's some kind of jungle juice cooked up in a stone crock and they are betting heavily on Pai Gow." Joshua waited for her response.

"And you have to be there for that?"

"Unfortunately, the boss requires my services. Why don't you get some good sleep?"

There was a long pause. "Remember what the old couple did in the hostel while we watched them?" Laurie didn't wait for Joshua to respond. "Just know I'll be doing that to myself for about an hour." She hung up the phone wishing she hadn't the instant the receiver hit the cradle. Joshua's feelings were hurt but he realized there would be a breaking point somewhere and they may be getting close. Frustration was running high.

Joshua brought a second giant yellow cast of Baijiu out of the back room and set it on the table. He watched as they drank, ate, slapped tiles around on the table and slid huge stacks of money back and forth. They looked like they were having the time of their lives if it hadn't been what they did every Thursday of every week of the year.

At three thirty in the morning, the boss paid Joshua a small wad of money from the winnings and told him to go home. The old man was drunk and would sleep in the office because that was as far as he could walk. Joshua helped him into a stuffed chair and shut the front door as he left. Laurie was going to kill him coming in this late but he did have one-hundred sixty pounds for the day's work. She should be proud of that.

At that hour, even for a city like London, the streets were relatively empty. Joshua pulled his jacket collar up around his neck and walked toward the Cavendish with his hands in his pockets. He had to walk very near Christie's to get to the hotel. He turned down the street and could see the auction house on the right. A black car was parked in front of the building. Two weeks ago, that would have meant nothing. Tonight, it made Joshua nervous.

Your body and mind tell you when you're doing something you shouldn't. Joshua heeded the warning and stepped into the shadows continuing to observe the car. "It's just a car," he tried to convince himself. Joshua stood in the cold London pre-dawn for an hour waiting for something to happen. And then it did.

A man got out of the car, stretched and lit a cigarette. Through the dark, the fog and with every lamp light giving off a halo, the man looked very much like one of Juliette's henchmen. The man got back in the car after tossing the cigarette butt into the gutter. Joshua waited another thirty minutes and nothing happened. It would make sense he thought to himself. Juliette knows the egg is at Christie's and the chances of us returning there are much better than a needle in a haystack.

Joshua was still mulling it over. Juliette is desperate to find us. She sends a guy to stake out Christie's. Good call. Juliette goes around all the antique shops. Another good call. What's the third guy doing? Canvassing the hotels? Joshua spun out of the darkness and ran away from Christie's. He had to alter his route to get to the hotel.

Joshua only exposed himself for a second, but the car lights popped on. He had been spotted. Joshua ran around the corner, down an alley and hid behind a pile of garbage sacks. The car lights came into view at the end of the alley. Ever so slowly, the car turned down the alley and crept forward. Joshua burrowed under the trash sacks. The car took forever to roll by and out the back end of the alley

Making his way back to Happy Chicken and calling Laurie to warn her was his new plan. Going to the hotel now may lead the bad guys directly to her and that wasn't going to happen. Joshua ran, looking for the black car around every turn. The problem with London was every car out that night was a black car.

Back at the restaurant, he went in the office and used the phone to call Laurie. The drunken owner never stirred. Joshua explained what happened and told Laurie to pack up and take a taxi to Happy Chicken. He didn't want her walking the streets with the henchman's car cruising around.

When the cab arrived an hour later. He hugged Laurie like he loved her. Which he decided, he did love her. They walked, wrapped in each other's arms to the alley and climbed up on the roof. Living on the roof together was destined to be their fate.

Chapter 34

On the roof, they built their respective sleeping pallets. Laurie laid out all the clean, but still wet clothes falsely hoping they would dry in the cool early morning temperature and ninety-eight percent humidity. When their roof house was in order, both went to sleep. The time was seven in the morning.

Joshua forced himself to wake up fifteen minutes before he had to be at work. He dressed without any of the usual bathroom regimen and kissed Laurie on the cheek. She woke enough to tell him bye. Joshua descended the ladder and presented for work right on time.

The boss was moving around and preparing for the day like he had gotten the best night's sleep of his life. Joshua was impressed the old guy could reboot so quickly. Joshua was dragging, but managed to keep up with the man forty years his senior.

At two thirty, Joshua brought Laurie a plate of potstickers, chicken potstickers, of course. Joshua said, "If you put enough dipping sauce on them, you can imagine they're made of pork." Laurie crinkled up her nose and made a face at him, but she ate the potstickers and liked them.

At eleven thirty that night, Joshua climbed the ladder and found Laurie already in bed. They both were exhausted. Joshua had enough strength to kiss her goodnight and retired to his pallet, way over there. At one in the morning the rains came, not a deluge but cold and continuous.

They scrambled around and consolidated all their things, including themselves, under the tarp. They were not getting rained on but they were damp and cold. Sitting side by side, backs to the roof wall, Laurie said, "Does this remind you of St Die?"

"It does," replied Joshua. "I think every time it rains from now on, it'll remind me of St Die."

Laurie held his arm and smiled in the dark underneath the tarp. She was wet, cold, filthy, tired and sick of eating chicken but somehow, she was happy. More than happy, content.

They dozed, heads bobbing up and down until they found a way they could stretch out and not get wet. When they went prone, both were asleep instantly. Laurie dreamed of St Die. Joshua envisioned nothing but chickens.

After a while, Joshua could see daylight through the open seams of the tarp. The rain stopped sometime in the early hours of the morning. Joshua felt good even after a couple of miserable nights. Laurie began to stir also. "Is it time for work already?"

"Just about. Come on, get up. We have enough time to go to the coffee shop if you want to."

"This sounds crazy but I think I want to sleep in."

"Nothing crazy about that. When you do get up, do you think you can try to get these clothes dry. I've been wearing the same thing for three days now."

"I know," said Laurie squishing up her face.

"Okay, okay, I stink. I get it." Joshua kissed her tenderly and climbed over the roof wall and down the ladder. Laurie watched his every move as he departed. She missed him already.

Chapter 35

This is the way the days went. Laurie stayed on the roof and Joshua went to work around the corner. They ate a lot of chicken. Joshua would bring things up with him every day that improved their circumstance. He made a frame for the tarp so Laurie had a house. It was more like a kid's club house but she could move around in it on her knees and not hit her head on the top.

Laurie had a small library of paperback books that Joshua commandeered from somewhere, she didn't ask. For an hour or two every day, Laurie would roll out the sleeping pad and do yoga. Joshua also affixed the rope to the ladder so Laurie could pull it down by herself in case she needed the facilities at Happy Chicken or the coffee shop.

They were spending less than twenty pounds a day. Joshua was making bank. He gave her all the money at the end of each day which added up to nearly two-thousand pounds saved with less than a week to go before the auction.

Their routine was smooth and comfortable but something was missing. That something was sex! Although they were close and tender with each other, it wasn't enough. She needed her world rocked and Joshua was the man to do it, if they could ever put this mess behind them.

Joshua came up the ladder at his usual time after the shift only to find Laurie crying. Joshua rushed to her and asked a dozen times what was wrong. Finally, she said, "Margerie." Joshua held her tightly. "I want to go see her. She got shot because of me and I abandoned her." Laurie cried into his shoulder. He could tell the breaking point was near.

"We'll find her when all of this is done. Keep it together for five more days and I'll get a hotel the night before the auction, we'll go shopping and buy new clothes appropriate for Christie's. You'll find Margerie and make things right. It'll all work out."

Laurie wiped her nose on Joshua's sleeve and resigned herself to the fact there was nothing they could safely do right now. After Joshua was assured Laurie was settled, he washed his face and hands in the bucket of water and they went to bed.

That next morning, they walked to the coffee shop and had their usual. Joshua decided some time ago he was making enough money to buy two cups of whatever they wanted and individual breakfasts. They felt rich. There was a time in Laurie's life, not so very long ago, a three-star hotel would have been slumming it in her eyes, but now, a roof top shanty seemed luxurious.

Breakfasts consumed and bathroom routines completed, they walked back to the Happy Chicken. Life was good, except for them being ever vigilant for Juliette and her henchmen. Joshua never let his guard down. Laurie seemed a little more relaxed, maybe because she relied so heavily on Joshua for providing security. She didn't really know what her role was but she figured if she soldiered on, loved Joshua and didn't complain, maybe that was enough. So that's what she did.

Chapter 36

The auction was to be held on Saturday. It was more than an auction; it was a gala. The news outlets and social media were filled with the event. This auction was more talked about than others because this one was catering to royals around the world. The European royals would never buy such a thing as a Faberge egg because it would be too expensive. Their crown fortune could be much better spent on themselves instead of a decorative egg. But maybe the royals in the Arab world would dare to spend so much because their subjects wouldn't complain. Plus, when there are hundreds of billions in your personal treasury, what's twenty-million. It's like five bucks.

The day was Thursday before the auction. Laurie hated Thursdays because Joshua worked late. However, tonight was going to be his last night of work. He would shop with Laurie on Friday and attend the auction on Saturday. Then it would be over, or at least, that's what they thought.

Laurie was on the roof, doing yoga and reading one of the books from their library when Joshua popped over the wall on his afternoon break. He brought her a box of orange chicken. "Have you forgotten what beef tastes like," he asked jokingly.

She took it sexually and replied in a double entendre, "It's been a while since I had any real meat."

The phrase went right over Joshua's head. "I'll tell you what. Tomorrow, when we're out shopping, I'll buy you a Quarter Pounder with cheese from that McDonalds we saw."

"Not what I had in mind," Laurie replied.

"Okay, how about a Beef Wellington from that fancy restaurant down from the coffee shop?"

She walked over to him and wrapped her arms around him, hands grabbing his butt. "I was thinking more of Joshua steak, medium rare."

"Oh," he said in surprise.

"This is coming to an end and I've been patient."

"You have," Joshua agreed.

"Just to let you know, I'm having Joshua steak dinner in the hotel tomorrow." She slid her hand around to his front and gave an angry squeeze to emphasize her statement. "Do you understand?"

Joshua's voice went up an octave, "Yep, got it," completely understanding her meaning. She let go and walked off to eat her orange chicken. Joshua went back to work, once again, feeling a surge of emotion for Laurie.

Chapter 37

At four in the morning on Friday, after the Pai Gow blow out at Happy Chicken, Joshua scaled the ladder for the last time. He was tired, bone tired. Not even bothering to say anything to Laurie, he just collapsed on his pallet and fell asleep.

At nine in the morning, Laurie awoke, fought her hair until she had it fastened in a pony with a rubber band and appeared from the tarp castle searching for Joshua. Once she saw him asleep on the pallet she relaxed. He was home. Laurie washed up using the bucket water and sat down to read one of her books, glancing up at the end of every page to gaze at Joshua. Each time, smiling for no reason.

An hour or so later, Joshua began to stir. Laurie moved over to him and sat on his pallet. He put his hand on her leg. "What time is it?" he asked.

She grabbed his wrist, turned it and looked at his watch. "Ten-thirty," she replied.

"Well I guess I better get up. Are we going to the coffee shop first or are we packing?" Joshua asked hoping Laurie would opt for the coffee shop. As usual, he was wrong.

"Let's pack, I want to get off this roof forever."

"Can't argue with that." He jumped up and they began scrambling around trying to decide what they would take with them.

When it was done, they had everything they were keeping in the pack. It was heavy but easy to transport. They looked around the roof. Joshua had his arm around her shoulder. Laurie was almost moved to tears. What she saw was the tarp house, the bedding, the books, the bucket… their home.

Joshua kissed her forehead and said, "Let's go."

They spun around and descended the ladder. On the ground, Laurie hugged Joshua like they lost something special. She was happy and sad at the same time. Joshua could tell she was struggling with leaving their roof home behind but he couldn't muster much strength help her. He was too tired. He wrapped his arm around her shoulders and pulled her close. She felt nearly limp in his embrace. Joshua kissed her once again on the cheek. "It'll work out."

Chapter 38

Joshua was glad to get to the coffee house because he was about to burst. He needed to pee from the moment he awoke. Things felt more relaxed after the bathroom break. Time slowed down like on a lazy morning in the deep south. They laughed, joked and played footsie under the table as they drank their coffee. Even dirty and tired, Joshua and Laurie were the best-looking couple in central London.

"Where do you want to stay tonight?" asked Joshua.

"You never got to experience the Cavendish. How about back there?"

Joshua thought for a minute and said, "I'm not sure. Juliette may have found out we rented a room there before. I think she's canvassing the hotels in the area. Just like the antique shops."

"So, no to the Cavendish?"

"I think it would be best if we got on a train and went somewhere else for the night. Some random place, like Southend-On-Sea."

"You're making that up!"

"No, I swear. I saw it on a map yesterday." Joshua held his hand up as if he were saying an oath.

"So, you want to go to Southend-On-Sea?"

Joshua shrugged, "I'm not saying I want to go there. I'm just saying we should go someplace that's not here."

"Southend-On-Sea sounds fine to me. How do we get there?"

"By train of course."

They took a taxi to the train station, bought round trip tickets costing a little over sixty pounds and were settled in a coach within the hour. Joshua and Laurie sat closely together, holding hands, excited about getting cleaned up, never having to go back up on the roof, buying new clothes and Joshua was especially excited he would never have to chop-a-chicken again. Even speeding through the London suburbs was exciting. They looked at one another and realized they were more excited about being together than anything else.

Arriving at the Southend-On-Sea station, they kissed before getting off the coach. Then they kissed again and again. The train lurched and they realized it was starting to move. Laurie cried out and ran to the door. Joshua, dragging the pack, was not far behind. They got the door open and jumped out on the platform laughing like crazy people for making out through the entire stop.

Regaining their wits, they exited the station to find a hotel. Not far from the station, there were numerous accommodations. They settled on the Gleneagles Guest House, a large but quaint lodging that served a boutique breakfast.

Laurie didn't much care where they stayed, she just wanted to get Joshua alone and naked. The rest would work itself out. Joshua wanted to please her. She seemed easily satisfied up to this point but eventually he would have to make love to her. Not that he didn't want to, he desperately longed for her. But Joshua didn't know what the money would do to them. He wanted to find out who they were before he made a move. Casual sex with Laurie was not on the agenda.

Checked in, they went to the room and unpacked their essentials. When done, Laurie stripped naked and took a shower. Joshua waited on the bed having some sort of doubt running through his mind. This was not a good thing. Laurie came out with towel wrapped around her. "Your turn," she said.

Joshua slowly got up and went to the bathroom. She could tell something was wrong. Joshua shut the door and began his shower. The whole time he was washing himself, he was thinking how could he possibly tell her.

Cleaned up and dressed, Joshua went out to the bedroom. Laurie was lying on the bed, naked. When she saw him fully dressed, she knew this wasn't going to go the way she wanted. "What's wrong?" she asked immediately.

"Nothing. It's getting late in the afternoon and we need to go buy clothes."

"You don't want to have some fun first." Laurie spread her legs ever so slightly.

The hardest thing Joshua ever did was turn that down. "We need to stick to business for one more day, okay?" He could see the disappointment in her countenance. She got up without speaking a word and dressed. Joshua felt like an ass.

They went to a shopping center close by and purchased new clothes that flattered them both. Laurie was sullen the whole-time making Joshua feel even more like an ass.

Back at the Guest House, they ironed their new clothes and hung them up for the auction the next day. Laurie sat on the bed in bra and panties while Joshua sat on the chair fully clothed.

Laurie chewed her nail and asked, "Why don't you want me?"

Joshua took a deep breath and exhaled. "Oh, I want you alright. I have since the first second I saw you at the station in St Die. It's just that we're so close to being finished with this. I'd like to see it though before our relationship changes."

"Changes into what?" Laurie asked, still chewing her nail.

"I don't know. Just changes. In twenty-four hours, you'll be a millionaire. Many times over. It won't be me and you on a roof top, in a hostel or even asleep on a platform at a St Die train station. It'll be you with millions of dollars."

"Is that what's bothering you? The money we're about to come in to?"

"Not we. It'll be your money."

"Nonsense! It's our money."

Joshua shook his head. "No, it's your money."

Laurie got up and went to him. They stood face-to-face for a moment and then they embraced. Laurie's lithe frame felt wonderful in Joshua's arms. Laurie was thinking how delightful it felt to held by such a strong man. They kissed deeply, soulfully, but Joshua never aroused like he used to in the past. He was resigned to staying chaste until the auction was complete.

Laurie was disappointed, deeply so, but was proud of Joshua for his resignation and honor. She wasn't too worried, feeling confident she could dissuade him by using her charms, to see his way into sharing the money. This will work out, who could turn down her and millions of dollars.

Laurie loosened up a little during the evening as they were eating their outrageously expensive steaks. She felt certain she could right the ship if Joshua's only concern was the money. She had no doubt in her mind he was the guy for her. Looking back, she couldn't find the exact point in time that she knew, but subconsciously, it was probably when he woke her up at the St Die train station. It seemed like such a long time ago. Maybe a month is a long time when you're in love. Everyday seems like forever, in a good way, and every night seems like forever in a bad way, waiting for the new dawn and spending time together.

After the meal, they went out on the patio for drinks. Laurie had a glass of wine and Joshua had a pint. They could smell the sea. The air was cooler than it felt on the roof top in London so Laurie snuggled up to Joshua. Laurie ordered a second glass of wine and Joshua had another pint. When finished, Laurie discovered she was a little tipsy. She hadn't consumed any alcohol in several weeks. Plus, she lost weight on the coffee and chicken diet augmented with two hours of intermediate yoga every day. She was thin to begin with but now she was like a rail, at least in her eyes. Joshua thought she had a lot more curves to her than a rail.

Back at the hotel, Joshua was trying to figure out how not to sleep with Laurie when she solved the problem. She passed out in the bed. What else was really going to happen after a month of exhausting austerity, a large meal and two glasses of wine. Joshua joined her. It was the perfect storm for sleep, tired, clean, comfortable, well fed and highly lubricated with alcohol. Good night.

Chapter 39

The next morning, Laurie awoke to Joshua laying on his side, propped up on his arm, staring at her. She pushed her hair out of her face and said, "Good morning."

He grabbed her and pulled her over to him. They spooned for a moment until Joshua started becoming aroused. Laurie smiled to herself thinking everything is going to be alright. In two or three minutes, Joshua spoke, "Do you want to go first or me?"

"You go ahead. I'm going to enjoy this bed for as long as I can.

Joshua arose and went to clean up. He took a long leisurely hot shower, a luxury. While he was soaping up, he thought about the shower he took under the scupper at St Die. He was fascinated about how he could one day be taking a shower in water from thunderstorm roof runoff, the next day be bathing out of a bucket on top of Happy Chicken and the next be enjoying a slow, hot shower in a guest house at Southend-On-Sea.

Laurie could hardly relax on the bed knowing this was the big day. The auction was upon them. Laurie had no idea what to expect. She hoped the dress they bought would be elegant enough for the task at hand. Or maybe it was too much, she didn't know about these things. Now she was worried.

As Laurie sat up in bed becoming fraught over her dress decision, Joshua was scrubbing his underarms in a steamy shower without a care in the world.

Joshua learned long ago to be yourself and everything else will fall into place. Joshua came out of the bathroom, shiny as a new penny, but saw the worried look on Laurie's face. "What's wrong?"

Laurie said, "I'm worried about my clothes, how to act, what to do…"

Joshua laughed and sat on the bed beside her. He hugged her tightly and said, "I don't think we'll have to worry about that stuff. It doesn't matter what you wear. You're so beautiful, you could wear that sweat pants outfit and be just fine. We won't have to worry about what to do, somebody will be there to tell us. And don't worry about how to act. Be yourself, like you are around me."

"Oh, how's that? Afraid and helpless."

"Far from it. You're the girl who rides trains across Europe to clandestine rendezvous with international thieves and assassins."

"When you put it that way, worrying about what strangers think of me at a party sounds a bit trifle."

"There you go." He kissed her on the forehead and got dressed in his fine duds.

They went to the eating area to get their brunch. Most of the Guest House residents were wearing casual clothes or even something resembling pajamas. Joshua and Laurie looked like royalty. As the gorgeous couple ate their crumpets, eggs and tomatoes, a matronly woman came to their table and asked them if they were people of importance.

Joshua nearly burst out laughing. Instead, he rose, taking a regal stance and said. "I'm Lord Lewis Arlington and this is Lady Delacroix." Laurie tilted her head towards the woman in acknowledgement.

The woman slightly curtsied and said, "I knew you were important. I have a nose for these things. What are you doing here?"

Joshua suddenly went on high alert. Is this a busy body old lady or is this Juliette's assassin grandmother getting in on the act? Joshua couldn't read people's character anymore.

"Come on Lady Delacroix. We must be going." Joshua ordered as he stuck out his arm.

Laurie looked up at Joshua like he was crazy. Laurie was only half finished with her brunch and she so dearly wanted to eat. She knew better than to argue and stood with grace and bid the lady a good day. They went back to their room, retrieved their pack and walked to the train station.

"What was that all about?" asked Laurie when they were clear of the Guest House.

"Who walks up to total strangers, ask them who they are and why they are here?"

"Completely innocent grandmother types who can't control their curiosity or…. Juliette's assassin grandma."

"I don't like it," said Joshua.

Laurie had a faraway look on her face. "Why's that bitch trying to kill us?" she said into space more than to Joshua.

"Unless you've done something horribly heinous to someone in the recent past, it has to have something to do with the egg."

"Yeah, I get that, but what? Do you think it's her egg and she wants it back?"

"Oh, I think she wants it but I'm not sure it's her egg."

"She's a murdering thief then? Are we thieves?"

"Someone gave the egg to you, right?" Laurie nodded her head. "You were supposed to pass it off to someone else, right?" Laurie was still nodding. "Those people are dead now? Juliette has been rather thorough and brutal, wouldn't you say?" Still nodding. "There's no chain of custody. There are no reports of it being stolen. If it were stolen, I guarantee you Ms. Vanderweerdt at Christie's would have known. We're not thieves."

Laurie thought for a moment as they walked to the station. "Juliette wants to steal the egg from us? How can she? We don't have it."

"I'm afraid she may be pissed and wants to kill us now because she's frustrated."

"But what's her connection? What enticed her to start stalking us all the way back in France?"

Joshua tossed the big pack into the baggage corner of the rail car. They sat facing the entrance. "I don't know," Joshua replied. "I think she was hired by somebody but I don't know who. Some Russian oligarch or mafia type guy. Just like we discussed before. I can't figure anything else. Why she hasn't quit chasing us is another story."

"Maybe she really is just pissed. Got to answer to the boss, failed mission and all of that."

"I hope not. That means she'll never stop. It's got to be costing her a small fortune to keep searching for us. I'm mean, hotels, transportation, food, paying two soldiers to do some dirty work. When I say dirty work, I mean the dirtiest of work, killing. That's not cheap."

Laurie held on to Joshua's arm as the train clickity-clacked down the track. For the rest of the journey, they were lost in their own thoughts.

Chapter 40

At the London station, Joshua asked Laurie if she had any preference about where to stay. The obvious answer was, "Not on the roof of Happy Chicken."

Joshua suggested, "Let's go to a random hotel, drop off this pack and tell them we'll be back to check in later. That way if Juliette is still canvassing hotels, she won't know we were there. We'll check in after the auction. What'd you say?"

"What are we going to do until the auction? It's still four hours until it starts."

"There's a multiplex at Piccadilly. Want to take in a movie?"

"Dressed like this?"

Joshua opined, "We could always wait on the roof at Happy Chicken."

Laurie grabbed his arm and pulled him down the street,

"What's playing?"

"Does it matter?"

"I'm with you, so…no, it doesn't matter at all."

They picked the first hotel they came to which was an older urban hotel with walk-up rooms. Joshua dumped the pack and gave the bell captain a few pounds to watch it. They walked on to the movie house. One of the many theaters was showing vintage movies. The 1942 World War II film called Mrs. Miniver was playing. Perfect.

The previews, old newsreels and a cartoon preceded the feature film. By the time the movie ended, there was barely enough time to get to the auction. Little did the young couple know but the Faberge egg was to be auctioned last so there was plenty of time.

Ms. Vanderweerdt met them at the door. She was wearing a long gown making her look elegant. Joshua thought she was quite striking, not Laurie sexy-cool, but the lady could win first place in her age group. Ms. Vanderweerdt made sure Joshua and Laurie had a drink and pointed out some of the important people in the room filled full of important people.

"See the lady in red." Ms. Vanderweerdt discreetly pointed. "That's a royal from Belgium. The lady in blue on the other side of the room is a royal from Denmark. The man with the purple sash." She pointed with her eyes, "is a royal from Sweden."

Laurie was mesmerized by what she was seeing. Ms. Vanderweerdt continued. "The girl in that fabulous jeweled dress…that's the young princess from Spain."

Laurie spoke, "I didn't know all these countries still did this stuff."

"It's amazing isn't it?" Ms. Vanderweerdt replied. "Those gentlemen over there wearing thawbs…."

"Thawbs?" Laurie cut her off.

"Yes, the robes are called thawbs or thobes. I'm not real sure about the correct pronunciation. Those men wearing them are princes from Saudi Arabia. We're hoping they bid for your egg." Ms. Vanderweerdt took a long drink to finish her cocktail and excused herself to begin the auction.

Everyone was gently and respectfully herded into an elegant room filled with chairs and a podium. The bidders were given paddles with numbers on them. Joshua and Laurie sat in the back of the room soaking it all in.

The auctioneer walked out and the crowd politely clapped. "Welcome everyone to the Christie's Fall Gala. We have some wonderful items up for auction tonight. I will reiterate that bidding will be in U.S. Dollars. Shall we begin?"

Laurie and Joshua looked at each other nearly giggling. They couldn't have been any more excited if they were about to board the Cyclone roller coaster at Coney Island. The auctioneer focused, "First up we have the 14 karat blue diamond earrings worn by the great Viscountess Nancy Astor. Bidding will begin at two-hundred thousand dollars." Two men carried out a stand with the earrings dangling from it.

"Do I hear a reserve bid of two-hundred thousand?"

A paddle with the number 77 went up in the right rear of the room. "Thank you, sir. Do I hear two- twenty-five?"

And so, the auction started. The earrings topped out at four and a quarter. Joshua and Laurie were amazed at the way money was thrown around. Someone paid 1.2 million dollars for a tea set formerly owned by one of the English Kings of the past. Joshua wouldn't have paid fifty bucks for it.

Halfway through the auction, Joshua got up to get them another drink. He went out into the now empty lobby and bellied up to the bar. The bartender happily poured him a stout and a glass of red wine. As Joshua turned around, he saw Juliette standing in the doorway, wearing a beige ball gown. Their eyes met.

Joshua set the drinks down and decided he was tired of running. He walked straight toward her. Her eyes widened at the unexpected move. She popped open her clutch purse and removed the little Beretta pistol. She made sure Joshua saw it.

Joshua did see it but was not deterred. He stopped within a few feet from her and said very calmly, "Hello Juliette." Joshua could see out the door and recognized the henchmen standing on the sidewalk.

"I see you brought the boys," Joshua said.

"A girl can't be too careful, you know."

"What do you want Juliette?"

"I wanted that fabulous Faberge egg that you got your hands on, but now, I think I just want a pound of flesh."

"Why?" asked Joshua.

"That's a good question, Josh." Joshua didn't like the shortened form of his name and especially didn't like Juliette using it. "You see, I was paid and exorbitant amount of money to intercept the egg in Tunisia. But missed the boat, literally, by that much. The guy who had it managed to escape on a ferry just minutes before I caught up to him. But I found him again in Barcelona. He was supposed to hand the egg off to an unknown party to take the egg to Switzerland. However, I found that unknown party first. He told me everything he knew before he expired."

"You killed him?"

"No Josh. Not really. He kind of died while we were talking to him."

"You tortured him to death."

Juliette smiled, "That's more like it." She continued. "I was going to use one of my guys to be the unknown courier to Switzerland but the original grease ball must have gotten wise. He gave the egg to your bitch. Can you imagine that? Giving a twenty-million-dollar trinket to somebody like Laurie from backwater Louisiana. He gave it to a random stranger with legs up to here. Men are so stupid."

"Who hired you?" Joshua asked.

"Just a guy. He lives in Malaysia."

"A crazy rich Asian, huh?"

"You got that right, rich and most definitely crazy."

"Why are you still after us? Revenge? Pay back? Why don't you just cut and run?"

Juliette grunted a little, "You can't run from this guy. He owns the world. He's in there right now, going to bid on the egg. If he can't steal it, he'll buy it. The money means nothing to him. He's worth billions."

"Why did you shoot Margerie?"

"Who?" asked Juliette, not really knowing the name Margerie.

"Margerie, the lady from the antique shop?"

"Oh, the old fat lady. She grabbed my arm trying to help your string bean. I never saw a woman run so fast as Laurie. Long hair flying behind her like a horse's mane."

"Why did you kill the Germans?"

"What Germans?"

Joshua thought, my Lord, this girl doesn't even know who she kills. "The people in the hostel."

"Oh them? They were witnesses. Got in the way, you know."

So, what's next?" asked Joshua.

"Are you worried?"

Joshua looked Juliette in the eyes, "I just want to know if I'm going to have to kill you before this is finished."

Juliette was a little stunned. She thought he was the one who should be worried. Now, he turned the table.

"I am pretty good at this," said Joshua. "You couldn't find us."

"Where were you hiding? I know you never stayed in a hotel or hostel or any other reputable establishment. I barely missed you at the Cavendish. That's the last I knew of you. Where were you?"

Joshua smiled back at her.

"Trade secret, huh? Where did you get the money to hide so well?"

Joshua smiled again. "I had to work for it. For thirty days I butchered meat." He stretched the truth a little. "I've gotten very good with knives and cleavers. Next time I see you, you better have more than that twenty-five-caliber pop gun because I learned how to slice through bone." Joshua towered over her and his body looked thick and muscular.

Juliette never showed it but she was intimidated. She didn't know which would be worse, looking over her shoulder for the rest of her life for Joshua or the crazy, rich Asian. Juliette strolled over to the bar, picked up Laurie's glass of wine and drank it straight down. She patted Joshua on the arm, noticing how firm it felt, as she walked out. "See you around stud." On the sidewalk, she made a motion with her hands and the two henchmen ran to a car. One held the door open for her. Once seated, the car sped away into the night. Joshua was hoping that would be the last he ever saw of Juliette and the murderers. He bought another glass of wine a went back to sit with Laurie.

Laurie was excited and told Joshua about a vinyl record by the Beatles selling for $15,000, a platinum watch bought for $27,000 and a Macedonian coin selling for $125,000. He could tell she was having a great time, choosing not to tell her about Juliette in the lobby.

The night progressed with Laurie's excitement being rekindled with every sale. After three hours, there were only two items left on the sale, a painting by Edouard Manet and the Faberge egg. The egg would be auctioned last even though the Manet may bring a higher price. The last Manet painting sold at Christie's went for 65 million dollars.

The auction continued with the Manet brought out. The painting looked like a mess to Joshua. It was a scene of some people standing near a pond, or at least, that's what he thought. The bidding began. The reserve bid was ten-million dollars and for a long time no one bid. Laurie was looking around anxiously, holding her glass of wine.

The auctioneer announced, "Last call on the reserve bid of ten-million dollars for the Manet."

Timidly a lady in the front raised her paddle.

"Thank you, madam. Do I hear eleven?"

The bidding went up a million dollars each bid until it reached 28 million. At that point the auctioneer expertly guided the bidders up in price at a half a million dollars each bid. The ugly Manet painting faltered at $30.5 million dollars.

Joshua sat stunned. He was having a hard time believing anyone would throw away thirty-million on a two-foot square painting. An ugly painting at that. He downed his beer. "Unbelievable!"

Chapter 41

The egg was the last item to be auctioned. Laurie was so excited she couldn't drink her wine. Joshua took it from her before she spilled it and set it on the table behind them. Joshua excused himself to go to the bathroom. Laurie would have pee'd her pants rather than leave at a time like this.

In the lobby, Joshua looked around for a pen and paper. Finding none, he ventured down a corridor and saw a young woman in her office. Joshua politely knocked on the door frame, startling the young miss. "May I help you?" she asked.

"Do you have a pen and paper?"

"Yes, of course." She reached in a drawer and handed him what he requested. She was stunned by how handsome he was. Joshua took the items and thanked her.

"Anything else I can get you? Anything at all?"

"No. You've been very kind. Thanks."

Joshua left the office. The woman sighed and went back to work.

Joshua quickly wrote a note to Laurie. He found Alastair, the security guard, and asked him to give it to her. Alastair remembered Laurie well and knew exactly where she was sitting. Joshua gave him the note and thanked him. Alastair went to fulfill his duty. Joshua left Christie's and disappeared into the night.

The egg was on the block and the auctioneer called for the reserve bid. Instead of the twenty million reserve, a man in front raised his paddle and said, "Thirty-million dollars."

Laurie squealed. After the ice was broken, there was a quick war among six bidders bringing the price up to 39 million dollars. The last bid was held by one of the Saudi princes. "Going once. Going twice…"

"Forty million!" hollered the Asian man in the front.

Alastair found Laurie and handed her the folded note. Laurie read it immediately.

Laurie

You're going to be rich beyond belief now. You'll go home and be welcomed with open arms. Every cousin and acquaintance will come out of the bayou backwater to be your bestie. You'll have to sort through who is true and who is not. Sharks will be circling so watch your six. I wanted to make sure I was with you for the right reasons. Initially I was attracted to you because you were beautiful and you were sleeping on concrete. My kind of girl. After a while, when we discovered the worth of the egg, I had my doubts. Money changes people.

If you're still the same person after experiencing obscene riches, meet me at the train station in Saint Die exactly one year from the night we met there. Maybe next time, it won't be raining.

I do love you but I've got to find out if we're meant to be.

Joshua

Laurie ran out into the lobby as she heard the auctioneer say, "Thank you ma'am. The bid is now forty-one million!" She frantically looked around for Joshua but couldn't find him. She did see Alastair come out of the auction and ran to him.

"Where did Joshua go?"

"He left, miss. He just asked me to deliver the note and left."

Laurie chewed her nail. She knew not to run after him. Joshua was too good at hiding. He was gone. "Damn it!"

Forlorn, she walked back into the auction. The gavel dropped, "Sold! For forty-eight million dollars. A new record for a Faberge egg." People were congratulating the Asian man. Laurie walked over to him.

The man saw Laurie and walked free of the small crowd surrounding him. He approached her and she smiled at him, not knowing Juliette was his agent. "Congratulations," she said. "I hope the egg brings you more joy than it did us."

"Oh?" he said.

"Yeah, our short time owning the egg was rather tumultuous."

"Oh?" he said again as he observed how beautiful she was.

"Just wanted to congratulate you and thank you for buying the egg at such a generous price."

"Thank you for bringing it to auction. And I'm sure your hard times are over now."

Laurie didn't know it but the man just gave her a free pass. No more sanctioned hits. All he wanted was the egg. As many billions as he had, he still didn't want to pay 48 million for it, but it was done. He would rather have stolen it for the two million he paid Juliette. Two million he basically paid for nothing. He would have to meditate over what to do about that.

Chapter 42

Laurie waited as the crowd cleared out. Everyone was talking about the price of the egg. The 30-million-dollar Manet painting was already forgotten. Ms. Vanderweerdt found Laurie and told her to come by Christie's on Monday and they would settle up, either by wire transfer to a bank or an old fashion check.

"How much will my end of the settle up be?" Laurie asked.

Ms. Vanderweerdt's eyes looked up and to the left as she were calculating in her head. "Somewhere around 41.5 million dollars."

Now Laurie's eyes rolled back in her head. "Okay. What time should I come by?" Laurie asked, barely managing to keep from passing out.

"Let's say around eleven, love." They hugged and Laurie walked out of Christie's.

With no better idea, she went straight to the walk-up hotel she and Joshua picked out earlier. Once there, she discovered the pack was present with all her essentials in it. Joshua's stuff was missing, which made her sad.

Laurie started to stay at the hotel but at the last second changed her mind. She learned a new word from Joshua… hostel. Since she had a few days before she could get the millions, her hundreds were going to have to tide her over.

The nearest hostel was only a few blocks away. With pack on her back and still wearing her evening clothes, she knew she looked ridiculous but she felt free and surprisingly happy. Somehow Joshua was with her, guiding her every step.

Laurie checked in to the hostel, made friends with everyone in the room and settled down for a good night's sleep and sweet dreams of Joshua. Joshua, on the other hand, was standing outside the Hotel Sofitel watching Juliette and the murderers unload luggage from the car and check in. He was lucky the hotel was only four or five blocks away from Christie's and the auction traffic clogged the streets, otherwise he wouldn't have been able to keep up on foot.

As soon as Juliette and her thugs went inside, Joshua rushed to the front door trying to determine what rooms they were staying in. From his vantage point, he could only tell a transaction was being conducted at the front desk. Juliette handed her men key cards and they went to the lift, followed closely by the bell captain and their luggage.

Joshua had no way of figuring out which rooms they occupied unless he went up to the desk clerk and asked, which may entail a hefty bribe. Since he was low on funds, that course of action was eliminated. His next thought was to wait them out. Joshua didn't really know what he wanted to do with Juliette and the murderers other than emphasize the need for them to leave Laurie alone. After he confronted them, he would like to see them get on a plane or train and leave London.

Joshua decided to wait in the lobby where it was warm until they threw him out and then he would wait outside in the cold damp London fog. It wasn't much of a plan but that's what he was going to do. There were a couple of stuffed chairs in the lobby and he planted himself in one, picked up the paper from the end table and started reading like belonged there.

Joshua lasted an hour and half before the clerk came over and asked him his business. Joshua said he was waiting for his party to show up. The clerk pressed with more questions which Joshua semi-answered. "Alright boy-o," the clerk declared. "It's time for you to leave."

At that moment, the lift doors opened and Juliette stepped out with her luggage. She appeared to be absconding in the middle of the night. The clerk ran over to the desk readying himself to hear her complaint as to why she was checking out at this hour.

Joshua wondered if the two murderers upstairs had been murdered themselves, tied off neatly by Juliette as loose ends. Joshua's assumption was correct. Earlier, after the bell captain put her big suitcase in the rack and left, Juliette joined the boys in their room with a small suitcase. She sat them down on the couch, found some dance music on her iPhone and blue-toothed it through a tiny but powerful speaker.

She kicked her high-heels off, dropped her evening gown to the floor and stood up on the coffee table in front of the couch. Wearing only elbow length evening gloves and lacy, matching see-through, black panties and bra, she started dancing seductively. The boys sat forward in their seats.

"Since you did so well, I thought I would give you a little reward." She continued dancing. One of the big men started to get up but Juliette jumped off the table and pushed him back down. "No, no, not yet."

She went to the small suitcase, pulled out two stacks of British pounds, each bound with a rubber band and tossed them on the table in front of them. Both men reached for the money in perfect choreography. Juliette pulled out her Beretta and Bam! Bam! Shot them in the head. The time between shots was a half a second.

One man collapsed, face first on the table. The other guy grabbed his head, stood up and said some unintelligible words because his brain was scrambled. He walked instinctively five steps to the door but fell in the middle of the room. His blood soaking into the cream-colored carpet.

     Bonnie Shiloh

Juliette scooped up the two wads of money, one was a bloody mess from the guy who died on the coffee table. She went to the bathroom and washed it off, threw it in the suitcase and pulled out a black stylish jumpsuit and slipped into it, then donned a pair of sensible loafers.

She rolled her high-heels up in her evening gown and stuffed them in the suitcase. The iPhone and speaker were inserted into a jumpsuit pocket. Juliette rolled her suitcase out the hotel room door, took off her evening gloves and stashed them in the suitcase side pocket.

Juliette went to her room like nothing happened, got her larger suitcase and took the lift to the lobby where she was now confronting the clerk. Juliette did not notice Joshua in the far corner of the lobby, sitting calmly, reading a paper.

The clerk was upset and apologized profusely for whatever was causing Juliette to check out of the hotel at midnight. Juliette didn't care about his fragile feelings. Escape was her only thought. The clerk refused to take any money for the room and Juliette snatched up her luggage and rushed to the front door. Joshua followed.

Juliette walked a block to the car park and threw the luggage in the boot. Joshua watched her drive off with no hope of knowing where she was going or what she was going to do. He should have confronted her again but sooner or later; she would use that pea shooter she had in her purse. To the dismay of the clerk, Joshua returned to the hotel. The clerk, whose name was Oliver, protested and ran from behind the counter to accost him. Oliver's approach slowed as he neared Joshua because Joshua towered over him by five inches and outweighed him by 45 or 50 pounds.

Joshua held up his hand and stopped the clerk in his tracks with the gesture. Joshua spoke in a commanding voice, "Check the room!"

"What?" queried the clerk.

"Go to the room she just checked out of and look at it."

"Why?"

"She is a known murderer and thief. A pile of bodies has followed her across Europe."

"Are you the police?"

"Not exactly," replied Joshua.

"Interpol?"

"Check the room now or I'll have you arrested as an accomplice."

"You're American? What authority do you have here?"

Joshua grabbed his collar at the tie knot, "Get up there and check the room or I'll authorize your ass all the way out into the street." Joshua let go with a little shove.

Oliver straightened his tie, appearance was important. He pulled a master key card out of his jacket pocket and turned to go to the lift. Joshua followed. At Juliette's room, Oliver asked, "Are you sure this is legal?"

Joshua put his hand on the nape of Oliver's neck. "Just think of yourself as a hero." Joshua squeezed, demonstrating the immense power in his arms. Oliver squeaked like a mouse and knocked on the door, "Hotel staff!"

No answer. "Just go in," Joshua urged.

Oliver swiped the card, the door light turned green and popped open. Joshua shoved Oliver out of the way and went in first. The room looked completely untouched. Joshua didn't need to see anything further. Juliette used the room as a ruse.

Oliver stepped in, "She better not have opened the mini-bar!" He took two steps toward the refrigerator. Joshua snatched his coat tail and pulled him back out of the room.

"Take me to the room occupied by the two gentlemen who checked in with her."

"It's just across the hall. Are you sure this is necessary?"

Joshua put his hand back on Oliver's neck.

"Alright, alright." Oliver knocked on the door. "Hotel staff!" Oliver knocked once more with the same announcement.

Joshua snatched the key card from Oliver's hand and opened the door. Joshua pushed it open slowly not knowing what to expect but quickly realized what happened when he saw the body on the floor with a pool of nasty matted blood in the carpet. Joshua stepped in and got the full image of the damage. Two men dead, both shot in the head with what he was assuming was Juliette's .25 automatic pistol.

Oliver rushed in behind Joshua and couldn't wrap his mind around what he was seeing. "Oh no, the carpet."

Joshua looked at him, amazement all over his face, "That's your takeaway from this? The carpet's ruined?"

Oliver had no response. Joshua shook his shoulder. "Oliver." Joshua read the name on his silver name tag. "Go downstairs, call the police and wait to guide them up. Got it?" Oliver made a slight head movement which Joshua took as confirmation. "Go!" Joshua pushed him out the door.

As soon as Oliver was out of sight, Joshua searched the room and the bodies. He pulled the wallet out of the pocket of the man on the floor. The man was identified as a Croatian with a name Joshua couldn't pronounce or spell. It had a lot of Z's, C's and K's in it. His name was inconsequential.

There was a large amount of euros in his wallet in 100-euro bills. Joshua had moral dilemma. Should he take the money? Was it stealing to take the money from the man who was paid to murder you? After a pause, Joshua shrugged and stuffed the money in his pocket. There was nothing else of interest on the dead man.

Joshua searched the second dead guy leaned over on the coffee table in a grisly position which would have been funny had the man been passed out drunk. Since he was shot at close range in the eye, the position of the body had no hilarity.

Joshua extricated the dead man's wallet and discovered his last name was Gashi from Kosovo. He too had a small fortune of 100 euro bills which Joshua confiscated. The rest of what was in the wallet was of no use except for a small folded piece of paper with the words, 'On the Cliff Suites', written on it.

Obviously, the reference was to a hotel, but where, the Cliffs of Dover where he a Juliette crossed the channel, the Cliffs of Moher in Ireland?

He'd figure it out later. Joshua wanted to search their luggage but was running out of time. The police would be here soon. He replaced everything, except the money and the note. He glanced around the room and it looked exactly like it did when he and Oliver entered.

Joshua left the room, walked down the fire escape stairs and exited the side of the building. He was gone. The police, in droves, rumbled out of the lift and cordoned off the room waiting for the Detective Chief Inspector.

Chapter 43

After blundering around and asking directions, Joshua found Internet City, an internet café. He paid his fee and looked up 'On the Cliffs Suites'. To his total surprise, the hotel was not in the United Kingdom or Ireland. It was on the island of Santorini, Greece. "I guess I'm going to Greece," Joshua said to himself.

For a short while Joshua contemplated how to get to Greece. He had money now. He hadn't taken time to count it but it was significant. He could take a train to the coast, a ferry to the continent, a train across Europe all the way to Greece. Then a ferry to the island. Or, a train through the Chunnel all the way to Greece. Or… "Screw it!" He went to Heathrow and bought a plane ticket to Athens. The plane was to depart first thing in the morning. Joshua left his meager personal items in Juliette's hotel lobby and didn't bother to get them because the risk-reward was not worth it. He bought a small backpack and toilet items at the airport. It was good to have money.

He purchased a pastry and coffee and settled into a very uncomfortable seat in the waiting area at the gate. After finishing his meager meal, he was fast asleep, dreaming of the beautiful auburn-haired girl he left behind and was now trying to protect.

At daybreak, Joshua woke with a start. It took a few seconds before he could figure out where he was, what he was doing and what happened last night. He went to the toilet, brushed his teeth, bought a gigantic cup of coffee and boarded his plane.

Laurie woke on her lower bunk in the hostel and rubbed the hair out of her face. She felt refreshed and happy. Joshua was the first thing on her mind. Laurie needed to kill a few days so plans were made to fill them with useful or otherwise time-consuming tasks. Laurie cleaned up and dressed in front of the other hostelers like she was a native European. Both guys and girls stared at her equally.

Laurie found herself sizing up each individual, but not like they were doing to her. The girls were looking at Laurie for flaws. Did her butt sag, were her boobs not perky enough, maybe her hair was dyed, clothes inappropriate? The girl guests found none of that. Laurie was close to perfection. The guy guest just stared because that's what guys did. It was easy to pass their scrutiny. She had them at "Good morning."

Laurie looked at the guests for traces of betrayal, deceitfulness, cunning and danger. She learned that from Joshua also. One of the better-looking male guests came from the shower wrapped only in a towel with the slit positioned in front. His genitals were partially exposed. He attempted to engage Laurie in a conversation.

Laurie was dressed in her Gucci outfit to the approval of all the females. Laurie shook her hair out and ran a brush through the long, thick locks. The flasher guy stuttered a little as he tried to strike up a conversation. The girls in the room giggled. The guy was six feet tall, weighed 180 pounds and looked like he hit the gym several times a week. His hair was cropped extremely short. Laurie could see a receding hairline and realized he shaved his head to get in front of his male pattern baldness.

The guy regrouped to make a remark. Laurie gave him the once over before he could speak and said, "The showers must have run out of hot water." She nodded towards his genitals. The man retreated in shame. Laurie's assessment of the group, no one here is a threat.

Laurie's first stop was a bank. It was a large, old bank building owned by some ancient British banking family. She paused at an information desk and asked to see the manager because she wanted to open an account. The male desk attendant was reluctant to call the manager for a simple opening of an account but Laurie was the most beautiful woman he'd ever seen and his will to refuse wilted in her presence. The attendant escorted her to an empty office lavishly appointed with wooden features. Most of them appeared to be from India.

The manager entered wearing a suit looking more appropriate for the 1970's rather than the 2000's. The man took a seat behind the large wooden desk. He pointed to the uncomfortable looking straight back wooden chair on which she was supposed to sit.

As expected, the chair was miserably uncomfortable. Laurie assumed this was the office designated for meetings which were not going to take a long time. "Now, young lady. How may I help you?"

Without hesitation Laurie stated, "I want to open an account, with the minimum amount of money."

"I am a very busy man. You could have done that at the counter. Why are you wasting my time?" The manager rose, straightened his five-decade out-of-date suit and left Laurie sitting in the hard, wood chair. Within seconds the attendant came to escort Laurie to the counter so she could open a low-end account the proper way.

The attendant left Laurie at the counter and assumed his position behind the front desk, guarding the family banking heritage from interlopers and low-end account openers. Laurie walked out of the bank. Both she and the attendant were thinking that was for the best.

Laurie felt the chill in the air as fall was upon London town. She wrapped her arms around herself and thought of Joshua. "Where is that boy?" she said out loud, maybe, or did she just think it. Laurie walked down the street with no particular direction in mind but ever on the lookout for another bank and Juliette and the murderers or their agents. She literally tingled all over thinking of Joshua, feeling free, flirting with danger and sensing the fresh breeze on her face.

Within three blocks, Laurie came upon another bank. It was more modern looking. Maybe this one won't have a stick up its butt, she thought. When she entered, there was no attendant to give her the bum rush back out. At the counter, Laurie asked the female teller if she could see the manager.

The young teller asked if something was wrong and could she possibly make it right. Good start, thought Laurie. "No, nothing is wrong. I want to open an account and I like to meet the people who are responsible for my money."

Without hesitation the teller closed her drawer, locked it and came around from behind the counter. The young teller motioned for Laurie to follow. "Come on with me. Mr. Belgrave is the manager. He's got an office around the corner."

Laurie followed the teller down the hall to an office with a closed door. The teller spoke. "Mr. Belgrave is the nicest man. He took the worst office in the building so those who do the work would have a good place to do business. He's the nicest man, or did I already say that?" The teller knocked on the door.

"Come in!"

The teller pushed the door open and said, "Mr. Belgrave, this woman would like to open a new account and wanted to meet the person in charge."

"Oh, my goodness," Mr. Belgrave said as he stood up, pulled a napkin out of his collar and shoved a sandwich into a desk drawer. "Sorry," he said, "I didn't know I had an appointment." He wiped his mouth with the napkin even though he hadn't taken a bite of the sandwich yet.

"I should be apologizing," said Laurie, "I interrupted your lunch."

Mr. Belgrave ran around the desk, shook Laurie's hand and said "John Belgrave."

Laurie replied, "Laurie Delacroix."

As Mr. Belgrave grabbed several books off a ratty chair he asked, "How can I help you? Please have a seat."

Laurie sat in the beat-up chair which was ten times more comfortable than the previous chair in which she sat. "I'd like to open an account at this bank."

"Okay," he said. "We can do that."

Mr. Belgrave picked up his desk phone and punched a button. "Mary, come back in here with all the paperwork you need to open a new account."

Laurie told Mr. Belgrave he could go ahead and eat his lunch, she didn't mind.

"If you really don't mind, I'm starving." He pulled open the drawer and retrieved the sandwich. He replaced his napkin bib, unwrapped the sandwich from its paper and set it in between them both. "You want to share. It's roast beef?"

Laurie hesitated for a long moment, sizing up the situation. This guy was like night and day from the other bank manager. "I am hungry," she said and grabbed the half a sandwich. Mary walked in with some papers and was pleased by the scene of them sharing lunch.

Mr. Belgrave stood up, reached in his pocket for his wallet and pulled out a twenty-pound note. He handed it to Mary and said, "Can you run over to Gil's and buy us a Coke, some chips and lunch for yourself. Bring it back straight away and we'll do some business." He nodded his head for Laurie's approval.

"By all means," replied Laurie. Mary laid the papers down on the desk and left with the money. Mr. Belgrave and Laurie continued to talk and eat. Before Mary returned with the food and drinks, Laurie learned Mr. Belgrave grew up in Liverpool and moved to London to attend university. After graduation, he began banking and a short thirty years later, he was now, manager of this small independent bank. He was married and had three children all in diverse fields of work except the youngest who is still in college, studying history.

Mary returned, with a cardboard tray of chips and drinks and a sandwich for herself. She also had three tarts for dessert. Mr. Belgrave was pleased. They continued to eat and get to know each other. When it came Laurie's time to speak, she told most of the story except for the last month and a half.

Finished eating with the trash cleared away, Mary sat with Laurie and went over each piece of paper needed to open an account. At the end, Mary asked, "How much would you like to deposit today? The minimum is twenty pounds."

Laurie reached in her pocket and pulled out a twenty-pound note. "Twenty," Laurie said.

"Perfect," replied Mary. Mary took the money, handed Laurie a receipt, a card with the account number and some routing numbers on it and some temporary checks. Mary got up to excuse herself to make Laurie an ATM/Debit card.

While Mary was out, Mr. Belgrave reiterated to not write any checks or try to use the ATM card until some more money could be deposited. "The ATM will not let you withdraw anything but the checks will bounce and generate a service charge. So be prudent."

"Gotch ya," Laurie responded.

Mary returned with the plastic ATM card and handed it to Laurie. Mary started to speak but Laurie stopped her, "I know. Don't try to use it until I deposit some more money." Mary pointed at her in approval.

Laurie left the bank after saying goodbye to Mr. Belgrave and hugging Mary. Mr. Belgrave had the most fun he'd had in months and Mary felt elated for no reason. Laurie had that effect on people. Laurie was feeling mighty fine too.

Chapter 44

Joshua stepped off the plane around midnight, not sure of the hour because of crossing a couple of time zones. He knew he was tired and it was late. Joshua talked to the taxi drivers at the stand. Only a few of them could converse in English enough to understand he was looking for a hostel or extremely cheap hotel. A particularly aggressive driver grabbed Joshua's pack off his shoulder, threw it in the trunk of his car and told Joshua to get in. This driver was fourth back in line and all the other drivers began shouting Greek obscenities at him.

Without words, the driver took Joshua to a white-washed area below the Parthenon. He pointed to a blue door and said, "Room rent." The driver popped the trunk so Joshua could get his pack.

Joshua paid the driver with a little extra for the service and knocked on the blue door. An older woman answered. She saw the taxi driver and blew him a kiss before he drove off. "My son," she said. The woman ushered Joshua into the tiny home and showed him a bedroom. The room was small with a bed a little bigger than a twin, a desk and a stuffed chair that had seen better days. There was also a 13-inch, small box TV on the desk. One picture hung on the wall of a harbor scene.

The lady nodded at Joshua asking for his approval. Joshua gave the thumbs up and dropped his pack on the chair. The lady smiled and took him down the hall to a bathroom with a small towel hanging on the rack. It looked like a dish towel. Joshua gave another thumbs up. The lady was beaming. She then led him to the kitchen-dining area where she served him a bowl of steaming hot beef stifado and a small glass of Kourtaki Imiglikos Nemea Red wine. One of the cheapest wines in Greece.

The stew tasted salty and sweet at the same time and melted in his mouth. Excellent Greek food. The wine… not so much. When Joshua finished, the lady said the room cost twenty euros and the wine cost three euros. The food, supper and breakfast the next day, was complimentary. Joshua gladly handed over enough British pounds to satisfy her and went to bed.

Lying in bed, Joshua's mind raced thinking of Laurie and planning the next day's moves which would involve getting to the ferry port, taking a ferry to Mykonos and another one to Santorini. Finding a cheap place to stay on Santorini may prove to be a problem. Before long, sleep overcame him.

Joshua became aware of sunlight breaching the flimsy curtains on the window and then heard a TV chattering in Greek somewhere in the household. He sat up in bed and rubbed his face while trying to fully wake up. Joshua pulled on his jeans and picked up his toilet kit. He checked the hall for activity and went to the bathroom to shower and prepare for the day.

While in the shower, he heard the bathroom door open and shut. He peeked out around the opaque plastic curtain and saw the lady in the bathroom setting out larger towels. He was pleased but felt encroached upon. He thought he heard the door shut again and continued to wash his hair. When completely rinsed, he pulled back the shower curtain surprised to see the lady standing there, offering Joshua a towel. Joshua didn't know what to think.

He wasn't sure if this was part of the Greek custom of if this was an old lady trying to get a good look at a young, well built, well-endowed man. He stepped half out of the shower, trying to stay covered with the curtain and took the towel from her hand. Once the towel was placed in Joshua's hand, the lady left the bathroom, leaving Joshua baffled.

After Joshua was dressed and packed, he came out into the kitchen-dining area to be greeted by the lady and her son. They were both eating staka me ayga. Basically, it's a pile of eggs enhanced with some creamy, flour concoction. They were tasty and plentiful. Finished eating, the son offered his taxi service to Joshua, never missing an opportunity to serve and rake in some low hanging British pounds.

Joshua told the driver he needed to get to the ferry terminal to go to Mykonos and then to Santorini. The driver acknowledged the request, grabbed Joshua's pack and ushered him into the taxi. At the ferry terminal, the driver parked and went with Joshua to buy tickets for both ferries. When finished, Joshua paid the driver for the fare and a generous tip for the extra service. The driver was most thankful. Greece recently fell on hard times and was appreciative of all the foreign influx of euros or in this case, pounds, it could get.

Joshua waited a short while for the ferry and then he was off. On the plane to Greece, during the taxi ride and even on the ferry, Joshua was always looking for Juliette. What were the chances of them being on the same mode of transportation at the same time?

They did leave the hotel where the two thugs were murdered at about the same time. They could have easily been on the plane together or one plane earlier or later or she could have taken the train. Maybe she flew into Santorini or maybe she was in Genoa or Budapest or anywhere else in the world. All Joshua had to go on was the name of a hotel written on a small piece of paper found in the dead guy's pocket. Joshua was starting to feel silly chasing this flimsy clue thousands of miles across Europe.

Chapter 45

The ride to Mykonos was smooth but the Aegean Sea showed some fury between Mykonos and Santorini. At the Santorini ferry port, Joshua disembarked feeling a little sick from bac-to-back ferry rides, the second leg being more carnivalesque. Once standing on tera firma, he cupped his eyes and stared up at the towering cliffs of Santorini. He fought a small crowd for a taxi and took the ride up the steep road to the top. The views were priceless. He wished Laurie could be here with him.

Joshua asked the driver to take him to the nearest bank. He wanted to exchange these British pounds for euros. The driver took him to Piraeus Bank. Joshua asked the driver to wait while he went in to exchange the pounds.

The banker counted the money and the total was a little short of eight thousand pounds. After paying the fee for the exchange, Joshua had over eight thousand euros. The rate was very favorable and as suspected, Joshua had been over paying for everything since he left England.

Joshua asked the driver to take him to an inexpensive hotel. The driver took him to Villa Manos. Joshua could stay there for less than fifty euros a night. Not bad for Santorini. Joshua paid the driver and checked in for an indefinite period. The hotel was luxurious according to Joshua's standards.

He jumped on the bed and overturned his pack on the spread. The contents were meager for an international traveler, a second change of clothes and toilet articles. That was meager even for homeless people. Joshua took a shower, washed the clothes he had on and changed into his new outfit he bought at the airport. He made a mental note to pick up some socks and underwear along the way.

His plan was to wander the island, especially the high-end tourist areas and keep his eyes peeled for Juliette. He'd inquire at the various hotels, especially the On the Cliffs Suites to see if Juliette checked in using the name Juliette. He didn't have a last name and she may use some other name. As he gave the plan serious thought, his decision to come here was starting to look like a bad idea. He decided he would leave Santorini when his money began to run out. He could try to get a job but jobs were scarce on an island. They were mostly reserved for locals who needed the work.

He left the hotel to walk to Oia, a beautiful cliff side enclave, to find the On the Cliffs Suites. He would get something to eat and observe the comings and goings. He thought about renting a motor scooter but they were too expensive and the island was only eleven miles long. He could walk the whole thing back and forth in a day, easily.

In London, Laurie was shopping for a new purse. The trusty tote she always carried was left on the roof of Happy Chicken. After discovering the exorbitant prices of name brand purses, she decided to walk back to Happy Chicken and retrieve her favorite bag. The distance was at least a mile from where she was to the Chinese restaurant. Before meeting Joshua, she would have taken a taxi or Ubered for anything that far away. Now a mile stroll seemed enjoyable.

As she neared the restaurant, a craving for sesame chicken overcame her. Sitting in the tiny restaurant, she tucked into her appetizer and savored every bite and couldn't help smiling the whole time. Laurie was not yet sad about Joshua leaving her. She still felt his presence, his strength and the wisdom he had beyond his years. She was forever changed and she liked the new Laurie.

After her three bites of sesame chicken, she returned to their alley and pulled the rope on the fire escape ladder, and easily climbed to the roof. Their gear was still packed away as they had left it, neatly wrapped in the tarp and tied off with the remnants of the rope. She found her tote bag and held it up in the sun to inspect it as if she were seeing it for the first time. She re-wrapped the rest of the supplies. You never know when one might need a hide-out with all the trimmings.

She descended the ladder and strolled down the alley sporting a tote with absolutely nothing in it. Happy as a clam, was a good description. Back at the hostel, she loaded her tote with what female necessities she had which weren't much… a brush, a light sweater, a pumpkin-red lipstick and a pocket book with all her personal information and new banking cards.

What to do now? There were a couple of nights before the money was available. The plan was to go to a movie every day at Piccadilly, that would kill three hours, eat at a restaurant once a day which would take another hour, walk at least two miles for exercise and do yoga with a shower afterwards would take another hour. A premier league football match viewed at a local pub would take two hours. After considering some of the many options, filling three days in London with little money would be a breeze.

As the afternoon progressed, Laurie went to Gil's, the restaurant-pub across from her bank. She bought a gift certificate valued at one-hundred pounds. Walking down the block, she found a clothing boutique and bought a gift certificate from them for the same amount of money. Laurie went to the bank just before closing and saw Mary behind the counter at her teller window. Mary waved, locked her drawer and ran around the counter as if she hadn't seen Laurie in years. It had been a few hours.

"Is Mr. Belgrave in now?' Laurie asked.

"Yes!" Mary grabbed Laurie's arm and the headed back to his office.

Mary knocked and heard an acknowledgement from the other side of the door. Mary stepped in the office and said, "Look what I found!" and dragged Laurie in by her hand. Mr. Belgrave jumped up from behind his desk, knocking over a stack of papers on the corner. He grabbed Laurie's hand and shook it profusely.

They took the same seats they had before and Laurie stated she was treated so kindly she wanted to do something nice for them. She handed each of them their gift certificates. Mr. Belgrave and Mary were overcome by her kindness and insisted Laurie should have used the money to increase her meager account. Laurie's reply was, "Too late now."

Mr. Belgrave, being one of the nicest men Laurie had ever met, decided to close the bank a few minutes early and reconvene at Gil's where he would buy everybody some chips and a pint. Mr. Belgrave made the announcement to his crew and all of them wrapped up business right smartly and they crossed the road to the pub. Mary walking arm in arm with Laurie.

There were six of them altogether and did some considerable damage to the gift certificate. They had Scotch eggs, sausage rolls, chips and the two men, Mr. Belgrave and the loan officer, had two pints a piece. Mr. Belgrave didn't care, he was having a great time and liked Laurie immensely, not in a creepy sense but like a friend or even a daughter. Mary liked Laurie too, more specifically, Mary admired Laurie. Laurie was a good person and out of this world beautiful.

In the middle of the reverie, Laurie saddened. Mary noticed and asked what was wrong.

"Nothing really. I just miss someone."

Mary easily guessed, "A bloke I suppose."

"Yeah, a bloke."

"Where is he?"

Laurie looked at her and responded, "I don't know."

"Did he run out on you?"

"No, not really. It's complicated."

Mary put her hand on Laurie's shoulder, "Do you want to talk about it?"

"I'll make you a deal. If you and Mr. Belgrave go to lunch with me on Monday, I'll tell you all about it."

The girls agreed feeling sure Mr. Belgrave would participate so they didn't bother to tell him. It would be a surprise.

The party broke up with sorrowful goodbyes and hugs, but with promise of reconvening on Monday.

Back at the hostel, Laurie recounted her money making sure there was enough to last the rest of the time. She had more than three hundred euros. A real tourist probably couldn't eat off that but Laurie thought it was a small fortune. No problem, plenty of money, even with an unfavorable exchange rate.

Laurie decided to stay in the hostel for the night. Finding a book worth reading in the lending library of the hostel was difficult. All the books were ratty paperbacks handled hundreds of times. She found one filled with short stories from various authors about the apocalypse. She didn't care about reading end-of-world stories but it was the only book that had complete stories. All the books had a few pages missing in the front or back making the beginning, ending or both a mystery. The apocalypse short story book had a dozen complete stories in the middle. The book was chosen by default.

Laurie slipped into her lower bunk and began reading. Within a few hours, she disrobed down to her bra and panties, slid between the sheets, thought of Joshua and said a little prayer for his safety. She was asleep in a matter of minutes. She awoke once when some young travelers came in from the pubs but she never stirred and easily fell asleep once more. Two months ago, she could never fathom sleeping in front of strangers.

Chapter 46

After Joshua watched the sun set over the Santorini caldera, instead of looking for Juliette, he walked back to his hotel to call it a night. What a wonderful island. He couldn't wait to bring Laurie to it. He hoped she was safe and wondered if he did the right thing by leaving her behind. Joshua began having doubts but would feel better if he could find Juliette just to know she wasn't after Laurie. Maybe Juliette was staking out Margerie's hospital room waiting for Laurie to come visit. Now, he was panicking himself. He needed to find Juliette soon. How long would he stay on the island looking for a ghost in the wind? Joshua's doubts had doubled.

Early the next morning, Joshua went to Oia and hung out near the On the Cliffs Suites all day. He did not find Juliette. When the sun set, he checked out several popular night spots but Juliette was still the unfound needle in a haystack.

On Sunday morning, he thought he would try something different. He would go to the beaches. Although it was late in the season, the sun shown brightly and the air was warm. He went to three nearby beaches but didn't see Juliette. As a matter of fact, he only saw a few dozen people. Surveilling beaches may not be the proper tactic. Determined to stick with the plan for the day, he went to Red Beach. It was about an eight-mile hike to get there, adding more reason as to why this was a bad idea.

To get to the beach, after the long walk, Joshua had to descend a small incline. He could see four women on the red sand. Three were lying on their towels, feet toward the water. One was walking toward him carrying a towel and flip-flops. All the women were topless.

Joshua's eyes focused on the woman walking. She was a long way away but he could tell she was well built and looked naked, because she was wearing the tiniest peach-colored thong. Her breasts bounced with every step. Joshua would have thought she looked world-class sexy except for the fact she was the sadistic, killer-bitch, Juliette!

Juliette reached the bottom of the hill and put on her shoes oblivious to the fact Joshua was watching. She was used to every man watching her especially when she was only wearing a thong. She began to climb up from the beach and noticed Joshua standing at the crest. She walked halfway up, stopped, shielded her eyes from the sun and realized who he was.

Joshua could tell she recognized him by her body language. She stopped and flinched as if she were going for her gun. Of course, she was nearly naked and had nothing to defend herself with unless she took off her shoe and slapped him with a flip-flop or snapped a towel at him.

She knew she was toast. She continued to walk up the hill and stopped in front of Joshua.

"How the hell did you find me?" She asked as she was still shielding her eyes from the sun.

"It was easy."

"Did you have help?" she asked.

"You mean the crazy, rich Asian? No, I found you on my own. If I don't kill you, you'll have to worry about him later He has a hell of a lot more assets than I do."

"I think you have plenty of assets. That egg of yours sold for nearly fifty million dollars."

Joshua snorted, "Not my money. I walked away from that."

"Well then, you're a stupid bastard. How did you get here without any money?"

"Your boy told me where you were going," Joshua lied.

"My boy? What are you talking about?"

"The guys you left for dead in the hotel room. One of them didn't die. He told me everything and gave me the money you paid him so I could come kill you for him. He's in police custody right now and singing like a canary."

Juliette was stunned at how wrong this was going. She wasn't prone to making mistakes and never failed at her assignments. "You're lying! I shot those idiots in the head!"

"The one you shot in the eye on the couch. Oh, yeah, he's dead. But the other one you shot in the top of the head and he started walking toward the door. He lived! When I went into the room, he sat right up on the floor, told me all about the On the Cliffs Suites and handed me nearly four-thousand pounds to fly out here and take care of you."

"You're lying!" she kept reiterating in disbelief.

"Think so? Then you tell me how I found you."

"I think the Asian put you on to me."

"Either way," Joshua said, "You're dead now."

"So, you're going to kill me and that's it?" Juliette was stalling for time, trying to figure a way out of this monumental mess. Her best chance she surmised, was to call his bluff.

Joshua was enjoying the power he lorded over her but wasn't sure what he was going to do. Killing her was out of the question, he was not a murderer. Turning her over to the authorities was the proper thing to do but he didn't know if the 'authorities' would take him seriously. The story of the egg and all international intrigue was quite unbelievable.

Juliette relaxed her arms at her side and said, "Okay stud, go ahead and kill me." She called his bluff.

Now Joshua was on the defensive, "In due time…." He never finished his thought. Joshua heard a thud and Juliette's left breast exploded, spewing blood vapor into the air and across Joshua's face. He blinked in bewilderment as he heard the report of the rifle a full second after the Juliette's chest burst open. The sniper was at least a thousand yards away on the other cliff across the beach. It was a professional hit.

Joshua spun and began running. After three hundred yards, he thought, this is crazy. Am I going to run eight miles back to the hotel? He slowed to a fast walk. He was heading down the only road to the beach. If they want me dead, I'm dead already.

After walking nearly half a mile, a car came up behind him and slowed to crawl as it passed. Two men were in the car, both wearing ski masks. Joshua could try to run out across the flat rocky terrain but anyone who could make a thousand yard shot dead center could easily gun him down on the run. Joshua stopped and stood his ground, deciding to go out like a man instead of a fleeing rabbit.

The car halted and the man on the passenger side rolled down the window. "I have a message for you, Joshua," the man said in a broken Slavic accent. "Go home. It's over." The window rolled up and the car drove away.

Joshua couldn't believe it but felt sure he was handed a free pass. This was not a get out of jail free card but a get out of death row card. He hoped Laurie also got a pass. This was a good thing, but he had to get some distance between him and Juliette's body. The only witnesses were the other three sunbathers on the beach and they were hundreds of yards away. Joshua felt it was unlikely they could identify him but he better get further away. Walking down the road felt highly conspicuous. In twenty minutes, he was over a mile from the beach, in forty he was two and half miles away.

When he was three miles away, emergency service vehicles flew past him headed for Red Beach. He kept walking, knowing the body had been discovered either by the sunbathers or others who wanted to sunbath. At the four-mile mark. Joshua nonchalantly ducked into a restaurant and calmly ordered some souvlaki. He took his time and consumed two beers with his meal.

The emergency vehicles passed by going the other direction. Joshua walked to his hotel and stayed there. He tried to sleep that night but was worried about escaping. He rose early and packed to take the ferry back to Athens.

Chapter 47

Joshua had a less bumpy ferry ride back to Athens by way of Mykonos. At the Athens airport, he asked for the first flight out to anywhere in Europe. The clerk sold him a ticket to Berlin, one of the last two seats on the plane. He settled in for a quick nap in the uncomfortable airplane seat.

Laurie woke on Monday morning so excited she had to pee several times before she realized it was just nerves. She kept telling herself, what was there to be nervous about, it's just money. "It's just money," she said aloud.

Dressed in her non-Gucci outfit, she walked to a café to get some breakfast, thinking it may settle her down. She even purchased decaffeinated coffee because she felt wired already. Eggs, a sausage and some toast did nothing to ease her nerves but it did make her stomach feel queasy. Great, she thought. Now I have something to throw up.

Approaching Christie's, she took a couple of deep breaths hoping to ground herself and not expectorate on Ms. Vanderweerdt's desk. At the front door, Laurie was greeted by Alastair who escorted her to see Ms. Vanderweerdt. The ladies greeted one another warmly and took their seats.

Ms. Vanderweerdt opened a folder and pulled out a check, slid it across the desk and sat back with her hands clasped. Laurie looked her in the eye and Ms. Vanderweerdt nodded approval. Laurie slowly reached out and pulled the check up to her eyes. Laurie couldn't focus on the numbers.

Laurie turned her head, blinked a few times and tried to refocus on the check. The numbers became clear, $41,520,000! Laurie stared in disbelief. It's strange because Laurie knew this was coming but now that it was here, she still couldn't believe it.

Ms. Vanderweerdt broke the silence, "To your satisfaction, I take it."

Laurie was numb. "Yes," she said in return. It was the longest sentence she could possibly put together at the moment. She did wish, with all her heart, Joshua could be here. This was his doing as much or more than hers. She'd probably be dead if it weren't for him.

Ms. Vanderweerdt came from around the desk and walked with Laurie to the door. "If you find any other trinkets in the attic, please bring them by. I'd love to look at them."

Laurie chuckled a little and said, "We do have some antiques in my family but we're still using them because we can't afford to buy new stuff."

"Not anymore," said Ms. Vanderweerdt. They hugged and Alastair escorted Laurie to the door. For some reason, Laurie leaned over and kissed Alastair on his ruddy cheek before she left. Alastair watched Laurie walk down the street. When she was out of sight, he ran to the security camera room and played the tape back three times to watch her give him the peck on the cheek. His year was made.

Laurie walked to the bank nearly skipping as she crossed the road. When she entered the bank, Mr. Belgrave and Mary were in the lobby waiting on her. They each grabbed an arm and took Laurie outside, "We're taking you to lunch today."

They walked two blocks and came to the Cat and Mouse Pub. Mr. Belgrave said, "They have the best bacon butty's in all of London."

Laurie didn't know what a bacon butty was but she was looking forward to having the best in London. When seated and lagers ordered, Mary recommended the BLT sandwich instead of the butty. Mr. Belgrave went for two buttys. Mary explained a butty was a bacon sandwich with butter slathered all over it. She thought the bacon sandwich with lettuce and tomato was much better. Laurie agreed.

They ate, talked and laughed like they'd known each other for years instead of days, but Laurie always made people feel at ease. After finishing their meals, Mr. Belgrave ordered sticky toffee pudding for everyone. Laurie didn't really need to eat that much but consumed most of what was placed before her. When she couldn't eat anymore, she leaned back and patted her stomach. Mr. Belgrave was pleased with the unconscious gesture.

They walked the two blocks back to the bank with Mr. Belgrave saying he was glad they could walk it off before sitting behind a desk for another three hours. Laurie smiled to herself thinking he'd have to walk twenty miles to walk off two bacon buttys and a sticky toffee pudding.

Back at the bank Laurie said, "I have some money to deposit to my account."

Both Mary and Mr. Belgrave were proud of her for starting to save so quickly, explaining a lot of people with first time accounts couldn't manage them properly. They went back to Mr. Belgrave's desk. Mary picked up a deposit slip on the way.

Mr. Belgrave took his place behind the desk and the girls sat in the two chairs with Mary on the edge so she could complete the form. "Okay," Mary said. "How much would you like to deposit."

Laurie reached in her pocket and pulled out the folded check. "Forty-one and a half…."

Before Laurie could finish, Mary interrupted, "Forty-one and half pounds is great! That triples your savings." Mary started to write an amount on the deposit slip.

Laurie grabbed her hand and stopped her, "No." Laurie handed Mr. Belgrave the check. Mary looked at Mr. Belgrave for him to relay the correct amount.

Mr. Belgrave looked at the check. Mary looked at Mr. Belgrave and Laurie waited to see what was going to happen. Mr. Belgrave held the check in front of him, frozen in position.

"Forty-one million, five-hundred twenty thousand dollars," said Laurie.

Mr. Belgrave cleared his throat. Mary silently began to write. Her hands were shaking. Laurie broke the silence, "How long will it be before I can withdraw some money?"

"By tomorrow," Mr. Belgrave said.

"That soon?" asked Laurie.

"Yes Ma'am."

Mary handed her the deposit slip copy. "Here you go Ma'am, for your records."

Mr. Belgrave stood and shook Laurie's hand, "Thank you for choosing the Mercantile Bank for your business. If you have any needs, please let us know and we'll try to accommodate them."

Mary left the office without saying another word. Mr. Belgrave walked Laurie to the front door. "Good day Ms. Delacroix."

Laurie stepped out on the sidewalk and thought, what the hell just happened. Is money going to change every thing that much? Maybe Joshua was right. It's going to take a while to figure this out. Laurie walked back to the hostel shedding tears the whole way. Her life would never be the same.

Lying in her bunk, hands folded behind her head, she thought this would be the last night she ever stayed in a hostel unless she wanted to for some reason. She could stay at the Ritz-Carlton every night for the rest of her life. She could buy a small yacht, an airplane, a new bass boat for Daddy, a new stove for Mom. Hell, she could buy a new house with a thousand acres. It was hard to realize she could do anything she wanted to do but was cursed because she didn't know what that was. She wished she could talk to Joshua.

Chapter 48

Laurie awoke the next morning filled with energy. She had a mission! She was going to find Margerie. Also, checking in to the Ritz London was on the agenda. Why? Because she could. Dressed and packed, she left the hostel forever, hailed a taxi and drove to the Ritz. It was a beautiful old hotel, with rooms costing over five hundred pounds a night. Young men fell all over themselves trying to be the one to carry her backpack. They thought it was strange for someone to travel with a backpack and stay at the Ritz. But there were no questions asked, they had seen eccentric millionaires before.

Once Laurie was checked in and sipping cognac from the minibar, she called around to the local hospitals and found Margerie admitted to St. Bartholomew's. Laurie brushed her teeth to try to mask the alcohol smell because it was early in the afternoon and took a taxi to the hospital.

Laurie waited in the lobby until visiting hours began, going up to see Margerie the instant they let her. Laurie knocked and entered when beckoned. Laurie was pleased to see Margerie sitting up in bed looking quite well for someone who had been shot in the solar plexus.

Margerie outstretched her arms and Laurie fell into the hug. They chatted like school girls with Laurie confessing every detail of the story. Margerie was stricken dumb by the tale. At the end, Laurie said, "Don't worry about the hospital bill. I'll pay for everything."

Margerie explained that they all got free medical care in the UK. "Then I'll make up for lost sales at the store. I need to do something. You got shot because of me."

"Then come work with me at the store. I know you're young and have all kinds of money now, but I sure enjoyed your company. I started to love my work again when you were around."

Laurie said, "I'll make you a deal. I feel like I need to go home for a while. Figure some things out, you know. But I'll be back and work with you for a month."

Margerie shook Laurie's hand and a bargain was struck.

Laurie rolled Margerie in a rickety wheelchair down to the hospital cafeteria and had an awful lunch. Back in the hospital room, Laurie said goodbye and left to make plans for procuring a first-class ticket back to the states. By the time she reached the airport and boarded the plane, Laurie spent over four thousand dollars in one day. "I'm ridiculous," she told herself.

Chapter 49

Laurie opened the door to her house on the wooded three acres outside of New Orleans. "I'm home!" she yelled. Laurie's little sister, Annette, came running down the stairs to greet her. The Mom popped out of the kitchen wearing an apron. Dad was on a two-day fishing trip on the Pontchartrain.

The Mom smothered Laurie with kisses. They went to the family room for Laurie to tell them everything. Laurie started at the beginning. When she got to the place where she and Joshua arrived in London, Laurie pulled out Hermione's wand from the pack and gave to Annette. The girl went nuts over it. Not only was it what she wanted, but it came from England, the land of Harry Potter which to Annette was a mystical place. Of course, Laurie knew better. Living on the roof of Happy Chicken didn't feel so mystical.

Their mother asked about Joshua as all mothers would. Laurie explained he was the best of men.

"Prince Charming," Annette said.

"Better," replied Laurie. "This guy is real."

Then the mother asked, "You said you sold this egg thing?"

"Yes."

The mother was anticipating, "So how much did you get?"

Laurie looked back and forth at them, "Guess."

"A thousand dollars!" offered Annette, being too young to really know the value of money.

The mother countered, "Ten thousand dollars!"

"Closer," said Laurie. "I got over forty million dollars." Laurie waited for a reaction. There was none. Annette kept playing with her wand and her mother stared blankly.

Laurie stood and said, "I'm going to go up to my room, unpack, take a shower and a nap." Laurie went upstairs leaving her mother comatose on the couch.

When Laurie came down the stairs after a long nap, her Dad greeted her with a bear hug. "I hear you got a big payday?"

"Yeah, with a little help from my friend. I'm a millionaire now."

"Good, good. That's nice. It couldn't have come at a better time."

"What do you mean?" asked Laurie.

Mom interrupted and pushed Dad away, "We don't need to talk about this right now. Let's go have supper. We're having gumbo, sweetheart. I bet it's been a long time since you had real gumbo."

"Since I left to go to Europe nearly four months ago." Laurie took her mother's arm and they went to the dinner table.

Over dinner, they discussed the family situation. Laurie's Dad purchased two shrimp boats when Laurie was born. They were fifteen years old when he bought them and now, they were thirty-five years old. One is dry docked with an engine which can't be repaired and the other breaks down so often they can't chance taking it out. The family business has come to an end.

Also, as with all lower middleclass families, they live like they're upper middleclass. They amassed a huge debt, credit card upon credit card rung up to the maximum. The house payments are two months behind and the roof leaks. The home owner's insurance long since lapsed to be frugal.

"Why did you let me go to Europe if we were in financial trouble?" Laurie asked in amazement.

The Mom spoke, "Well Dear, we told everybody you were going."

Laurie put her face in her hands trying to comprehend the enormity of the situation.

"Now that you're back…." The mother interrupted herself. "We're going to have a welcome home party. This weekend! We'll invite everybody."

Laurie shook her head feeling uncomfortable in her own home for the very first time in her life.

Chapter 50

The next Saturday, the party was in full swing. It wasn't a cake and ice cream get together around the kitchen table, it was a yard filled full with over a hundred and fifty people, a giant crawfish boil and a Cajun band with accordion and washboard players. Laurie was paying for everything. The party cost eleven thousand dollars. That did include the liquor, tables and chairs, catering, the band, decorations and clean up.

The Mom also told all one-hundred fifty guests her daughter was richer than sin. Therefore, the family was richer than sin. By Sunday afternoon some of the cousins came over wanting to discuss their ideas. All of which included Laurie giving them obscene chunks of money. By late Sunday, more than a dozen family members came over requesting a piece of Laurie's money.

On Monday, several strangers, who knew some of the cousins, came over wanting a hand out of some kind or another. Finally, the Dad said, "We're not letting anyone else in this house before we discuss what we're going to do with the money."

They sat at the table to discuss the situation and the situation was this…the Dad wanted his money before anyone else could have theirs. The Dad needed a cool half million to get the shrimp boats going again. He needed to pay off the house so they wouldn't risk getting behind on payments…that was another hundred thousand. He needed house repairs and renovations for another hundred thousand. He needed a new crew cab truck and a small Cadillac for Mom. Plus, baby sister needed a college fund. That was just the start.

He didn't really ask for the money, he stated he needed the money. He added it up in his head several times and spoke, "Let's just say a million dollars. For now, that will be enough."

Laurie became circumspective. She was being had by her own family. It took them less than a week to ask for a million dollars. She felt sure this would only be the first go round too. However, until this very moment, she was well cared for, loved and never doubted her parents. The money changed them.

After a long moment of silence, Laurie said, "Okay."

The Mom and Dad eased from their tensed positions. "I knew you would see it our way," said the Dad with confidence. Laurie went to her purse, got the tiny book of temporary checks and made one out to her Dad for an even million dollars. Laurie felt strange writing such a large check. Then she missed Joshua so badly she began to cry.

The Mom and Dad, having no idea why she was crying, tried to comfort Laurie by telling her she was doing the right thing. Laurie was thinking how Joshua turned his back on the money until she could figure out who she was as a millionaire. He knew money would change everything. She wondered how he got so smart. "Joshua…." She hoped he was well.

Where was he, she thought. I hope he's safe. She had no way of knowing the murderers were dead by Juliette's hands and now Juliette was dead by the hands of the crazy, rich Asian who she actually spoke to. Little did she know, Joshua was in Berlin, living it up. That is if you call living it up repairing boilers in residential buildings. Winter was coming and the boiler business was booming, at least for two months when they shook off the dust and got them ready for use after six months of inactivity.

Joshua hollered for Finn to bring him the big pipe wrench. Finn responded in half German and half French. Joshua understood the French part which he interpreted as "Get it yourself." Joshua walked out of the basement and up to the street where their truck was parked only to find Finn chatting up several schoolgirls. Joshua didn't know Finn's age but figured it to be around nineteen. Finn was acting fourteen.

Joshua said hello to the girls who were super impressed with his maturity and rugged good looks. This irritated Finn to no end. Joshua suggested they get back to work and Finn basically told Joshua he could go have sex with himself. The girls giggled. They thought the boys were fighting over them. In this case, Finn was trying to impress the girls. Joshua just wanted the damn pipe wrench.

The guys squared off. Joshua said, "You don't really want to do this." Finn was almost six feet tall but weighed two-hundred fifty pounds of solid muscle. He'd been working in the boiler business for over a year and worked himself into good shape. Joshua was six foot two and weighed two-hundred fifteen pounds. Joshua was not in good shape; Joshua was chiseled out of granite.

Finn sized up the situation and wanted to back out but couldn't lose face. He smiled at the girls and took a sucker punch swing at Joshua. Being a former military policeman and having broken up a hundred bar fights, Joshua easily stepped aside, performed a judo move to use Finn's own momentum and weight to spin him around. Joshua put the surprised man in a choke hold and rendered him unconscious in three seconds. Joshua gently lowered him to the street. The girls were stunned and wildly impressed. Joshua went back down to the basement with the pipe wrench. Finn woke with the girls standing over him laughing. Finn mentally vowed to get even with Joshua but didn't know how. However, he was sure he didn't want to pick another fight.

Chapter 51

Joshua got fired from the boiler repair job. It turns out Finn was the boss's wife's nephew. Joshua was given his last check and an apology from the boss who knew Finn was a dumbass but couldn't do anything about him. Joshua understood and moved on.

He went to Geneva, Switzerland and knocked on the door of MSC Shipping. After some fast talking and a severe vetting process, Joshua was hired on a cruise ship based on his experience. He hoped to be part of the security team but his ability to chop-a-chicken won out and he was hired as part of the food service staff.

The cruise ship sailed on a seven-day cruise of the Mediterranean, departing from Naples, Italy. Every morning at the 'crotch of dawn', Joshua would wake from slumber in a tiny room down in the bowels of the ship by the propellers. He would clean up and dress in his whites and proceed to the buffet line to prepare for breakfast. His job for the first three hours was to cook eggs to order.

After breakfast, he would help prepare the line for the lunch service. During lunch he was assigned to the sandwich window. He would easily slice pounds of meat and prepare a hundred sandwiches, each individually specified by the guest. After lunch, he would clean up and help prepare for the supper service.

When in port, the sandwich window was closed and the pizza kitchen was opened. Joshua got six hours of shore leave at every port. This was a good job for him. He got room and board, woke up in a different country nearly every day, didn't have to pack and unpack, he got paid and best of all, it was a six-month contract. At the end of the job, he would be that much closer to the time to meet Laurie at St Die. He thought about her every day and hoped on high that she was coping with her new fortune. Not that he had experienced it but he knew it could be overwhelming.

Joshua's life settled into a routine. Sunday was bon voyage day. Monday was in Genoa, Italy where he'd take the bus to Portofino or one of the many quaint urban beach areas. Tuesday he was in La Spezia, Italy where he liked to take the train to one, or all the Cinque Terre's. The pesto was perfect. In Cannes, France he would hang out along the Boulevard De La Croisette. The road name reminded him of Laurie Delacroix. He couldn't wait to walk the ocean front boulevard with her. While in Barcelona, he went everywhere. The subway made it easy to get around. In Palma Majorca he shopped for the perfect pearl for Laurie. He never bought one because he couldn't find one that did her justice. In Ajaccio, Corsica, he just hung out and watched the tourist flock to Napoleon Bonaparte's birth place. Sometimes he would go to the citadel and stare out across the ocean dreaming of Laurie.

Every bon voyage was another week closer to the girl he loved. He was praying she would be at St Die on the anniversary and still be the same beautiful strong young woman she had been when he met her. Money changes people drastically. That was his big worry.

Laurie stayed with her family. It was miserable. Her Dad had to fight off several people every day wanting money for their wife's operation, to buy food or because they were greedy. Dad granted the local paper reporters an interview with Laurie but that was all. Many magazine and television news outlets sent representatives but none got to talk to Laurie unless they paid Dad a hefty sum of money, which they didn't. Laurie felt like a prisoner in her own home.

Mom soothed herself with shopping. With a million dollars, her entire wardrobe needed to be upgraded. Dad got his shrimp boats fixed and back in the water. He also took the money for the new truck and Cadillac and bought a cabin cruiser so he could be a guide for deep sea fishing. The money for the new roof was now in Mom's closet and the renovation money was a small office at the marina for Delacroix Charters.

Annette's college fund was spent on eating out every other night, a housekeeper and a new riding lawnmower-tractor for the yard guy. Mom and Dad had just enough left over for the swimming pool they always wanted. Construction would start the first week in December.

Laurie dressed upstairs for their Thanksgiving dinner. The meal was catered this year. Mom didn't have to lift a finger. Laurie was sad because she always enjoyed cooking with her mother. It took two days to prepare all the food.

Laurie walked down the stairs extremely hungry because she starved herself in the preceding days for preparation to gorge on turkey and dressing. The table was impeccably set with every kind of food one could imagine. However, there were two strangers standing at attention near the kitchen door. They were a young man and woman. Laurie thought she knew the girl. "Do I know you?" she asked.

"Yes Ma'am. I was two years ahead of you in high school."

"Fran? Right?"

"Frances but everyone called me Frankie."

"So, you work for the catering company?"

"Yes Ma'am."

"The table looks beautiful and you don't have to call me Ma'am. I'm nineteen years old."

"I do, if I want to keep my job."

She never broke from her position of attention.

"It was good to see you again. Here comes the rest of us," Laurie said as the family descended the stairs.

"Yes Ma'am." Was Frankie's response.

Dad was dressed in a suit and tie. Laurie couldn't remember him ever wearing a tie before. Mom had on one of her many new dresses and jewelry. Annette was dressed in a skirt and blouse with a belt. Hermione's wand tucked comfortably in the belt. The kid hadn't let go of the thing since Laurie gave it to her.

The two catering employees pulled out the chairs for Mom and Dad. Laurie seated herself and Annette jumped into a chair ready for some mac and cheese instead of dressing. Dad leaned over and grabbed a beer out of the new $400 Yeti cooler he had by his chair. He touched a button on the remote and the 65-inch TV freshly installed on the dinning room wall came to life with a football game. Mom opened one of the three bottles of wine on the table. Now it was time to eat.

Laurie was underwhelmed, ready to scream and run out of her own house to the nearest hostel. She thought how wonderful it would be to eat a turkey sandwich under the portico with Joshua at St. Die. A much-preferred scenario to what she was witnessing.

At the end of the meal, the family retired to the living room to finish the game while the caterers cleaned up. After Mom inspected the dining room and kitchen to make sure all was to her satisfaction, she walked with Frankie to the front door. Frankie ran the credit card through her phone device and asked Mrs. Delacroix to please sign it. Frankie held the phone sideways to make the signature area bigger. There was a line to add a tip but Mrs. Delacroix skipped over it feeling the $678 she was paying for the meal was enough. When signed, Mrs. Delacroix shut the door in Frankie's face and went to finish the first bottle of wine in front of the new 75-inch TV in the living room.

Laurie sat with Annette on a love seat and told stories about living in London. Laurie spun them like a fairytale. Joshua was the good prince; Juliette was the evil sorceress and the roof of Happy Chicken was a castle. The two murderers didn't need to change character, they were still assassins in the fairytale. Karl was a kindly old wizard while Reinhardt his assistant was like a court jester. Mrs. Vanderweerdt was the good queen and the Faberge egg was a priceless piece of magical art that could save the kingdom in the right hands. Laurie was the damsel in distress.

Laurie had to tell the story twice and Annette corrected Laurie if she couldn't remember how she told it the first time. This was the best part of Thanksgiving, being with her little sister.

Joshua spent Thanksgiving cooking eggs on the buffet line in the morning but in the afternoon, instead of making sandwiches, he was asked to carve the giant turkey in the main dining room. Joshua got this assignment of honor because of his chop-a-chicken experience. Joshua stood on a raised stage, poised with knife and fork. On command, he made the first slice of the holiday bird to thunderous applause.

When it came time to remove the drumstick, Joshua held up a cleaver so everyone could see. There were audible 'oohs' and 'aahs' coming from the crowd. He raised the clever above his head. The audience of diners sucked in a collective breath. Joshua ever so slightly twisted the cleaver in his hand so the reflection of the spotlight off the blade would shine back to the crowd. In one fell stroke… Bam! He held up the drumstick to a standing ovation. Chop-a-chicken experience just reaped its rewards.

Unknown to Joshua, a cool customer named Paolo Sorrentino was in the dining room that night. Mr. Sorrentino was an up and coming Italian film director who couldn't keep his eyes off Joshua. Not in a gay way but in a professional way thinking this guy would look good in one of my films. Joshua continued to carve the turkey with more aplomb than anyone should ever be allowed. Mr. Sorrentino absorbed every move and Joshua was well built and world-class good looking.

At the end of the meal after Joshua butchered no less than four turkeys, Mr. Sorrentino approached Joshua holding out a business card in his hand. Joshua reluctantly took the card and read it. It had Mr. Sorrentino's name in the middle with the word DIRECTOR underneath.

Joshua said, "Okay, I'll bite. Director of what?"

Mr. Sorrentino's English was broken but understandable. "I direct films in the cinema."

"Yeah? What can I do for you?"

"Have you ever acted before?"

Joshua looked at him sideways. "Ah, no."

"I have a part for you in my next film. Are you interested?"

"Is this a porn thing? If it is, I'm definitely not interested."

"No Signore, it is legitimate film making."

"You're serious?"

"Si Signore. A film about the world war. You would play an American soldier."

"Well, I have been an American soldier before so maybe I could act like one." Joshua laughed to himself.

"Benissimo! We shoot in Sicily in a month."

"I have a six-month contract with the cruise line."

Mr. Sorrentino waved his hand. "We'll buy out your contract. Not to worry."

They chatted a few more minutes and shook hands on the deal.

"Joshua Lewis Arlington, movie star," he said to himself as Mr. Sorrentino walked off.

Chapter 52

In Naples, Joshua walked off the cruise ship a free man. He had less than half the money he was expecting from the shortened contract and he needed most of it to get himself down to Sicily. A train and a boat took care of that. In Sicily Joshua found the hotel Mr. Sorrentino told him about and he checked in. It was free! The studio paid for the actors to be on location. The food was free too! Joshua thought he might like acting if this is how all actors were treated.

In the wee hours of the morning after Joshua enjoyed an evening in his spacious room. A young assistant knocked on his door. It was four in the morning. Joshua opened the door standing in his boxer briefs. The assistant was a woman in her early twenties with dark hair in a bun, black horned rim glasses and a mousey look. Although she was not unattractive.

"Mr. Arlington, you need to be at make-up by five." The woman couldn't rip her eyes away from Joshua's perfect body.

"Okay," he said wiping his eyes. "Where is that?"

"If you go to breakfast, I'll meet you there and take you."

"That's very kind of you. I'll see you in just a little bit."

The assistant fanned herself as she walked back to the ascensore.

Joshua cleaned up, dressed in his best clothes and went down to breakfast where he met the assistant whose name was Violetta. The two ate together and Violetta told Joshua he would be taking some random screen shots today. He would be given a script of the movie, his few lines highlighted and would have about three days to learn his lines before they started shooting his scenes. He would also be visited by an avvocato to sign a contract.

As they were walking to make up, Joshua asked how much this job paid. Violetta didn't know those things. Her job was to make sure everyone got to the right place at the right time.

Joshua entered the makeup area. It was a small residence they rented and he went to a room which looked like a master bedroom. Joshua was greeted by an army of people with blush brushes, hair spray and scissors. It was frightening. Not like Juliette and the murderers frightening but more like a carnival ride thrill. Violetta said she would come get him in an hour.

"An hour!" Joshua exclaimed.

"That's about the usual time it takes them to get an actor ready."

In an hour and fifteen minutes, Joshua was 'ready'. The ordeal took longer this time because it was his first time. Tomorrow would be much easier and less stressful to the makeup artists. He looked fine but his face and head felt as if glue were all over them. Violetta nodded in approval and led him down a street to the building where they were going to do the screen tests.

Violetta sat in one of three a director's chairs along with two real assistant directors. Neither one spoke English. Violetta translated. They wanted him to shout some military orders in one scene and tell a girl he loved her in another. He thought he could bark out a few orders but the other stuff he wasn't so sure about.

They stood Joshua up in front of a green screen and Violetta translated from the directors that he should say some military sounding things. Great direction, thought Joshua. These guys were second assistant directors, unpaid interns in charge of the screen tests of unknown actors. Fair enough, Joshua would try to deliver the performance of his life.

The one camera guy focused on Joshua's face. The lead assistant director yelled "Azione!"

Joshua took that to mean 'Action' and started to act. Joshua peered out as if he were looking a thousand yards away. "They're here," He said. "They'll be on us before you know it." He looked around. "We've got to move!" He crouched down, "Get that machine gun up on the line. Rocky, you take two men and don't let them get up the trail. Balboa, take the rest of the men and form a skirmish line. We'll hold this ridge. We'll hold this ridge if it'd the last thing we ever do. Let's go, move!"

"Tagliare!" the assistant yelled. Joshua looked at Violetta for translation. She held up her fingers like scissors and made a snipping gesture.

"Cut, I suppose," said Joshua.

The assistant directors set Joshua up for the next scene. A love moment with the Italian girl. Joshua was supposed to adlib since he hasn't seen the script yet. The assistant directors offered Violetta as the counterpart.

Violette stood, laid her clipboard down, took off her headset and microphone that had been pasted to her face since she met Joshua and removed her glasses. She unpinned the bun from her hair and shook it out. She strikingly resembled a young Audrey Hepburn. The two assistant directors were stunned. They were seeing Violetta for the first time. Joshua was quite aware of the chrysalis to butterfly transformation. Violetta positioned herself a few inches away from Joshua.

The assistant hollered, "Azione!"

Joshua closed the gap between them. He wrapped his arm around Violetta and pulled her close. He thought of Laurie and said, "I love you with every breath I take." Their faces were inches from each other.

"My Darling," Violetta said. "Do you have to leave me. I love you so much."

"I have to go. We're shipping out. Moving north to the Gustav line. I don't know if…."

Violetta put her fingers to his lips. "Don't say that. You'll be back. You'll come back to me."

"Oh Violetta," Joshua said and he kissed her. She went limp in his big strong arms but it wasn't acting.

"Tagliare!"

"How was that?" asked Joshua to Violetta as he stood her back upright.

She straightened herself and responded. "You'll be a big star one day."

Joshua was visited by the avvocato later that evening and signed his contract and was given a script. The lawyer spoke English well. "I understand your screen test was exceptional."

Joshua didn't know how to respond because he had not gotten any feedback and what the lawyer said wasn't a question, just a statement. "I wouldn't know about such things. I tried my best."

The lawyer laid out some papers and told him it was a standard contract. Joshua's room and board will be paid until his acting services were no longer needed; at which time he will be paid the sum of eighteen thousand euros. "The actual time to film your scenes will be about three days but you have to stay here until they're ready for you. Stay close to the hotel so Violetta can find you."

Joshua shook his head up and down in acknowledgement, still stunned at the 18 G's he would earn for three day's work. He tried to compare it to the salaries he had earned before. His three-day acting salary would equal a year in the army, eighteen months on a cruise ship or endless mind-numbing days performing chop-a-chicken.

Joshua signed the papers and shook hands with the avvocato. Joshua collapsed in the plush easy chair when the lawyer left. Is this what I'm supposed to be doing? It's too easy, he thought. Maybe I can earn some big money doing this and Laurie and I will be more on the same footing. As he was thinking, there was a knock on the door.

He opened it to find Violetta standing there, hair back up in a bun, glasses and headset in place. "Mr. Arlington, you're needed in wardrobe."

"Call me Joshua please. Where is wardrobe?"

"A block down in another house we rented. I'll take you there."

Joshua and Violetta entered the house which was packed from stem to stern with World War II uniforms and period clothes. "Wow!" Joshua mustered.

"A bit much, huh? You'll be in this room." She pointed to an area that looked like a dining room. "Alphonse will be in shortly. I'll be right outside if you need anything."

Joshua looked around at all the costumes and wondered if this was what every movie was like.

In a moment, a short pudgy man entered with pins sticking out of his sleeve. He gestured for Joshua to stand on a wooden step. Joshua obliged and Alphonse began taking measurements. When Alphonse got to measuring the inseam, Joshua felt him take a few extra liberties in that area. Joshua grabbed Alphonse's arm and twisted slightly making the pudgy man squeal like a pig.

Violetta ran in to see what the commotion was all about and Joshua explained Alphonse was a little grabby in the wrong place. Violetta came over and held Joshua's arm and made him let go of the little man and then shook her finger at Alphonse.

"I should have warned you," Violetta said. "He is all hands, this one." She shook her finger at him again.

Alphonse cowed like a whipped puppy and finished his measurements quickly. Violetta's finger shaking did little to deter the man but Joshua's imposing figure and vice grip hold on his arm was enough to compel him to stick to business.

Joshua finished up with wardrobe after trying on several uniforms. Alphonse grunted in approval when the correct fit was discovered. Violetta also approved in a much different way. After the fitting, Joshua was released to go to the hotel to relax until his call.

Chapter 53

Laurie decided to stay home until after the new year, at which time she would take her money and leave to places yet unknown. She contemplated remaining in the United States, maybe New York or somewhere quiet like Charleston or Savannah. Maybe she would spend a couple of weeks or a month everywhere she ever wanted to go. With forty million dollars her every wish could be fulfilled. All she knew for certain was she was leaving.

As early December rolled around, Laurie's Mom and Dad sat her down to have another talk about what she needed to do with her money. As Laurie suspected, what they suggested was to give some more to them. Evidently, they miscalculated the amount they needed. The million dollars wasn't quite enough. They humbly asked for a quarter million more but a half million would be better.

Laurie wrestled with her conscience about gifting them the money. After an agonizing five minutes of her Dad pacing and her mother pleading with her eyes, Laurie agreed to a half million dollars more. Her parents were ecstatic.

After Mom and Dad settled down, they wanted to further discuss the plans for Christmas. Laurie wondered why they needed to talk about plans, they always had grilled cheese sandwiches and tomato soup on Christmas eve, followed by exorbitant amounts of candy, games and hot chocolate. They would watch a Christmas movie and go to bed after leaving a plate of cookies and milk out for Santa.

On Christmas morning they would tear into presents, eat pancakes and bacon and wait for Mom to fix the big Christmas dinner in the early evening or late afternoon. Laurie thought it was perfect, what did they need to discuss?

Dad started the discussion by stating, "Since there is so much money available…." The gist of the conversation was Dad wanted about twenty thousand dollars for his gifts, Mom needed thirty thousand for hers and of course, Laurie could buy herself anything she wanted.

"What about Annette?" asked Laurie.

"I don't know," said Mom. "Let's ask her. Annette! Come here honey."

The little girl came in to the room still holding her magic wand. Mom took the ten-year-old in her arms and said, "What do you want for Christmas? You can have anything you want. We have a lot of money now."

The young girl thought while inspecting her wand. Eventually she whispered something no one could hear. Mom asked her what she said. The girl simply said, "I want Laurie to stay here forever."

A gusher of tears rolled out of Laurie's eyes as she hugged little Annette to pieces.

Chapter 54

Joshua finished shooting his scenes and was paid the amount promised. Mr. Sorrentino gave Joshua a card with three phone numbers on it and told him to call those numbers in April to discuss coming to France in May. The movie they were shooting, Tears in the Sea, would initially be shown at the Cannes Film Festival. Joshua was invited if he wanted to come.

Joshua thanked Mr. Sorrentino for the opportunity, gave Violetta a hug she would remember for a decade and left Sicily for the mainland. He made his way to Sorrento and then took a ferry to the Isle of Capri where he spent three days in relative luxury. The views were fantastic and the food was scrumptious but the whole experience was hollow without Laurie. He missed her deep in his soul.

After his three days on Capri, Joshua slowed way down and started his austerity living again, a string of hostels and menial jobs back across Europe to Amsterdam where he was working as a bouncer in the Amsterdam Banana Bar in the heart of the Red-Light District. The pay was exceptional.

Management let him stay in one of the back rooms for a reduction in salary. Most of the rooms were occupied with sex workers, dancers and live performance entertainers. After a month he was completely oblivious to the parade of swinging male parts and bare female breasts parading up and down the hall.

While Joshua was awash in flesh peddling, Laurie left home without telling her parents until the day before she called the cab. Mom and Dad cried for their loss which was the money. Annette cried for her loss which was her big sister. Laurie cried because it was all changing. She realized life would never be the same.

Laurie was at the Louis Armstrong International Airport sitting at a coffee shop trying to decide where to go first. She rolled her medium sized suitcase through the crowded corridors thinking how she wished she could get her stuff trimmed down to what would fit in her tote. A medium sized suitcase seemed excessive. She laughed to herself as she thought that.

Laurie walked up to a Delta window and asked for a ticket on the next plane going anywhere.

The lady asked, "International or Domestic?"

"Don't care," was Laurie's reply.

The lady typed about ninety words a minute into the computer and said, "Okay, the next available flight is two hours from now, going to…. Montreal with a few stops in between."

"I'll take it," Laurie said.

"Going on vacation?" the lady asked as she typed in the information.

"No, not really. It's just a whim."

Laurie's adventure started. She would spend as much or as little time in her chosen place as she wanted and then move on. Hopefully, the time between now and getting back to Joshua at Saint Die would fly by.

Chapter 55

In April, Joshua called the number on the card given to him by Mr. Sorrentino. Joshua received his official invitation to the Cannes Film Festival for the screening of his movie. The secretary gave Joshua the time and place of the opening.

Joshua got himself to Cannes a few days early and was surprised to find out how expensive the hotels were. He tried, but couldn't let himself pay what the hotels were asking. He had money but nearly two thousand dollars for three nights was too much. He found a hostel that would let him stay on their floor in the common room because all the bunks were occupied. He took the deal at twenty-five euros a night.

Joshua was told he needed to wear a tux or a fine suit to the opening. It was a red-carpet affair. Joshua thought he looked pretty good in his jeans and denim shirt but social rules prevailed. He went to a tux rental store to get an outfit for one night for three hundred euros plus deposit! He decided he couldn't afford to be a movie star and laughed to himself.

The man helped him dress and said the tux they picked out was perfect for the red carpet. Joshua took his garment bag and went back to the hostel. He could stay in a hostel for two weeks for the amount he paid for the one-night rental of the suit!

On the day of the screening, Joshua dressed in his tux to the applause of everyone at the hostel who donned cargo shorts and T-shirts for their day in Cannes. He took a taxi to the waiting area and found some people from the movie set. They instructed him to wait until the guy in the headset called for him. All he had to do was relax a few minutes.

An hour and a half later, Joshua was still waiting and needed to pee…badly. He started looking for the restroom when the headset guy called his name. Joshua hopped up and marched over to the man who shoved him around the corner and told him to walk to the announcer at the red-carpet threshold.

Joshua shrugged and began his walk. Each side of the walkway was lined with bleachers filled with fans trying to see someone famous. Joshua stood in a short line waiting for his turn to talk to the interviewer. There were three people working microphones, all from different networks.

The guy in front of Joshua moved to one of the interviewers for his fifteen minutes of fame. Joshua didn't know what to do so he started to walk on down the red carpet to enter the theater. The last interviewer, a woman, called him over.

She spoke French, "Now, who is this handsome gentleman?"

Joshua answered in French, "My English is much better than my French. Can I speak in English?"

"Of course," the woman responded.

"I'm Joshua Arlington. I'm here for the debut of the film, Tears in the Sea. I have a very small part in the movie."

The interviewer reached out and subconsciously squeezed Joshua's bicep. "I say, you do look quite handsome in your tux. Who's it by?"

Joshua wasn't sure what she was asking not knowing fans all over the world cared about who made their clothes. "You mean who made the tux?"

The woman shook her head, "Yes, who made this gorgeous outfit."
"I don't really know."

In one quick movement, he shrugged off the jacket and looked at the label inside. "I rented it yesterday but the label says, Armani." Joshua held up the jacket, turned it inside out so the camera could see the label which in fact read Giorgio Armani. He put the jacket back on and waited for any other questions.

"Here he is," she said. "Joshua Arlington, wearing rented Armani, with a small part in Paolo Sorrentino's new movie, Tears in the Sea." Joshua wasn't sure if she was making fun of him or not so he let it go and walked into the theater. Joshua didn't know that the short clip of him disrobing would be an internet sensation and he would become the darling of the Cannes Film Festival. Mr. Sorrentino couldn't be happier.

Joshua sat where they told him to sit, which was so far back it was barely in the theater. The good news was, the seat was close to the restrooms, he still had to pee. When everyone was seated a Master of Ceremonies came out to introduce the film. Joshua couldn't wait any longer and excused himself passed two couples on the end of the row.

While Joshua was in the restroom the credits began to play on the screen. The film was shot in black and white to resemble the films of the period and to give it a gritty look. The audience applauded. The last credit read: 'Introducing Joshua Arlington as Sergeant Rick Thorne'.

When Joshua returned to the last row of the theater the two couples seemed put out by his lateness. "Who do you think you are?" one of them said in French.

Joshua answered, "I'm Joshua Arlington. Who are you?"

All four people stood up and said, "Excuse us. Please come on through."

Joshua wondered what transformation took place but was glad there wasn't a confrontation over a seat. He had no idea his name flashed up on the screen. He was a movie star and felt the first effects of its privilege.

Joshua watched the movie, enjoying a good wartime love story. It had enough action to keep him interested and enough love interest to make it appeal to the ladies. During his on-screen time, Joshua heard several sighs from the audience. He wasn't sure if they were caught up in movie or bored out of their minds. He thought this film business may be too nerve racking for him.

When the movie was over, he stayed in his seat long enough to see his name roll across the screen. "That was fun," he said to himself. The two couples next to him asked for selfies with him. Joshua obliged thinking it was silly.

A lady in the lobby asked for a selfie with Joshua. She wanted to text it to her daughter in Copenhagen. One look at Joshua in the flesh, in his tux and remembering his love scene in the ruins of the village with the beautiful Italian woman and she knew, Joshua would be a mega star. This was a special night for her. Joshua Arlington was about to explode across movie screens everywhere.

When Joshua removed himself from the lady, he was swarmed with reporters, paparazzi, as he would call them later. They wanted to know who he was and where he had been all their lives. One reporter asked him to take his coat off and show him the Armani label inside. They were pulling his chain but he didn't know it. He took his coat off and proffered the label. The cameras zoomed in and yet another GIF was born.

By the end of the day, Joshua's exposure on the internet was greater than anyone's at Cannes. His first disrobing had over three million views. The second had about the same and someone blended the two together in a five second montage which had over six million hits. He was famous and not the fifteen-minute kind either. He became one of the most sought-after men in Europe. His life changed that quickly. His only worry was if Laurie would still approve of him.

Cameras followed him back to the hostel and practically watched him change clothes. They did get a good shirtless shot which hit the internet with even bigger views. By the time Joshua was returning the famous tux, the paparazzi was down to one guy with a movie camera, one guy with a professional still camera and two women with phones following him around.

When midnight rolled around, Joshua lost his followers and retired to the hostel for a good night's sleep.

Chapter 56

Laurie spent her time moving from city-to-city. It was fun and she tried to really get to know the city, shying away from the tourist areas. However, the lack of purpose played heavily on her mind. After spending a week in Belize, she decided she'd had enough.

Laurie booked a flight to London and went to Once Again, the antique store, to find Margerie. With suitcase in tow, Laurie entered the shop. The bell on the door announcied her presence. Margerie came around the corner, looking a dozen pounds lighter and fully fit. She looked wonderful.

Margerie was holding a trash can filled with paper rubbish recently removed from a shipment of Waterford crystal. Margerie dropped the can, its contents floating helter-skelter on the floor and ran to Laurie. They hugged like long lost friends.

"How long are you going to stay?" asked Margerie.

"As long as you'll have me."

They hugged again. "Perfect."

They sat at an old table cluttered with gewgaws, as Margerie called her novelties, and Laurie confessed her entire story.

Margerie's response when she finished was not about the forty million dollars but, "Where's Joshua now?" Margerie could instinctively ascertain Laurie was suffering from a hole in her heart.

Laurie almost cried and confessed she didn't know where he was, what he was doing or if he felt the same way she did. Margerie tried to console her with the promise Joshua would be at Saint Die on the appropriate date, which was still months away.

As they sat in silence, Laurie's eyes drifted to a jewelry box behind the glass in the cabinet. Margerie tried to follow her line of sight to determine what she was seeing. "Ah," she said. "You have found the most interesting thing in the store." Margerie stood up and brought the box over to the table. "Go ahead and open it."

Laurie gingerly lifted the top of the ornate box. Music began playing Ave Maria. Margerie injected, "It's a music box and jewelry box from the early nineteenth century. It's the earliest combination box from this period I have ever seen."

Laurie stared at it as if it were alive. That feeling of being home again creeped over her and made her eyes well up. Margerie could see the transformation. "Welcome back, Love," she said. Laurie hugged her once more. They made tea and ate a lot of biscuits, promising each other they wouldn't keep count.

Laurie confessed she was a little lost and needed a purpose and wondered if that purpose could be working in the shop. Margerie welcomed the help and the company. Laurie's only demand was due to her recent found fortune, she would work for free. Margerie wouldn't hear of it but Laurie insisted. "Margerie, I have forty million dollars!"

"Okay, you're hired." They laughed and hugged once more.

Chapter 57

Joshua settled in Rome. He rented a cheap apartment for a month and went to look for gainful employment. What he found was a job working for the Metropolitana di Roma. Joshua was paid a very low wage to walk the subway tunnels and police up trash.

Working underground was not exactly what he wanted but it was an honest job…steady, there was no shortage of trash in Rome. He went to work early in the mornings and got off at three in the afternoon. His evenings were free to spend in one of the most interesting cities in the world.

On Wednesday, he found himself sitting on the Spanish Steps early in the evening, eating a coffee gelato in a cone. He traveled everywhere using the metro because he could ride for free as an employee, plus the rails got him close enough to anything he wanted to see or do.

The gelato was melting in the sun and was getting the best of Joshua, dripping all over his jeans. He gave up on trying to finish because it became too messy. He threw the remnants in a trash can thinking some poor schlub would have to empty that thing later today. He brushed his hands on his pants and started walking down the steps through the crowd. There was always a crowd at the steps.

At the bottom, when he started to slice through the tourists to ride the metro home, he heard his name called out. Joshua thought maybe he was imagining it. He stopped and listened carefully and heard it again, this time recognizing the voice. He turned and Violetta was running toward him.

She stopped short of running into him and they held each other's arms for a brief moment as Violetta steadied herself. "I finally caught up with you," she said out of breath.

"Where on earth did you come from?" asked Joshua in amazement.

"I have been searching for you for a week. Mr. Sorrentino sent me after you. No one knew where you were. We did exhaustive searches on the internet and hacked into several data banks we shouldn't have but we found you were employed by Metropolitana di Roma. I was waiting for you after work but you hopped the train before I could stop you. I followed you into the underground but didn't see what car you entered. I jumped on the train not knowing at which stop you would exit. I saw you get off from several cars behind you and had to ride to the next station and take the train back to this stop. I've been wondering around for thirty minutes trying to find you. That's all I could do."

"Why did you want to find me?" Joshua asked.

She subconsciously straightened her hair and clothes as if to say 'isn't it obvious' but what came out of her mouth was this, "Mr. Sorrentino wants you to star in his next movie, Signora Garibaldi. He wants you to play the other man in a marriage tringle. The other young, virile man," she added.

Joshua was deep in thought. "When does it start shooting?"

"Next month."

"Where?"

"Lake Como. A little village called Bellagio."

Joshua weighed the pros and cons. It took all of two seconds, "I'll do it."

Violetta was pleased and took his arm and started walking him toward the station. She outlined the details and Joshua promised to get himself there at the right time. Joshua and Violetta rode the train back to Joshua's neighborhood. He exited the metro to go to his apartment to plan and think of Laurie. Violetta rode the train two more stops and went to her four-star hotel to pack for Lake Como to scout for accommodations and services and think of Joshua while she laid on her bed. He's not like most men, she thought. He didn't even suggest we get a drink or go back to my place. Maybe he's gay. What a shame that would be.

Chapter 58

Joshua exited the train at Lecco and caught a taxi to Bellagio as he was instructed. Violetta met him at the mansion on the lake at which they were staying. Joshua's room was a master bedroom, one of three in this mansion. The other two lead actors were in the remaining master bedrooms. All meals would be served in the dining room unless they were on location, in which case the meals would be delivered. Acting's a tough job but somebody's gotta do it. Joshua laughed to himself. Just yesterday he was picking up trash in the subway for a living.

Violetta stuck her head in the door and asked if he was settling in okay. She gave him a script with his lines highlighted and suggested he learn the first few days' worth of lines and then add a day as the shooting progressed. He said he'd get right on it.

Violetta waited to see if he would invite her to stay but he stared at her, not in a lustful way but more like saying, 'Anything else?'

"Oh, makeup is at five in the morning. I'll knock on your door at four."

"Okay," Joshua said waiting for her to finish.

"Alright then, I'll see you in the morning." Violetta left but was even more determined to let her intentions be known. She would have him as surely as her name was Violetta Francesca Marino.

Joshua read the script and was pleased to find a lot of his on-screen time was showing him staring lustfully at Signora Garibaldi or brooding while plotting to steal her away. Although Signora Garibaldi's character seemed to be a relatively nice and a very attractive person, she was also rich, which was his motive for seducing her. Joshua's character was a broke American gold digger. He became introspective and assured himself that's why he wasn't with Laurie. He didn't want to be thought of as a gold digger.

Studying his lines into the late hours, the words began to blur on the page. He put down the script and pulled up the covers, allowing himself to think of Laurie one last time before the day ended.

All too soon there was a knock on the door accompanied by Violetta's voice. "Make up in an hour!"

"Okay," Joshua hollered back. Violetta waited to see if he would open the door but he didn't. She went to breakfast as Joshua cleaned up, not remembering a single word he studied last night. He had the feeling of impending doom, or more likely, embarrassing failure. Maybe last time was a fluke, he thought.

Make up took about an hour and Violetta came to get him after the crew gussied him up. They went to the edge of the lake to a small ferry dock. The ferry took locals and tourist around the lake or in this case, the ferryman took the actors and movie people to the day's shooting location. Joshua was amazed at the way the lake looked in the sunrise. Violetta was thinking the same thing about how Joshua looked.

Mr. Sorrentino greeted Joshua cordially but formally. The director introduced Joshua to his two co-stars, Aida Greco and Luca Lombardo. Joshua didn't know either one of them even though they were popular Italian A-listers. Both were at least ten years older than Joshua. They may have been twenty years older but actors in makeup have a way of turning back the clock.

Aida was impressed with her young co-star from America and was thinking of ways she could be caught by the paparazzi arm-in-arm with Joshua. Luca didn't like Joshua because Joshua was younger and better looking, but that is what the movie was all about.

Mr. Sorrentino asked Joshua if he knew his lines and Joshua confirmed he went over them but didn't promise they would come out the right way. Mr. Sorrentino took that as a yes. They set up the first scene of the movie which was Joshua bumping into the couple on the shore line. When they were in position, Aida asked Joshua if he was nervous. "I'm not really nervous but I feel different than I did the first time."

"I saw you in Tears in the Sea. You were great. Just be great again." Trying to break the tension Joshua was feeling, Aida said, "Do you know Villa Oleandra is only a half a mile in that direction." She pointed down the shoreline.

"No," Joshua responded trying to determine if he should know about Villa Oleandra.

"That's George Clooney's lake house. If you want to, we'll go down there after shooting and see if he's home."

"Just like that?" Joshua asked.

"I know him," Aida said. Then under her breath, "…a little."

Joshua was skeptical but completely forgot about being nervous.

The shooting began and Joshua said his meager lines perfectly. Aida and Luca retired to the mansion before lunch. Joshua remained another couple of hours because they shot a hundred different close ups of him looking at Signora Garibaldi, although Signora Garibaldi was played off camera by Violetta.

Joshua's glances and expressions were captured expertly by the camera men under superb direction. Actually, no matter who was directing or which guys took the shots, the camera loved Joshua. He was the most photogenic person with whom Mr. Sorrentino had ever worked. Violetta could testify to that. Joshua's pretend attention made Violetta feel queasy and girlish.

When Joshua's day was wrapped, Violetta escorted him back to the ferry explaining the avvocato would be by this evening to sign papers like last time. Joshua didn't ask about a salary because of his experience from Tears in the Sea, he knew remuneration would be more than fair and would sure beat the hell out of sweeping garbage down the subway.

Joshua met Aida and Luca at the dinner table for an early supper. Aida was wearing a bathing suit with a cover up. Luca had on typical dark European garb. Joshua had on his tight jeans and denim shirt, which sorely needed washing.

Once seated, Joshua asked. "Does anybody know where I can wash my clothes?" Luca laughed to himself as if he were saying 'dumbass'. Aida was more cordial.

"Sweetheart, tell the girl what you want and it will get done."

"The girl?" Joshua asked. "You mean Violetta?"

"Could be." said Aida in her broken English. "I don't remember her name but every set has one."

"Or two!" added Luca. "They'll do anything for you if you're a big enough star."

Joshua was getting the drift and figured Luca had sex with his share of Violetta's during his career. Probably the only way he can get a girl, Joshua thought. Aida was thinking the same thing.

"Okay, I'll talk to Violetta tonight."

Chapter 59

After dinner, Joshua went to his room to study lines. About twenty minutes into the study session, Joshua's eyes crossed. He took a break and went looking for Violetta who was assigned the last bedroom on the left on the third floor. It was the maid's quarters.

Joshua lightly rapped on the door. Violetta cracked open the door expecting to see lecherous Luca Lombardi standing there. To her pleasant surprise, Joshua filled the hall with his six-foot two broad shoulder body. "Joshua!" she said subtly astonished.

"I'm sorry. It's obvious you were expecting someone else. I can talk to you in the morning."

"No wait." She opened the door a little more. Joshua could see she was wearing a long sleeve red and black vertical striped soccer jersey with A C Milan on the front. He looked closer and saw it was a thin night shirt which barely covered her essentials. Her long her hair hung down to her shoulders. "What can I do for you," she said with the double entendre barely noticeable.

"It's a little embarrassing to ask, but I was told you would know where I could wash my clothes."

Violetta was disappointed in his excuse to come see her. "There is a washer and dryer in the basement. If you leave your clothes on the floor outside your room in the hall, I'll wash them for you."

"No. That won't be necessary. I need to wash my own clothes. But thanks. I better get at it. Goodnight." Joshua turned and walked down the hall to the staircase.

Violetta shut the door and leaned on it asking herself what was she doing wrong? Was he gay? He might be married or have a girlfriend but that never stopped any man she ever knew.

Of course, Joshua noticed how sexy Violetta was. But every time he saw a girl that made him think twice, a big picture of Laurie jumped into his head and the feeling dissipated as quickly as it came on. Laurie…. now she was a beautiful, sexy woman.

Joshua found a big puffy white robe in his room along with white slippers like the ones you find in swanky hotels. He took off his clothes because they all needed washing and went down to the basement with his dirty laundry and movie script.

Half way through the dry cycle, Violetta came down the stairs to the basement. She was wearing the thin jersey night shirt and a pair of fuzzy purple socks. Joshua sat up straight in the second-hand chair he found in the corner.

"Hello," said Violetta. "I just came down to see if you needed any help."

"No thanks. I've been washing my own clothes for a number of years now," he said lightheartedly.

Violetta moved closer to him. Joshua looked down at the floor. "You like my socks," she said and kicked her leg up to Joshua's eye level, letting him know beyond a doubt there was nothing under the jersey.

Joshua put his hand to his eyes like one would do if they had a headache. Violetta could tell he was trying not to look and she didn't know what to think about that. She wasn't real familiar with American men but thought there would be more of a response. Both people were young, attractive, half dressed and alone in a room together late at night. She was doing everything but throwing herself at him. But if that's what it takes…

She walked over to where he was sitting and sat down in his lap. Joshua's robe spread open because that's what she wanted it to do. There was the unmistakable feel of flesh on flesh as her bare bum ground into his thigh.

In a flash, Joshua stood up dumping Violetta on the floor with that bare bum now having an exchange with the unfinished, cold, dirty, concrete basement floor. She held her hands up for Joshua to help pick her up saying, "That wasn't what I expected."

Joshua apologized and explained he wasn't interested in her that way. Violetta, after being thrown on her ass on the floor, got the picture. She didn't even ask why he wasn't interested. "My apologies," was all she said and ascended the stairs. Joshua sat back in the chair and began studying his lines again as if nothing happened, which in his mind, nothing did happen.

In a few minutes, Joshua heard the door open again. He did not want to confront Violetta again.

"Mr. Arlington?" It was the lawyer. "I've been looking for you for hours."

"I'm here." Joshua stated and the avvocato descended the stairs with briefcase in hand. Once face-to-face, the lawyer spread some papers out on a table used for folding clothes.

"Same standard contract as before. We pay you for the work, put you up and feed you while you're working. Anything else is on your own." The lawyer handed Joshua a pen and pointed to three places he needed to sign.

"How much am I paid for this job?' Joshua asked.

The lawyer flipped through the multipage contract and pointed to a figure.

Joshua blinked a few times. "Is it acceptable? We're not going to have problems this late in the game, are we?" asked the avvocato.

Joshua said, "No, we're not," and signed the contract.

The lawyer wrapped up the papers, stuffed them in his briefcase and scurried out of the basement.

Joshua sat in the second-hand chair, watching his clothes spin around in the dryer wondering what he was going to do with $450,000.

He smiled and thought, I can hold my own with Laurie now.

Chapter 60

Laurie spent a day finding a reasonably priced apartment near the shop. She could have lived anywhere and flown to work on a helicopter if she so chose but she wanted to act like a real person. On her first day at work, Laurie ordered a new computer system tied into the cash register and inventory. The next three days, Laurie and Margerie took inventory and bar coded everything in the shop.

They were sitting at the work table when Laurie got the music jewelry box off the shelf. "We still have a couple of dozen items we haven't priced. Let's do that next, starting with this box." Laurie held it up for Margerie to gaze upon.

"Right-o," Margerie responded. Laurie fired up one of two new lap tops and began searching for early to mid-nineteenth century music/jewelry boxes that played Ave Maria.

"When was Ave Maria written?" Laurie asked nonchalantly.

"I have no clue, Dear," Margerie responded as she drank tea.

Laurie looked it up and said, "1825. So, this box cannot be any older than 1825."

"Alright." Margerie was going with the flow, watching Laurie do her work.

"It's Swiss," said Laurie excitedly. "Mid-century, cylinder works, some on e-Bay are listed for eleven hundred U.S. bucks!" Laurie pushed the computer away and sat back on her chair, satisfied with herself.

Margerie was quite proud too. "This is going to be fun; you know. You and me." Margerie reached out and stroked Laurie's hair.

Laurie was still in work mode, "I think we need to clear off a space in the front window and set up table and chairs. Serve coffee and tea while we show our customers all your fine pieces. We'll advertise, get a website, a mailing list, Twitter account, Instagram…. get you up on Tik Tok."

"Hold on. I'm too old of a dog to be doing all that." At her age, she didn't really want to learn any new tricks.

"Don't worry, I'll handle the IT and marketing. That's what you pay me for."

They looked at each other and laughed.

Chapter 61

Once Again, the antique shop, was buzzing with people after Laurie completed a round of advertising and converted the front display area into a coffee and tea room. They had to get a permit from the city to serve consumables even though they didn't charge for them.

Laurie's next project was to search the world over and find the most unusual and rare antiques possible. Laurie loved this job! Her first trip was going to be to Switzerland to see Karl and listen to his sage advice. Plus, she liked the old man and wanted to visit.

Margerie would stay in the shop and share tea and biscuits with the customers. One of her favorite things to do. Margerie was enjoying this job again. She would miss Laurie for the few days she was gone but young kids had to run wild.

In four long days, Laurie came back to London followed by two men rolling a giant crate stuffed with shiny baubles and bangles just right for Margerie's store.

After the women hugged it out, Laurie wanted to show Margerie what she procured. The two men pried the lid off the crate and were rewarded with a handsome tip before they departed. When alone, except for a half dozen customers in the front, Laurie started pulling the packing out of the crate and one after another the treasure boxes were revealed.

Margerie was speechless, only able to render and 'ooh' or 'ahh' at the appropriate time. There were jewels, books, crystal, snuff boxes, a golden scimitar and autographed pictures from a few well-known actors like Hepburn, Guinness, Burton, O'Toole, Quin and many more. There was a gold lame scarf once worn by Queen Victoria with the provenance. Halfway through the crate, Margerie exploded in tears and couldn't quit hugging Laurie.

They spent days cataloging and pricing their new inventory. If this stuff sells, Margerie would be solvent again not that Margerie cared. She was content with the coffee klatch and Laurie in her life. Laurie felt she owed Margerie something special. The lady took a bullet for her. How many other people would do that?

In six weeks, the ladies sold most of the newly procured items. Never having a quarter of a million pounds pass through her cash register in such a short time. Margerie insisted on paying back everything Laurie spent on the shop. Laurie couldn't argue her way out of it and was repaid in full. Margerie said, "I don't mind being helped, but I don't like taking charity." Laurie didn't want to insult the wonderful woman so she accepted the repayment.

Life was good, Laurie was happy and time was passing. Only a few more months and Joshua would be waiting for her at Saint Die. She got giggly thinking about it. However, on the days when it rained and the fog was persistent, Laurie would let a sliver of doubt creep into her mind. What if he doesn't show? What if he's found somebody else? Laurie would have to sit with Margerie, eat biscuits all day and talk it out until Laurie was convinced everything was going to be alright.

Chapter 62

Joshua finished shooting and the cast and director went to Milan for a wrap party. Paparazzi were everywhere. Aida finally got her chance to be seen with Joshua arm-in-arm. The studio picked up the enormous tab. Joshua lived for weeks, high on the hog, and hadn't spent a penny. Maybe he needed to get an agent and do this full time. How was he going to do that? He sure wished he could talk to Laurie.

When the party broke, Joshua went on his way with one back pack, a wad of cash and a check for $450,000 in his pocket. He decided living in hostels and doing menial labor may be a thing of the past. Renting an apartment in Rome near the Metro allowed him to easily get around town. Every time he rode the train, he was thankful he was riding the train instead if sweeping up after it.

Joshua found the movie studio, Cinecitta. It was hard to miss. The grounds were massive, nearly a hundred acres of sets. Joshua was going to ask some of the employees where he might find Paolo Sorrentino. The secretaries in the lobby had seen every kind of pretty face come through the doors of the studio anyone could ever imagine, but when Joshua walked in, business came to a halt. There was no typing, no talking on the phone and no conversations. The place went crickets.

"Ciao," said Joshua to the first secretary. She slightly nodded her head. "Do you speak English or French?"

"Si Signore, English."

"Can you tell me where I might find Signore Paolo Sorrentino?"

She batted her eyes until she came back to reality, "Si Signore. He is in building twelve."

Joshua looked at the front door and was about to ask where that was but the lady offered to take him. The secretary jumped up from behind the desk and led him to the door, barefooted, forgetting to put on her shoes. She had been sitting shoeless behind her desk for the last several hours. When she went back to put her heels on, another secretary rushed to Joshua and escorted him out of the building, successfully kidnapping him from the first secretary. "I'll pay for this later," she said in perfect English.

Joshua walked with Concetta to the door of building twelve. She told him she saw Tears in the Sea and fell in love with him. It was a shame he died.

"I wanted to live," Joshua said comically. Concetta smiled.

"You'll find Signore Sorrentino in there. Just ask anybody."

"Thanks," Joshua said waiting for her to walk off, but she didn't. He waited and awkward few seconds and then said, "I'm going in now." He walked in the building leaving Concetta standing there. When the door shut, Concetta snapped out of it and went back to face the music with girls in the office.

Joshua was in another plush lobby with a receptionist behind a large counter. On the wall was a screen with digital images flipping continuously showing movie posters of every film made at Cinecitta. There were hundreds of them. Joshua knew this because he was asked to sit and wait for Signore Sorrentino and wait, he did. The receptionist said the wait may be a long while since Joshua didn't have an appointment. Joshua watched the posters flip curious if he would see Tears in the Sea or Signora Garibaldi.

Three hours later, Joshua was still waiting. He was about to stand up and stretch when a familiar face entered the lobby…. Violetta. She saw Joshua immediately, after all, who could not notice a man like that.

"Joshua!" she cried out, sincerely excited. "I was hoping to see you again. I didn't want to track you down and chase you through the subways like before."

"Why did you need to track me down again?" asked Joshua.

"Signore Sorrentino wants to cast you in his next movie and we didn't know where you were."

"Already?" Joshua asked. "The other film has only been wrapped for a couple of weeks."

"Your test audience reviews are off the charts and Tears in the Sea is doing well at the box office since Cannes. He wants to strike while the iron is hot."

"When will this happen?"

"I'm not sure. He and the producer are working out the details and the cast. The only person he knows for sure is going to star in it is you. That is, if you agree to it."

"Actually, that's why I'm here. I never gave you a way to contact me because I didn't have a phone or an address for that matter. I have an apartment now. Right here in Rome."

"Good. This's where we'll be shooting. The film has a working title of…. I shall translate…. An American in Rome. Based on a non-musical version of An American in Paris. You know that film?"

"Oh, Lord, it's another love triangle, right? I'm going to be type cast as the third wheel."

"Amore mio, the third wheel is special." Violetta was starting to get that look in her eyes she had at Lake Como. Violetta started to move in when the receptionist interrupted.

"Signore, no see Signore Sorrentino today. He has appointments."

Violetta looked up at the receptionist and back at Joshua. "How long have you been here?"

"A little over three hours."

Violetta went ballistic! Not ballistic, but more badger, wolverine and Tasmanian devil all rolled into one. She ripped the poor receptionist a new orifice and threatened to throw her out in the street for not recognizing Cinecitta's newest star, Joshua Arlington. She also accused the poor girl of being a lesbica for not responding to Joshua's obvious masculinity.

Violetta wrapped her arm around Joshua and said, "Come on, let's go see Paolo." She pointed an accusing finger at the receptionist as they walked right into the director's office without knocking.

"Look what I found," Violetta announced as they walked in. Signore Sorrentino startled but gained composure quickly with a big smile crossing his face.

"Joshua Arlington, just the man I've been looking for." Paolo Sorrentino lit a cigar and downed the rest of a cognac that was sitting on his desk. The smile on his face went from ear-to-ear.

Chapter 63

Being a star in this movie meant Joshua had a lot of lines. Violetta made sure he got a script well ahead of shooting. Joshua's obligation would be for eight weeks of set time. They would begin shooting in early June. That was perfect for Joshua. He needed to be in St. Die in late August and wanted a little time to wander around Europe and find himself again before he met Laurie.

Two days after Joshua received the script, Mr. Sorrentino called him in to the studio office. There he met with Mr. Sorrentino, Violetta and the smarmy little avvocato, who had a rack of papers Joshua was to sign.

The lawyer explained all of Joshua's obligations and outlined what the studio would do for him. The last point of the contract is what all contracts boiled down to, the money. "I hate to ask," said Joshua, "but how much will I make?"

Violetta, the lawyer and Mr. Sorrentino all looked at each other in anticipation. "Three million euros," said the lawyer. The three waited for Joshua to be excited and jump at the chance. But Joshua did not.

"I'll have to think about it," Joshua said to their total amazement.

"What is their to think about?" asked Violetta incredulously.

"I honestly don't know if that's a good number or a bad number. I think I need to get an agent."

All three of them chimed in simultaneously stating there was no need for that. They could work something out. "What amount of money were you thinking about?" asked Mr. Sorrentino as he poured another cognac.

"I don't know. I think I need to talk to some people first."

"People?" said the lawyer. "People?" he said again. "What people?"

"People in the business. Those with a little more experience than me."

Mr. Sorrentino piped in, "How about we sweeten the pot a little. What would you say to four million euros?"

"That sounds a million euros better but I think I still want to get an agent."

It was the lawyer's turn to reason with Joshua. "An agent will take at least ten percent, maybe more for someone so new as yourself."

Mr. Sorrentino struck again, "I'll add ten percent to the salary. A 'no agent fee' so to speak. What do you say Joshua? How does 4.4 million euros sound?"

Joshua stuck out his hand and he and Mr. Sorrentino shook on it. The lawyer adjusted the contract and Joshua signed in a dozen different places. Everybody seemed happy afterward.

"There is one favor I'd like to ask," Joshua queried. Mr. Sorrentino waited for the other shoe to drop. "I'd like for all of us to get something to eat. I'm starving. I've been here over four hours."

The group smiled in unison, glad that the favor wasn't Joshua picking his own co-stars or wanting a luxury trailer for the shoot or some of the other things major stars request.

"Oh," Joshua added. "There's a young secretary in the front lobby who doesn't seem to wear shoes much. Can you ask her to go with us to eat? She missed an opportunity earlier."

Mr. Sorrentino looked at Violetta and she nodded her head reluctantly. Mr. Sorrentino's car picked all of them up and drove them to the main lobby. Violetta got out and went into the building. All the secretaries stopped working and looked at her. Violetta was well known as a wicked witch of Cinecitta.

In Italian Violetta said, "Which one of you shameless bitches is the barefoot whore?"

The young girl in question meekly raised her hand.

"Come on," Violetta said. "Mr. Arlington asked that you join us for a meal. And for God's sake, put your shoes on."

They had a late lunch-early supper in the studio cantina but not in the main dining hall with all the extras and bit players. They ate in the private club room reserved for the big names of the industry. During the meal, Mr. Sorrentino admitted to Joshua that he was authorized to offer Joshua five million euros.

"If I'd had an agent, you would have paid the 5 million but the agent would have taken ten percent leaving me 4.5 million. You paid me 4.4 million. So, I lost a hundred thousand and you saved the studio six hundred thousand. I'll get you next time," Joshua said teasingly. But Mr. Sorrentino swallowed hard at the friendly threat.

Joshua bid his farewells and said he would be in the right place at the right time for the shoot. Violetta said she would come by his apartment and get him if he wanted. Joshua declined. Joshua hugged the barefoot secretary and left the group to go home and study his lines. His thoughts were on the movie An American in Rome, a non-singing An American in Paris rip off. What a bomb this was going to be.

Chapter 64

Joshua arrived at the location of the shoot. It was on a rural street on the outskirts of the city. Several blocks were cordoned off by the Carabinieri. Joshua had three co-stars. His old friend Aida Greco was his first love interest, Andrea Rossi was the tough guy and boyfriend to Chiara Jilani who played the young women who stole Joshua away from Aida's character.

All the introductions were made on the street by Mr. Sorrentino and the cast was whisked off to make up and wardrobe. Two hours later they met again and began shooting scene one. The picture progressed with very few hiccups but Joshua was amazed at how hard and long the days were.

About three quarters of the way through the shoot, Andrea, the man playing the tough boyfriend was to shoot a scene with Joshua. Andrea was going to confront Joshua about seeing his girlfriend behind his back. It was an intense scene where two grown men nearly come to blows.

During the scene, Andrea got bent out of shape about something and the argument they were supposed to have in the script turned into a real argument. Joshua never understood what they were arguing about.

Mr. Sorrentino never yelled "cut" and the cameras kept rolling. At the apex of the argument, Andrea took bitter offense to something Joshua was doing. Joshua didn't understand half of what Andrea was screaming at him because he switched back and forth between Italian and English and every now and then something French would come out.

Andrea snapped and punched Joshua in the chest. Joshua thought why in the hell would he punch me in the chest of all places. Andrea immediately clutched his hand because punching Joshua in the chest was somewhat like punching Superman. Joshua felt like steel.

Joshua looked Andrea in the eye who was still holding his broken hand and said, "Is it my turn to punch you or have you had enough?" Andrea surrendered and went to seek medical attention. Joshua spun and looked at Mr. Sorrentino, "I'm sorry. I think I blew that scene."

"Cut!" yelled Mr. Sorrentino. The director called for the writers to come and add that scene into the movie just as they said it and to rewrite every scene thereafter with Andrea's character having a broken hand. This was priceless stuff. Mr. Sorrentino saw euros flashing before his eyes because he was going to leak out that the two co-stars had a real fight on camera and it was kept in the movie. Even if the movie ratings were low, it would be a box office smash because the masses would pay to see a real fight. Not that Andrea put up much of a fight. Mr. Sorrentino laughed to himself.

Chapter 65

Joshua stumbled over at least one of his lines every other day and he apologized abundantly but Mr. Sorrentino would yell 'cut' and they would back up a few sentences and start again. For as many mistakes as he made, the shooting went smoothly.

Andrea eventually apologized to Joshua about becoming angry and the two of them hit it off well after that. They even had occasion to drink a beer with each other after the day was done.

Aida and the younger actress, Chiara, stood mesmerized as Joshua took his shirt off to shoot the beach scene. They had traveled almost an hour to Ostia where the studio cordoned off a half mile of beach for their private use. Chiara was the woman to act opposite Joshua at the beach so she dropped her robe in front of Aida and sashayed down to the beach in her thong and string top to roll around with Joshua on the sand.

Aida was not in any scene that day and was only on set to watch Joshua act in his bathing suit. She felt a little slutty but didn't care. Mr. Sorrentino called for 'action' and the actors took their places

on the beach. The shot was an almost identical shot to the one in
From Here to Eternity, where the lovers were on the sand kissing
as a wave begins to lap over them. However, the shot did not go as
planned. There were no waves that morning. The two actors lay next
to each other and when a wave looked like it was going to roll in,
Joshua would get on top of Chiara and begin kissing her until Mr.
Sorrentino yelled "cut."

This happened repeatedly because the waves would not break
properly. Mr. Sorrentino was furious because he was a control freak,
although he would not admit it, and he couldn't control the waves.
After a frustrating hour and a half, Mr. Sorrentino decided to shoot
the scene with Joshua carrying Chiara out of the water and deposit-
ing her at the edge with their legs in the water, then he would mount
her and kiss.

Chiara, like Mr. Sorrentino, was also frustrated. She had been kissing Joshua for over an hour with him rolling on her every few minutes
and she could feel every inch of him through his bathing suit. What
girl wouldn't be frustrated?

On the third take of the 'carrying out of the water' scene, Mr.
Sorrentino hollered "Cut!" for the final time. They packed up the
whole truck load of equipment and bus load of people and went back
to the studio to call it a day. There was no sense trying to shoot any
other scenes because it would take Chiara too long to wash the sand
out of all the crevices of her voluptuous body and to fix her hair. She
looked a mess. Joshua looked like he was ready to shoot a GQ com-
mercial. Aida sat in the back of the bus smiling at Chiara's wet rat look
and took clandestine pictures of her on the iPhone.

At the studio, Joshua and Chiara got off the bus still wearing their
bathing suits. Violetta met them there and started wiping dried sand
off Joshua's broad back. Joshua spun in a circle and she wiped off the
front too. Chiara spat out a grunt, stomped over to her Mercedes
with her fur lined flip-flops snapping with each step and sped off
the studio lot.

"Shooting go well?" asked Violetta facetiously.

"The ocean waves wouldn't listen to Mr. Sorrentino's direction but I thought everything else went fine. I didn't have any lines to say so I aced that part." Joshua laughed.

Aida stepped off the bus and locked eyes with Violetta who asked brusquely, "What are you doing here?"

Aida smiled and replied, "Just along for the ride. I like the beach."

Violetta was furious and stormed into the building. Joshua looked at Aida and asked, "What's going on. Everyone is leaving mad and I don't know why? Is something going on?"

Aida grabbed his bare arm and walked him to her car. "Yes, my boy. You are going on." Joshua slipped his pants on over his bathing suit and put his shirt on so he wouldn't get her car sandy. Aida gave him a ride back to his apartment as she tried to explain the female temperament.

Joshua's brain nearly boiled over attempting to understand the juvenile jealousies that evidently abounded in the show business world. Joshua was doing his job for which he was being paid a great deal and everyone else had some other kind of agenda which he didn't understand. God, he wanted to be with Laurie.

Chapter 66

Laurie was sitting with Margerie in the window coffee klatch drinking a cup of mocha latte with extra cream and sugar. She thought of Joshua making fun of her for drinking a coffee milkshake instead of real coffee. She was smiling as she held the large cup to her lips.

"I know that look," Margerie said. "You're thinking about that man again. It's been eight months. Do you think any man would wait that long?"

Laurie was in deep thought for a moment. She held the cup with both hands feeling the warmth all the way down to her toes. Or maybe that was the thoughts of Joshua. Laurie smiled again, "You don't know him like I do. One look at him would buckle your knees…."

"That's just looks, Dear. Don't you think by now he may have spread those looks around a little. Do you know what I mean?"

"I guess anything is possible but this guy had honor. Does that sound corny?"

"I think he may have been a little light on his feet if you get my drift." Margerie looked at Laurie out of the corner of her eye. "Any man who spent a month with you and didn't get any may be playing for the other side."

Laurie was staring out the window at the grey summer morning. There never really was a summer in England, at least not as Laurie knew a summer to be. "I don't think he's gay if that's what you're insinuating. He responded biologically to my touch if you get my drift."

"You mean the lipstick came out…"

Laurie smiled at the analogy, "Yes. I can quite say it came out a long way."

"How long?" asked Margerie.

Laurie laughed at the older lady getting fresh and said, "Now you're just being nosey," and got up to wash her cup.

Margerie tried to take another sip of her tea but said she was too hot to drink any more. "I'm burning up. It must be the change of life washing over me."

Laurie responded, "I don't think imagining a parade of unfurling lipsticks is synonymous with the change of life."

"Right-o. Leave an old lady to her troubled mind and let's get to work." She and Laurie laughed about it all day. It's been many months and she was missing Joshua terribly.

Chapter 67

Joshua worked hard at his new craft. He was proving to be a very good actor. Pretending to be someone else was easy. However, he wished he could play more characters like the soldier from Tears in the Sea instead of womanizing playboys.

At the end of the shoot, the wrap party took place at the studio in a warehouse called Lot 21. There was an orchestra made up of studio musicians and the singer was a lady named Giorgia. Joshua didn't know the singer but was told she was a big deal in Italy. After she started singing, Joshua knew why. Her voice was magnificent.

Violetta took Joshua to meet Giorgia during a break. Violetta clung to Joshua as if he were a life preserver and she was in the middle of a raging sea. Giorgia noticed Joshua's awkward stiffness as Violetta adhered to Joshua like Velcro.

Joshua was trying to give Giorgia sincere compliments but Violetta kept interrupting with compliments about Joshua and how big a deal he was going to be. Giorgia nodded her head in agreement and said she had to do another set. Joshua was embarrassed and pulled away from Violetta. He complimented Giorgia one more time and took his leave.

Taking his leave meant he walked out of Lot 21, marched down to the front gate of the studio, hopped a taxi to his apartment, packed his stuff in a back pack and went to France on a train. He'd had enough of Violetta, Chiara and Aida for a while.

By this time, Joshua had a bank account, one of those Swiss numbered jobs. After all, he was a multimillionaire. He had a check book, debit card, credit card and a wad of cash. And what did he do? Stayed in a hostel near the Paris train station. He was comfortable again. The only thing missing was Laurie. It was only a matter of weeks before he was supposed to be in Saint Die. He couldn't wait.

Joshua occupied his time with museums, movies and plays. He had good meals at fine restaurants and partook of street food enjoying both equally. The only thing he didn't do was go up the Eiffel Tower. He was reserving that experience for when he was with Laurie.

Some days he doubted if Laurie would show up at Saint Die. It had been nearly a year and she was rich now. As far as he knew, she was back in Louisiana living it up down in the Big Easy. She was nineteen years old when they met. No telling who she would grow into.

Joshua was trying to convince himself he hadn't changed very much since the last he saw Laurie but he was now rich also. How did that happen? A year ago, he was performing chop-a-chicken eleven hours a day for less than minimum wage and now he's carrying a credit card with a hundred fifty-thousand-euro limit.

After several weeks in Paris, Joshua couldn't take it anymore. He caught the train to Saint Die des Vosges. He arrived a week early but felt closer to Laurie being in Saint Die than in Paris. He got a room at the hotel on the corner with the good pub he remembered from last visit.

He spent most of his time there watching football, drinking his beer and trying to pass the time. Joshua took long hikes into the surrounding hills when he wasn't at the pub or in his room. The countdown to the anniversary of their meeting was going glacially slow.

Laurie was still in London working on a public auction to be held at the shop. Once Again, had to be remodeled to accommodate the group of people they anticipated. The project was almost more than Laurie could handle, especially with the anniversary bearing down on her. A semi-nude Joshua under the portico in Saint Die was clouding her thought process.

Two days before the anniversary, Laurie packed her special stuff in a medium sized suitcase, road the Chunnel train to Paris and spent the night at a hotel near the train station. She didn't sleep a wink. On the anniversary day, Laurie took the train to Saint Die. Her stomach was doing flip-flops all the way.

She wanted to eat something but was too nervous to try. What if he didn't show? How would she handle that? What if he did show? Laurie had to force herself not to think about it too much.

Chapter 68

Laurie arrived at the Saint Die passenger station and immediately began scanning the area for Joshua. She knew he wouldn't be there because he said to be at the freight train station. Joshua had some short-comings, although Laurie couldn't think of one at the moment. He was a man of his word. He would be at the freight train station. He had to be.

The time of day was approaching sundown and she wanted to get there before dark. A taxi scooped up Laurie and her one bag and hauled them off to her destination. She dragged her bag up to the little freight office and literally ran around the corner to the portico. Joshua was not there!

"Oh, Dear God," she said to herself trying to calm her nerves. She chewed her nail for a second and then sat on the edge of the porch and decided to wait until he showed up. How long would she wait? Until midnight. That was the deadline she gave him. If the clock turned to the next day, then Joshua missed the anniversary and he would not be showing.

She pulled out her fully charged cell phone and tried to get reception. It was spotty at best but gave her enough internet time to stay occupied. After an hour the darkness crept in like a shroud and filled her with even more doubt.

In another hour, the light on the single pole flashed on completing her feeling of déjà vu. She put her phone into her tote and leaned against the column, shutting her eyes for just a minute. Her nerves had worn her out and she fell asleep.

"Bonjour!" came a familiar voice. Laurie jumped to an upright position and saw Joshua standing at the corner holding his backpack over one shoulder. He was wearing jeans, a denim shirt, a leather jacket and hiking boots. He was sporting a perfect five-o-clock shadow beard and his hair was windblown. He was gorgeous!

Joshua stared at Laurie. She was wearing a pink short dress with long sleeves and pink high heels. She looked exactly like she did a year ago except she had gained seven pounds. She weighed one-hundred fifteen back then and now she weighed one-hundred twenty-two. She was no longer a skinny high school kid. Those seven pounds were in all the right places and Joshua took notice.

Joshua said, "I've got a lot to tell you but first things first." He dropped his pack on the ground and approached. He never made it to the porch because Laurie ran forward and jumped off into his arms. He caught her and spun in a circle. She wrapped her long legs around him and kissed him from somewhere deep in her heart.

The kiss was strong and passionate with tongues rolling at super-sonic speed, hungry to make up for the lost time. When she slid down his leg and they opened their eyes to gaze upon one another, lightening flashed in the distance. The both laughed and kissed again.

Joshua was holding her tightly, as if he didn't ever want to let her go. Laurie noticed the lipstick was out and smiled to herself. Joshua said, "I love doing things for old times sake but I really don't feel like getting drenched and taking a shower under the scupper again. I'm staying at a hotel in town. Are you game?"

Laurie smiled, "Is it on the roof?"

Joshua smiled back and kissed her again. He couldn't make himself stop. "No, not this time."

Joshua pulled out his cell phone and said, "I'm calling a taxi. If we walk back, I don't think we'll beat the rain."

Laurie looked at him with her head cocked sideways. "Joshua Arlington, twenty first century man."

"Together five minutes and you're already giving me a hard time."

She looked down between his legs and put her hands on her hips.

"I didn't mean it that way…" He never quite finished what he was going to say before it was Laurie's time to kiss him.

The taxi came and whisked them away to the hotel where they stayed, locked in the room for three days. Room service left the meals at the door and retrieved the dirty dishes fr om the hall. No one saw them.

On the morning of the fourth day, they exited the room to go explore. The only reason they stopped making love was because their muscles were sore and their flash raw. They needed at least a few hours of recuperation.

As they were walking around town, Joshua explained how he followed Juliette to Greece and saw her murdered. He also told her about the crazy rich Asian who orchestrated the whole sordid affair. Joshua told her the crazy rich Asian bought the egg at the auction!

Laurie chimed in, "I talked to that guy after the auction. I told him thanks for buying the egg at such an exorbitant price. Asshole!"

Joshua told her about being a bouncer, working in the subway in Rome and working in the boiler business and being a cook on a cruise ship but left off the movie star part. Why? They were going to the movies that evening to see Tears in the Sea. Joshua was going to surprise her.

Chapter 69

Joshua bought tickets, popcorn and sodas. He was afraid she would see his name on the movie poster but she was too busy looking at the man himself. Laurie never questioned why he wanted to see this movie. It was an Italian movie dubbed in French subtitles. Laurie wouldn't be able to understand a single thing going on. She knew the movie would be a bust but her plan was to fondle Joshua from opening scene to closing credits. He could have asked her to take a two-hour bus ride to nowhere or sit on a park bench but as long as she could physically touch Joshua, she didn't care what they did.

Joshua sneakily kissed her during the opening credits so she wouldn't see his name. After the credits, they sat back, her hand on his thigh and munched on popcorn as the movie unfolded. About ten minutes into the movie, Joshua's first scene was about to take place. He told her to pay particular attention to this part.

The screen showed a close-up of Joshua's face. The camera panned away revealing a large gathering of soldiers on a dock and ships preparing for a voyage. The camera zoomed in on Joshua's face again as his character on screen called out. "Okay men. Grab your gear and get ready to board. We're going to Italy!"

Laurie sat bolt upright in the seat. Popcorn spilled in the aisle. Laurie's head snapped over to Joshua and back at the screen. She pointed at the movie but no words came out. Her head snapped over to him again. She was frozen.

After a minute of screen time, the film cut to the soldiers on the boat in tight quarters. Joshua's character, Sergeant Rick Thorne, was standing in an aisle between two rows of closely configured bunks, filled with soldiers. Sergeant Rick Thorne was not wearing a shirt. His muscles had muscles.

A few ladies in the theater gave short applause. Laurie finally got over the shock enough to be able to speak. She pointed to the screen. "That's you!"

Joshua smiled, "Yep."

"You're a movie star?"

Joshua leaned back in his seat with his hands behind his head.

"You made a movie?" Laurie was really having a hard time getting wrapped around the idea of Joshua being a movie star.

"No. I didn't make a movie. I made three."

"Three!"

"Tears in the Sea, Signora Garibaldi and Un Americano a Roma. Not a remake of the 1954 movie of the same title but a non-musical version of An American in Paris."

Laurie stared at him stunned. "I thought you were a bouncer, a subway janitor, a cook on a cruise ship, a guy who worked on boilers, when did you have time to become a movie star?"

Laurie was getting loud, not in anger but more in surprise. Some of the audience shushed her.

Joshua put his arm around her and whispered in her ear. "It just happened. I was butchering the Thanksgiving turkey on the cruise ship when this guy named Sorrentino saw me. I never thought all that time I worked at Happy Chicken would pay off but evidently, I cut up a turkey with enough flare to get noticed. He offered me the part of Sergeant Rick Thorne right on the spot. The test audience liked my acting and he offered me two more movies."

Laurie was standing in the aisle. Amazed.

"Oh, by the way, I'm a millionaire now. Not like you but I do have millions of dollars." Joshua felt he needed to say that. Not that Laurie would mind if he was broke as a church mouse but he felt better being more on equal footing.

A couple behind them told her to sit down, she was blocking the screen.

Laurie sat alright, she straddled Joshua in his seat and began kissing him and rubbing herself on him. If she didn't quit soon, Joshua was going to have the lipstick out. The couple behind them hollered to get a room.

Laurie stood up again. "Do you know who you are talking to?" she said to the couple.

They couple expressed their total indifference to who she was and told her what she needed to do was sit down and shut up.

Laurie pointed to the screen just as a close-up of Joshua's face was on. "You're talking to Sergeant Rick Thorne!"

The lady and half of the couple leaned forward in her seat to look at Joshua's face. "Oh my God, George. It is him!"

"Him who?" asked George.

"The half-naked man on screen. George, it's him!"

It was George's turn to lean forward and look at Joshua. Joshua proffered his best profile. "I do believe it is, Nellie. What's your name?"

Joshua replied, "Joshua Arlington. It is me playing Sergeant Rick Thorne in this movie."

Now the couple, an expat American duo, stood up and went all giggly. Pretty soon everyone in the theater was getting in on the act. Within a minute, the manager burst into the theater to see about the commotion. When the manager realized the hubbub was about one of the stars being in the theater, he ran out and called the local news.

Within thirty minutes, a local newspaper reporter and a local TV channel reporter with cameraman were on the scene, live.

The manager couldn't be more thrilled. Joshua and Laurie were standing in front of the theater being interviewed while the manager was trying his best to be in every picture the newspaper reporter was taking.

When Laurie tired of the attention, she called a taxi and the young lovers made their escape. Laurie was laughing the whole time. Joshua was pretending to be mad at her but mostly what they were doing was making out in the back seat as the taxi drove to their hotel.

"Let's go to Rome. I'll introduce you to the man who discovered me." Laurie was all in. They left for Rome the next day.

Chapter 70

In Rome, after one night in a hotel, Joshua and Laurie took a taxi to the Cinecitta studios. Joshua skipped checking in at the front lobby and had the taxi drop them off at Building 12. The receptionist behind the counter recognized Joshua, this time, and rolled out the red carpet. Joshua and Laurie were ushered into Mr. Sorrentino's office immediately.

Violetta was in with Mr. Sorrentino discussing their next movie. Joshua walked in first. Violetta jumped up and started to run to him. Then Laurie walked into the room. The room lit up. Violetta took a step backwards.

Mr. Sorrentino walked around his big desk and hugged Joshua. Joshua introduced Laurie and Mr. Sorrentino bowed and kissed her hand. "Oh my," said Laurie looking at Joshua. Violetta mustered the courage to come forward and Joshua introduced her to Laurie. Laurie put out her hand to shake it but Violetta couldn't take her eyes off Laurie.

Laurie was stunningly beautiful. Tall, thin but curvy, big doe eyes and shiny long auburn hair wrapping around her shoulders like a royal cape. When Violetta didn't shake her hand, Laurie pulled it back and said, "No? I'm sorry. I'm afraid I don't know how to great people in the Italian culture."

Violetta shook her head and apologized. "I understand now," said Violetta.

"Understand what?" returned Laurie.

"Why Joshua was never interested in me."

Laurie looked at Joshua and back to Violetta who said, "I threw myself at him but he would not respond. I thought he was gay for a while. I didn't know he had such a beautiful girlfriend."

Laurie wasn't sure if she was supposed to be mad at Violetta or not. Europeans had a different outlook on sex and Violetta did say she was beautiful. How can you be mad at that? Violetta was right. Laurie was beautiful beyond measure, somewhere above the scale. Violetta was a solid 7.5 to 8 on a scale of 1 to 10. Standing next to Laurie, Violetta looked like a 4, less than average.

Mr. Sorrentino was glaring at the couple wondering what he would have to pay to get these two in a movie together. Euros were bouncing around in his head and his eyes were spinning like a slot machine. They decided to have lunch together and get to know each other.

They went to the canteen VIP section and had more pasta than they ever dreamed possible. Joshua pushed back and rubbed his six-pack belly and said, "I struggle with living in Italy because the food is so good. I think I'm already getting fat."

Violetta's and Laurie's eyes met, they smiled at each other and shook their heads in the negative. Mr. Sorrentino asked Laurie if she had ever done any acting. Besides playing a Christmas tree in the church cotilion when she was a child, she had never acted before.

Mr. Sorrentino and Violetta agreed it didn't matter because Joshua never acted before either and he was going to be a big star. "In two more movies, Joshua will be a household name in Europe."

Joshua sat up a little straighter, "About that," he said. "I'm not sure I'm cut out to be an actor."

Mr. Sorrentino nearly chocked on his tiramisu. "What are you talking about. You're a natural. Everybody loves you."

"I don't really care if everybody loves me or not. Just one person is all I care about." He looked at Laurie. Violetta sighed and nearly busted out crying.

"Is it the money? There will be more next time, I promise. No less than ten million euros!"

Even though Laurie was worth forty million euros, she was still amazed that numbers like that existed. Laurie spoke, "Joshua, do you like acting?"

Joshua thought for a minute as Mr. Sorrentino held his breath. "It's not very manly. They dress you, put make up on you, comb your hair for you. Tell you what to say, how to say it and what to do with your body."

"But do you like it?" Laurie asked again.

"It was better than scrapping human sludge out of the subway."

"Think of the good we can do with all of the money."

Violetta assumed Laurie was after his money. Oh, what a bitch, she thought. Violetta wanted to like Laurie but anyone that beautiful didn't need to be liked especially if they were a gold digger.

"I don't have to make up my mind right now do I?" Joshua's question was rhetorical because he wasn't going to decide anything now no matter what Mr. Sorrentino said.

They bid their good bye's and Joshua took Laurie to Naples, Pompeii, Sorrento and then a ferry to the Isle of Capri. At each Location, they had to force themselves to get out of bed and go see the sights. On the third night on Capri, Laurie told Joshua she had to get back to London to help Margerie with an auction.

They flew to London the next day.

Chapter 71

Laurie and Joshua walked into the Once Again shop. The little doorbell rang to announce their entrance. Margerie came out of the back room wiping her hands on a rag. She saw Laurie and lit up. The two women hugged for a long while until Margerie opened her eyes and saw Joshua standing in the doorway.

She whispered in Laurie's ear, "Is that him?"

Laurie shook her head up and down. Margerie let go of Laurie like a hot potato and went to Joshua. Joshua smiled at her and said, "Hello Margerie."

Margerie giggled and looked back at Laurie. Laurie pointed with her head, "Go on. You can touch him."

Margerie squealed a little and hugged Joshua but wouldn't let him go. Laurie had to rescue him by prying Margerie off. "I'm sorry," the older lady said. "I don't know what got into me." They all laughed and went to the coffee klatch to catch up. Margerie was most definitely living vicariously through Laurie.

Margerie gave Joshua a tour of the shop and caught Laurie up on what they still needed to do before the big auction. Joshua liked their set up and felt comfortable in the shop. It felt like Laurie.

After an extended break, Margerie indicated she needed to go back to work. Laurie said she would help and Joshua rolled up his sleeves to pitch in. Laurie liked working with Joshua and Margerie was pretty stoked about it too. At the end of the day, Laurie went to her tote and removed three DVD's and gave to Margerie.

Margerie could tell they were Italian movies but still said, "What are these?" thinking they may be something rare for the shop.

Laurie said, "Take them home tonight

and watch them. They're dubbed but stick with them and we'll discuss them tomorrow."

"Don't you want to spend time with Joshua instead of coming to work?"

"Oh, I plan to spend some time with Joshua." Laurie used air quotes. Joshua and Laurie looked at each other, "He will be living here with me so we'll have plenty of time together. He'll help us at the shop for a while because he's in between jobs."

Margerie looked at Joshua with sympathy. A good-looking man like that out of work. Margerie wouldn't know until tomorrow Joshua was a successful actor.

Back at Laurie's flat, Joshua and Laurie sat down at the table with a cup of tea to discuss their future. The three main topics were, when would they go back to America to meet her parents, what were they going to do with all their money and did they want to get married now or wait a while because there was no doubt in either one of their minds they wanted to be together forever.

Before they even got a chance to discuss much of anything, Joshua kissed her neck and Laurie responded by bouncing up out of her seat and returning a full body hug-French kiss, resulting in the lipstick coming out. They retired to the bedroom to continue their 'discussion'. An hour and a half later they resumed their conversation at the table, this time wearing only the bare minimum necessary to keep away the

London chill. Laurie was wearing Joshua's shirt and Joshua had on boxer briefs with a small throw blanket wrapped around his shoulders. They would fly to Louisiana immediately after the auction at Once Again to meet her parents, they would start small businesses and employ under privileged people and conduct other forms of philanthropy and they would be married after meeting her parents. Plus, Laurie would continue to help Margerie in the shop. That was a given.

As they were drinking the tea and contemplating their decisions, Joshua said, "I'm sorry it wasn't a real proposal."

"You mean you would have preferred to get down on your knees with a ring?"

"I think we will regret not having a moment to brag about to other people. It won't bother you?"

Laurie contemplated for a moment. "I think we are beyond that. If anybody feels the need for us to brag about something, we can tell them the story of the egg chase, the Gentleman, Juliette and the murderers, the crazy rich Asian, the Happy Chicken roof and falling in love at the Saint Die train station. I think at this point if you were to get down on your knee and ask me to marry you, I wouldn't throw my hands to my face and shake, mouthing the word, 'yes' in exaggerated shock."

Joshua nodded his head and took a sip of tea. "So, my asking you to marry me on the Eiffel Tower idea is out of the question?"

"You're an ass," she said playfully.

"Seriously, I've never been to the Eiffel Tower. You want to run over there after the auction and fly to Louisiana from Paris? It's not like we can't afford to do this kind of stuff."

Laurie thought for a moment and said, "Why not? What's the use in being rich of you don't splurge every once in a while?"

Tea finished; they went to the bedroom to continue what they started before. The only way they could tell the act was complete was when they were asleep side-by-side or one of them passed out.

The next morning at Once Again, they met Margerie who looked tired. "What's wrong?" asked Laurie.

"I stayed up late watching movies. You didn't tell me Joshua was an actor and a good one at that."

Laurie said, "I wanted you to see for yourself." Joshua stood in the background shuffling his feet.

"Can you do something for me?" Margerie asked Joshua.

"Sure."

"Can you sign that paper on the counter? I want to frame it. A genuine Joshua Arlington autograph."

Joshua approached the counter and saw a piece of off-white paper with a border around it. Joshua picked up the sharpie lying next to it and wrote:

To my good friend Margerie. Joshua Arlington, my first autograph. And then he dated it. "Okay, it's done," he said and then added, "For what it's worth."

"Oh, I think in about ten years, this is going to worth a great deal. But I'll never sell it." Margerie picked up the paper and shook it as if she were trying to get the ink to dry faster. She placed it in an ornate frame and hung it on the wall behind the counter. It was now Margerie's prized possession.

Laurie and Joshua kept their hands off each other most of the time, at least long enough for them to complete the auction plans. The day of the auction, Ms. Vanderweerdt from Christie's showed up to congratulate them on a job well done. She also made some jokes about them being competition now. Also, she spoke with them about a business deal where Christie's would slough off some of their lower end items to be auctioned at Once Again for a commission but everybody would make money. Margerie agreed and the deal was struck.

Margerie was beginning to make more money than she ever had before. She'd worked all her life and never had two pence to rub together. Now that Laurie was on board, it was raining money. All Margerie had to do was get shot. If she'd known that, she would have shot herself decades ago. Laurie laughed at her every time she said that. Laurie loved the lady. Joshua had great respect for her also.

Chapter 72

The auction was a huge success. They sold everything except a cameo brooch which they gave to Ms. Vanderweerdt because she showed some interest in it. Mrs. Vanderweerdt was astounded by their kindness. In business, she mostly met people who were greedy. Ms. Vanderweerdt loved Laurie. Everybody loved Laurie!

Two days after the auction, after every pound had been accounted for and all the inventory adjusted correctly, Laurie and Joshua took the train to Paris. They spent three days there visiting the 'must see' attractions. All but the Eiffel Tower. They were saving that for last.

The day finally came when they ascended the tower with all of Paris sprawled out before them. Laurie remembered the last time she tried to see the tower. It caused the worst and best things to happen in her life. She told Joshua if it hadn't been for her desire to see the tower a year ago, she would have never missed her train and gotten sent to Saint Die by mistake. The tower would always be special to her. She was saying this as she was looking out over the park.

When she turned to face Joshua, he was on his knee with a ring offered. "Will you marry me?" he asked with confidence that made her tingle.

She didn't want to do it but she did…her hands went to her mouth, trembling and she uttered a barely audible 'yes'. The other visitors at the tower politely applauded with every girl thinking 'who wouldn't marry that guy' and every man thinking 'lucky bastard'. Joshua stood and placed the ring on her finger. They hugged forever whispering "I love you" many times into each other's ear.

Back at the hotel, Laurie stripped all her clothes off the instant she walked in the door. The only thing she was wearing was her ring. "I hope you have a seatbelt," she said. "This is going to be a bumpy ride."

They were only supposed to stay in the hotel one more night but that turned into three. Laurie didn't remember getting dressed during the entire time but Joshua reminded her that she put his shirt on twice when she was cold.

"Does that really count?" she asked.

"It made me want to take it off of you, so, yeah, it counted."

Laurie was content with the answer.

After the front desk personnel extended their stay, sent food up regularly, arranged for transportation and rescheduled their overseas flight, Joshua and Laurie were beginning to figure out that any simple problem could easily be solved if you threw money at it. This is something they would discuss on their long flight to Louisiana.

Chapter 73

On the morning the couple departed their hotel love nest, Laurie texted Margerie to tell her they were getting a late start on going to America. Laurie explained they got hung up in Paris because Joshua proposed and they spent three extra days in the hotel room!

Margerie texted back an eggplant emoji. Laurie thought it was the funniest thing ever. She laughed all the way to the airport.

They boarded the plane and turned left into first class which was extremely expensive. They reminisced about living well on thirty dollars a day. Now they could spend three-thousand dollars a day and never run out of money for the rest of their lives which wasn't counting investment interest and earnings or future income. They would need to get accustomed to the fact they were rich. No crime in that.

Joshua said he'd like to open an arts and sciences academy where smart and talented people could come together and change the world. Laurie said she wanted to start a business employing physically challenged or underprivileged individuals.

"The Arlington Arts and Sciences Academy," Laurie said. "It has a nice ring to it."

Joshua responded with, "Delacroix Cosmetics?"

Laurie wrinkled her nose and shook her head.

"Delacroix Clothing?"

Laurie shook her head again.

"Delacroix Custom Cabinets?"

Laurie smiled at him being silly.

"I'm running out of alliteration here."

Laurie laughed, "I'll figure it out." She patted him on the thigh. They were nearly lying down in their sleeper seats and Joshua started getting ideas.

"No, no, no," she said as she shook her finger at him and turned away to take a nap. Joshua laid back thinking about how he would start an academy but all he could really think about was Laurie. He may be ruined for everything but being reserved for stud. It was difficult to get that woman out of his mind.

Their plane landed at JFK in New York. "Dare I suggest we stay a few days in New York before we go to your house in New Orleans?" Joshua asked..

"You must have read my mind," Laurie winked at him.

They took an Uber all the way to the Plaza Hotel. Laurie made the hotel decision in the Uber. Still trying to get accustomed to her wealth, she wanted to practice being rich. They laughed pretentiously mocking rich people even though they didn't really know any. They walked in the expansive Plaza lobby with a medium sized suitcase and a ratty back pack.

Laurie and Joshua looked very touristy. The clerk decided or was instructed not to wait on them. Joshua stood patiently while several other customers were checked in. Realizing they were being snubbed, Joshua butted into the next customer's conversation. The customer was appalled at such behavior and the clerk shrank in fear.

"We were here first," Joshua said, waiting to see what the clerk would say.

The clerk didn't say anything but a doorman, a security officer and the manager came out to oversee the situation. Joshua could have easily inflicted severe chop-a-chicken on all of them but chose not to. He turned to Laurie and said, "Come on. I think I see what it's like to be rich." They hailed a cab and had the driver take them to the Times Square area. They walked a few blocks with their luggage until the came to an urban hotel.

"Laurie, what do you think of this place?"

"I like it." They went in to be greeted by a young male clerk.

"How can I help you?" he asked cordially.

"Do you have a room for the night or a few nights?"

The clerk went into warp speed working on the computer. "I am sorry to say we don't have any vacancies."

"None at all?" asked Laurie.

The young clerk tackled the computer again, "We have one room vacant but I'm not supposed to rent it out. The room doesn't have a window covering."

"Window covering?" Joshua said as a question.

"Yeah, you know all of our other rooms have curtains or plantation style blinds. This room doesn't have any. The workers who installed the new window features broke one putting them up and this is the room that got shorted. We aren't supposed to rent it out for fear of getting a sub-par rating on Trip Advisor or Yelp. But…." The clerk looked around as if he were about to steal from the register. "Management didn't say anything about letting you stay there for free. If you don't mind a bright sun scalding your eyes early in the morning the room is yours."

Laurie and Joshua looked at each other and said in unison, "We'll take it."

The couple entered the room and were pleased with the ambiance. It was a very cozy room. Joshua did what Joshua did best and rigged a spare blanket over the window which blocked out most of the light. He brushed the dust off his hands and turned to Laurie for her approval.

She was on the bed with her clothes off. He took three slow steps to the bed, shedding a piece of clothing with every step. At the edge of the bed, he still had on his boxer briefs. Laurie scooted forward and sat with Joshua directly in front of her. She started removing his briefs to give him his reward for being…. well, for being Joshua.

Chapter 74

After three days in New York, they had fished out most of the water as far as going to tourist spots. The only place they didn't go was museums. Laurie was afraid they'd get hung up in museums all day and not get to see anything else.

On the last night, they were strolling down 7th Avenue. Joshua stopped at a street vendor's cart and got Laurie a hot dog. He wasn't hungry but she insisted he take a bite. Mustard dripped on his shirt. "Oh, you'll have to take that off. I can't be seen with a man dressed like that."

Joshua took off his shirt right there in the sight of Times Square. He picked her up and carried her towards the hotel. Laurie continued to eat her hot dog. A good looking, shirtless man carrying a good-looking woman eating a hot dog through the streets of New York near Times Square was far from the most unusual thing to be seen.

Joshua carried her several blocks before he began to show signs of fatigue. "You better put me down," Laurie said. "I don't want you worn out before we get to the hotel."

Joshua set her feet on the ground and put his shirt back on, mustard stain now completely soaked in Laurie shoved the last bite of hot dog in her mouth and took his hand to walk the rest of the way. Joshua inhaled one deep breath and appeared to be fully recovered. He was a beast. He carried a hundred-twenty-two-pound girl in his arms for a half a mile and only took one deep breath. What a guy.

At the hotel, the usual happened. They were naked and rolling in each other's arms before you could count to ten. Somewhere between the second and third act, Joshua's cell phone rang. He never used it and had a hard time finding it buried in his back pack. After numerous rings, Joshua found it. The thing only had four percent charge because it hadn't been plugged in for one or two days, he couldn't remember.

"Hello," he said looking at Laurie as he said it.

"Joshua, it's Violetta."

Joshua held his hand over the phone as if it would block out the sound and told Laurie it was Violetta.

"What's going on?" he asked.

"Mr. Sorrentino is casting his next movie. He wants you to star in it as promised."

"Okay," Joshua said. "When and where?"

"He will be shooting on location in Africa, we'll start in Nairobi." She waited for his response. When he didn't say anything, she continued. "He'll start shooting in one month. Is there a place I can send you a script and other details?"

Joshua handed the phone to Laurie and said, "Give her your address. She wants to send me a script."

Laurie took the phone and said, "Hi Violetta," She made a horrible face at Joshua when she said it. You can send the manuscript to my house in New Orleans." Laurie gave Violetta the address and cut her off abruptly to finish what she and Joshua started. "Where were we?" asked Laurie.

"About to start act three if I remember right." Joshua moved in needing to be fully recharged. He lost his excitement in the short conversation with Violetta. Joshua fell on top of her pressing her against the bed. Within seconds, he was rising to the occasion and the phone call with Violetta was forgotten.

They checked out of the hotel which meant they just left because they never actually checked in. They did leave the young clerk and envelope with a €500 thank you in it.

The big day, at least for Laurie, was upon them. They arrived in New Orleans. Joshua asked her, "Do your parents even know you're coming home?"

Laurie looked bewildered for a moment. "I never thought about that. I've always lived there and never once considered I needed to tell them I'm coming back to my own house. Since I gave them one and a half million dollars last time I was here, I don't think they'll kick us out."

"Maybe they won't be there? With that much money they may have flown the coop."

"Then we'll have the house to ourselves."

They rented a car at the airport and drove to her home on the very outskirts of the city. As they pulled into the driveway, Joshua took note of all the toys in the yard, not bicycles and balls but canoes, kayaks, a bass boat, two ATV's, two wave runners, a golf cart, a 30-foot airstream travel trailer and a Winnebago RV. All of them were brand new. "Your Dad's been busy I see."

Laurie could do nothing but roll her eyes. "I gave them the money for house repairs and to get the shrimp boat business up and running again. I also think my little sister's college fund is on the lawn."

"That's two or three hundred thousand dollars' worth of toys," Joshua said. "I think you still need a new roof too," he pointed to a patch of missing shingles. "Maybe I can help him get started doing some of the things he needs to do." He leaned over from the driver's seat and kissed her. He started to pull away but she held him close feeling the warmth of his tenderness soak into her body.

They were abruptly brought back to reality by a banging on the window. It was Laurie's little sister Annette. Laurie jumped out of the car and hugged the girl. Joshua got out more slowly and made his way around to them. Laurie introduced them. Joshua noticed Annette had Hermione's wand tucked in a belt around her waist. Annette was dumbstruck at Joshua's presence. She was too young to fully appreciate Joshua's sexiness but Annette understood Laurie certainly had herself someone to be reckoned with. Even at her tender age, Annette realized Joshua was all of it.

"Are Mom and Dad here?" Laurie asked Annette.

"They're in the back arguing about the pool."

Laurie and Joshua looked at each other and Joshua shook his head. Laurie wrapped her arm around her young sister and they all went into the house.

Chapter 75

The three of them went to the back yard where they saw Laurie's dad pacing off a distance as Laurie's mother watched. "We can get a fifty-footer in here easily!" he hollered over his shoulder. Then he looked up and saw the three of them on the back porch.

He waved and trotted over to them wearing flip flops, khaki cargo shorts and a T-shirt. Her mother hustled over too. She was wearing no shoes, shorts and a tank top. Laurie hugged her Mom. Her Dad sized up Joshua before he stuck out his hand and said, "Ed Delacroix."

Joshua shook his hand and returned. "Joshua Arlington."

"I'm Betty," Laurie's mom said.

"Nice to meet you ma'am."

Betty said, "This is our youngest, Annette, but I guess you have already met."

Joshua shook Annette's hand in a grandiose gesture and said, "You know I was with your sister the day she bought that wand. We were at a magical place called Platform 9 ¾ in London, England."

Annette's mouth was open. Betty reached out her hand and gently pushed it closed. "Let's go have some tea." It was not the English hot tea Joshua had become accustomed to but iced sweet tea like all good southerners drank.

They had the 'get to know each other' discussion and the parents grilled Joshua about his upbringing. Annette already gave the Good Housekeeping seal of approval. Ed asked Joshua what he did for a living and he said Joshua wasn't sure. Ed and Betty sat forward in their chairs to hear the rest of the story.

"I'm in between jobs right now but I may have something lined up in Africa but I won't really know until I get some more information."

"Africa?" was all the parents could focus on.

"I'll go to Africa next month if it works out. Sign contracts or whatever needs to be done."

"Where in Africa?" The parents couldn't get past that part.

"Not sure," said Joshua. "I'll fly into Nairobi and the rest will become clear."

Betty asked, "Is Nairobi in South Africa?" Betty didn't really know what she was asking because she didn't know if South Africa was a country or place like North Africa.

"No, Nairobi is in Kenya."

"Oh," Betty said not fully believing Joshua's story.

Sometime later when the guys went out to inspect the toys, the ladies went to the bedroom to talk privately about Joshua. When they were sequestered properly, Betty said, "He's after your money!"

"What?" Laurie was wondering how she got to that conclusion.

"He's after your money. I can feel it. All this Africa crap. He's nothing more than a good-looking gigolo."

"Gigolo? Mom, do people still use that word?"

"Okay, you make fun of me but I know what I'm talking about."

"Mom, you don't know what we've been through. He's saved my life I don't know how many times. He provided for me when I had nothing. He's a good man, Mom."

"Well, you just be careful, you hear? I don't like it. No I don't. Not one bit."

"Would you like it better if he had money?"

Laurie's Mom didn't hesitate at all, "Of course I would. But he doesn't even have a job."

"Mom, I don't either and I have forty million dollars!"

"So, does he have money or not?" Betty wouldn't let it go.

"It doesn't matter to me. I love the man."

"Love! What do you know about love? You get rich and then you fall in love, it's all happening too fast. You're getting used!"

"I loved him when we had nothing." Laurie started to cry.

Her mother came to her side and hugged her. "Oh, don't listen to me. I just worry."

After Laurie finished sobbing, she told her mother she wanted to tell the whole story to everyone after supper. That night after eating delivery pizza because Betty didn't cook anymore since they were rich, they all sat in the living room and Laurie started her story when she was in Barcelona. The parents listened in rapt attention. Annette wanted to know when they first kissed. Betty had to shush her several times.

An hour and a half later when the whole story was out, Ed and Betty both asked, "Joshua, you're a millionaire too?"

Laurie exploded, "Good grief ya'll! That's your take away from this story? I was chased by murderers, lived on a roof over a Chinese restaurant, fled across Europe and all you want to know…." She got up and left the room in tears.

Joshua stood to go after her, "If it's that important to you…Yes, I am a millionaire." He too, left the room. Joshua caught up to Laurie as she was going out the back door. When Joshua got close, she threw herself into his arms for one of his hugs. She was not disappointed as his strong arms blanketed her.

She apologized to Joshua for her parents turning into money grubbers. She'd never known them to be like that before.

"Money does strange things to people. That's why I wanted to take a break after you became rich. I wanted to see if you would change or maybe even, I would change."

"Did I change?" she asked.

"Well, you're cleaner than you used to be."

Laurie punched him in the shoulder nearly hurting her hand on his rock-hard muscles. "Let's get out of here."

"Where we going?" asked Joshua.

"Vegas!"

"You want to gamble and see some shows?"

"I want to get married! Tomorrow. What do you think of that?"

Joshua responded, "I asked you to marry me and you say when. Sounds fair to me."

They got on the new home computer to book flights and rooms, spending only one night at Laurie's childhood home. That's all she could stand. They didn't tell her parents where they were going or what they were going to do. They promised Annette they would stay in touch.

Joshua and Laurie left the next morning with little fanfare. Laurie loved her parents but didn't like them very much now. She was hoping they would grow out of the money hungry phase. Dad needed to go back to work, real soon.

As they were sneaking out of the house at five in the morning, Laurie's mom came out on the porch wrapped in a robe. "You're just going to leave? Without this?"

Betty handed Laurie a package that came in from Italy. Laurie took the package which must have been Joshua's script and responded with, "Yes. We're leaving. We thought it would be best."

"I wish you could have stayed a little longer, we had some things we wanted to talk to you about."

"Money, I suppose."

"Well, yes. Your Dad is thinking about retiring and selling the shrimp boats. With that money and a couple more million from you, we should be able to retire comfortably." Betty quit speaking to let that soak in.

"Mom, Dad is only forty-six years old. He should work another sixteen years at least. He's bought all these things and still hasn't fixed the roof or renovated the house. For what he spent on the RV he could have put Annette through college."

Betty wrapped the robe around her tighter, "What are you going to do with all that money?"

"I don't know yet," responded Laurie. "All I've done so far is give some away to my family. And evidently, it wasn't near enough. I know you won't understand this but if I give you any more money, I won't want to see you again."

Betty was trembling a little. Laurie could see it in the ends of her fingers. "I hear what you're saying. I do, but I think we're going to need the money. You'll be upset with us for a while but when you realize how much money you have and remember we are family; you'll see your way through to come back. If you can't give a little money to your Mom and Dad, who can you give it to?" Betty's eyes were pleading.

Laurie was pissed. "I can't believe you're hitting me up for more money already." Laurie went out to the car where Joshua was standing and got her tote bag out of the front seat. Laurie glared at Joshua.

"Jeez, what did I do?" he asked.

She pointed her finger at him, "Not one word out of you."

Laurie went back to her mother and wrote out a check. Laurie held it out and said, "If you take this, you will lose me forever."

Betty trembled even harder, "Oh well. What are you going to do? I have to have the money." Betty gently took the check from Laurie's hand, looked at it and said, "Another 1.5 million? I was hoping for at least two million."

Laurie turned and walked away, got in the car and they drove off. Two miles down the road, Joshua pulled over and Laurie cried in his arms for thirty minutes. Joshua was thinking they might miss their flight but had the good sense not to say a word. He just held her.

Chapter 76

In Vegas, Laurie's mood improved immeasurably. They checked in to the Bellagio, went shopping for appropriate clothes for a wedding and got hitched in the chapel. They didn't pay the going rate because it would have been an eleven day wait, so they bribed the manager to let them "look the chapel over" for thirty minutes while the minister was there. Both the manager and minister were compensated graciously. The couple went back to their room and weren't seen for two days.

During one of their sexual lulls, Joshua told her about shooting his second movie around the real Bellagio on Lake Como in Italy. "That settles it," said Laurie. "Lake Como is a must see for me on the next trip to Europe. You promise to take me?" Joshua shook his head affirmative as he lay exhausted on the sweaty sheets.

When they checked out of the resort, Laurie asked where did he want to go next. Joshua thought for a moment and asked her, "Do you think we ought to buy a house somewhere? A place to call home."

"I was thinking the same thing, but where? We can live anywhere in the world we want."

"Can home to be in the good ol' USA. I don't feel like being an expat."

Laurie agreed as long as it wasn't in Louisiana.

"I like the southwest," Joshua added. "Maybe northern Arizona or northern New Mexico."

"Never been to either," Laurie replied.

"Sounds like we need to go have a look."

They rented a car at the airport, one way to Albuquerque. Joshua purchased an atlas at the truck stop as they ordered meatloaf from the café. Joshua drew on the map with an ink pen where they were going to go. They drove through Kingman, down parts of old Route 66, Williams, took a detour to the Grand Canyon, on through Flagstaff, stopped at the Meteor Crater and paused in Winslow to stand on the corner. They drove on through the painted desert and up into the majestic Monument Valley, played at Four Corners, stopped in Durango and rode the train to Silverton and back. Then they dropped down to Farmington, Gallup and into Albuquerque. Finally, they drove up to the Enchanted Circle and visited Taos, Angel Fire and Red River. At last, Joshua pulled into the Inn of Five Graces in Santa Fe New Mexico.

It took them five days to see every tourist attraction and back road in the northern part of the two states with a splash of Colorado added to the itinerary. Laurie got out of the car a stretched her long limbs and bent over to put the palms of her hands on the ground without bending her knees. Joshua's two thoughts were, I would split in two if I tried that and if she bends over again, I'm going to sprout horns.

In the room after exactly twenty-two minutes of extracurricular activity, Joshua was breathing hard in the recovery mode. He had been extra vigorous. Laurie was lying flat on her back, eyes closed with a smile on her face. Joshua was quite pleased with himself but if she didn't cover up, he was going to have another go.

Laurie eventually pulled the sheet over her lovely nakedness and Joshua could think again. They planned to drive around town getting into everything and anything they wanted since this may be their new home, they immersed themselves. At noon, they found something called the Railyard. It was an arts district and farmer's market with the namesake, a train called the Rail Runner Express that traveled up and down New Mexico from north to south and back again. Being suckers for trains, Laurie and Joshua jumped on with tickets back down to Albuquerque. Joshua loved riding trains with Laurie. It reminded him of the freighter at St Die and it afforded him the chance to hold and fondle her while transiting. Lord, they knew how to have fun.

After a week in Santa Fe, they were in love with the area. They picked out a large hacienda out of town at the foot of some rolling hills. Two-thousand acres came with the sprawling house. The price was in the millions and both took pause because they were still getting accustomed to the fact, they were rich.

After some serious thinking interspersed with tension relieving lovemaking, they bought the hacienda. Laurie was beaming with excitement. Her first home and what a doozy it was. Along with their new estate, they purchased an SUV and a pick-up truck. Joshua returned the rent car to Albuquerque and rode the Rail Runner up to Santa Fe. Laurie picked him up at the train station and they went to their new home and had sex in three different rooms including the main kitchen. There were two kitchens in this hacienda. The second kitchen had a horno in it. It was a clay oven designed for cooking bread over an open flame. Laurie couldn't wait to try cooking a giant pizza in it.

About the time they were ready to settle in and play house, Joshua had to go to Africa. This made Laurie sad because as much as she wanted to go with him, she wanted to be at home, decorating, furnishing and remodeling. They agreed on her staying at the house for six weeks and then flying to the shoot while they were finishing up the movie. They would spend a while in Africa together and return home. Home, was a nice thought.

Chapter 77

Joshua left on the Rail Runner to catch a flight out of Albuquerque to Nairobi with a half dozen stops in between. He hadn't once looked at the script until he was on the train. Laurie threw herself on their bed and cried a river. After a nonsensical period of self-pity, she bolted up right and went to work. Laurie hired a general contractor to help with renovations, repair and the construction of some out-buildings. She also hired an estate manager to deal with the general contractor and to look over the two-thousand acres to see what needed to be done in order to produce something useful with the land.

Joshua arrived in Nairobi and was met by Violetta at the airport. Joshua really wished Mr. Sorrentino would hire someone else to escort him around. They drove to Amboseli National Park where the crew was housed in a safari lodge. They must have passed a hundred elephants along the road. Joshua was overwhelmed at the beauty and took a little over a hundred pictures on his iPhone before they arrived at the lodge.

From the back patio of the lodge, Mount Kilimanjaro stood grandly in the background, across the border in Tanzania. Joshua's thoughts were of wanting Laurie here to see this with him. Everyone went to bed except the die-hards who met in the bar. Those guys drank until the wee hours. Joshua slept on a chair out on the balcony not wanting to miss anything, even the smells.

In the morning, Violetta knocked on Joshua's door and they pulled their duffle bags down to the lobby. Violetta tugged him into the main dining hall of the lodge for a large breakfast and introductions to the rest of the cast and crew. His leading lady came as no surprise, it was the spoiled brat Chiara Jilani from his previous movie. She and Joshua nodded but didn't speak.

Chiara and Violetta glared at one another as Joshua rolled his eyes thinking, here we go again. Mr. Sorrentino had them all sit while he explained how the shooting schedule would work. After the lecture, they packed up their belongings and boarded two large buses. After a long drive, they pulled over at an unremarkable intersection where twelve safari vehicles waited for them. Once all the personnel and gear were loaded, they drove down a road that was mostly paved but only for a mile or two until the road became completely unpaved.

The vehicles drove at what Joshua thought was an excessive speed for the road conditions but what did he know. The ruts and ridges were impassable for anything but a high-profile four-wheel drive vehicle. Maybe if they slowed down it would be worse but he didn't see how it could be much worse. His teeth were rattling and his kidneys were bouncing up and down like a basketball being dribbled. Hours later, they arrived at their destination, the Maasai Mara National Reserve. It looked every bit of what Joshua hoped it would look like. It looked like Africa.

Forty-five more minutes and they arrived at the lodge, a four-star resort. There would be no roughing it on this shoot. Once checked in and unpacked, they were to meet in the main dining hall for a briefing and their first buffet meal. Shooting would start at daybreak so the wakeup call was four in the morning.

On the first day of shooting, after makeup and wardrobe, the initial scenes were of a group of vacationers loading vehicles for a game drive.

Joshua was making small talk with the other safarians. Once they got into a safari vehicle, Mr. Sorrentino yelled "cut!" All the actors jumped out like a Chinese fire drill and switched to a safari vehicle loaded with mounted cameras. This switching back and forth kept up all day. Long distance shots were done in and around the regular vehicles and inside shots were done in the camera mounted vehicle.

By the end of the day, they had switched vehicles no less than half a dozen times. During the time when Joshua was not on camera, he was consumed with the beauty of the area and the majesty of the wild animals. Most notable were the massive herds of wildebeest, cape buffalo, zebras, giraffes and an occasional lion. The only thing missing was Laurie. Then it would be perfect.

Laurie was busy hiring staff and making plans with architects and designers to make their home something special and personal. Time flew by for both and before either one of them could get too lonely, Laurie was on a plane to Kenya. First class sure made traveling across the pond a lot easier.

At the Nairobi airport, Laurie hired a large Land Rover to take her to the lodge in the Maasai Mara. She was bursting with excitement. Seeing this place was amazing but getting to see this place with Joshua made her nearly cry. She couldn't be happier.

Hours later and with both breasts sore from bouncing around so much on the rutted dirt road, she arrived at the lodge. It was late and Joshua was off work and available to greet her properly. He was standing at the lodge's front entrance looking ever so dapper in his safari chic outfit. Laurie stepped out of the vehicle wearing her best khaki and they hugged until tomorrow.

Joshua got her to the room and immediately all the safari chic and khaki clothing landed in a pile on the floor. Joshua had his way with her in a passionate, wild way, quite fitting under the circumstance. Violetta, in a room just down from Joshua's, heard a wailing sound, several times coming in through the balcony screen. Violetta assumed it was an animal, maybe a large cat in the night, out stalking its prey.

But it was only Laurie crying out in pleasure as she was pounced upon and ravaged by Joshua. They didn't sleep much and Joshua knew he was going to suffer through the day's shooting.

Joshua woke at three in the morning so he would have time to welcome Laurie to Africa again before he had to got to work. Violetta, while getting dressed heard the wild cat cry out one more time in the night. When Joshua was finished with Laurie, he had to hurry to get ready so he could go down to make up and wardrobe and get ready all over again. Laurie with hair in a mess could hardly raise her head enough to tell Joshua she would stay at the lodge today and catch up on sleep from jet lag and his almost criminal abuse. Joshua wanted to stay with her but he was getting paid eleven million euros to do the work. He kissed in the vicinity of her lips, he couldn't tell for all the hair but she grunted approval and he left to earn his money.

The shoot that day was mostly around a campsite with a big fire and roasting meat. This is the day Joshua and Chiara were to sneak away from the rest of the safari and begin to get frisky in a grove of acacia trees. In the scene, Joshua was supposed to back Chiara up to a tree and lean into her to kiss her with a full body press. There was a seriously large bug on the tree and Chiara refused to do it. They changed trees but she saw termites on that tree. Mr. Sorrentino, very familiar with working with divas, changed the scene to where Joshua would gently lay her down on the ground and get on top of her. There was a smattering of Thompson's Gazelle dung in the grass and she wouldn't lie down.

Joshua suggested she lie down on top of him. They tried that but her decent onto his body appeared as if she were looking for bugs and dung on the way down. It was a most unnatural movement. Mr. Sorrentino was perplexed but didn't show it. He called for her stunt woman/body double, Alessandra. In one shot, perfectly directed to not show a closeup of the woman's face, Joshua pressed Alessandra against the tree and they appeared to kiss the living daylights out of each other. Chiara was jealous and stomped off to the vehicles.

Alessandra's knees were a little week after Joshua finished with her but she was the consummate professional. Alessandra was doubly pleased because she was paid an extra two thousand euros for any scene not already in the script.

They finished their shoot for the day and drove back to the lodge. It was Laurie's time to be standing at the lodge entrance looking all Karen Blixen. Joshua went straight to her and kissed her hard. He started to pull her away to the room but she stopped him, "Oh, no you don't. You're feeding me before we do any of that funny stuff."

They went to the dining hall and loaded up on the buffet of Kenyan food. Mr. Sorrentino joined them as did Violetta. Chiara chose to go to her room and get out of her dirty clothes before she ate. She couldn't stand the feel of Africa on her one more minute.

After dinner, Joshua and Laurie walked the grounds, holding hands listening to the night sounds. There were a couple of resident black face monkeys leaping through the tress. Every time the monkeys jumped from one branch to another in the dark, Laurie and Joshua also jumped. The couple giggled each time they were startled. The grunts and animal moans from the distance could easily be heard. Joshua couldn't tell how far away the animals were but he estimated they really weren't very close.

Joshua was leading Laurie farther and farther away from the lodge, more by accident than design. He just wanted to get as close to Africa as he could. Laurie thought he was trying to get her alone so he could have his way with her so she followed willingly. When the sounds of the movie people drinking in the outdoor bar became a distant murmur, Laurie stopped and said, "Don't you think this is far enough?"

Joshua turned to look at her and she was unbuttoning her blouse. Joshua pulled her to him and unsnapped her bra like he practiced it a thousand times. Her breasts were exposed in the moonlight as they heard a lion roar in the distance. They embraced. Laurie's bare chest buried against Joshua.

"Jambo!"

Laurie hooked her bra and buttoned her blouse in less than three seconds. Joshua and Laurie spun around to be greeted by a lodge security guard armed with a flashlight and three-foot-long thin stick. The stick looked more like something a mother would use to switch an unruly child instead of protection against wild animals.

"Sorry to intrude but I must ask you to return to the lodge. Guest are not allowed off the sidewalks at night. It's hotel policy. For your own safety."

Joshua nor Laurie argued with the guard. They probably were doing something stupid. The guard guided them back to the walkway with his flashlight. Laurie and Joshua apologized and thanked him for taking care of them and went to their room to continue what the African night started.

Chapter 78

The next morning Joshua and Laurie were eating breakfast. Joshua was telling Laurie about the day's shoot. This was the day the safari members were going to be attacked and captured by the Al-Shabaab terrorists. Joshua explained how the script set up the scene so Laurie could watch it unfold. She was going out with them today as Mr. Sorrentino's special guest. Violetta was not happy about it and Chiara was livid. In their minds, Laurie had no business on the set because she was not a professional. In actuality, the girls thought Laurie was too damn good looking and sexy to be there. They thought she diminished the value of every woman out there.

Once in the bush, the three vehicles were set up in a line, a copse of acacia and croton were a hundred yards off in the background. The terrorist would attack out of the bushes and kill the National Reserve guards with them and take the rest of them prisoner. There were three actual Reserve guards with them to protect them from animals and to make sure the cast and crew didn't take any liberties with the wildlife or vegetation. The guards agreed to fall dead on cue for a fee.

Mr. Sorrentino set up three cameras out wide to capture all the action and he had two hand held cameras with the safari group to get close ups. The terrorists were to charge out of the bushes, kill the Reserve guards first and then manhandle Chiara and the other older women in the safari group. Joshua was going to take a beat down when he stepped in to save Chiara. When Mr. Sorrentino told Laurie this she laughed.

"Why are you laughing?" he asked feeling a little insulted.

"You don't know Joshua. I know he's acting, but I don't think there's anybody alive who can give Joshua a…what did you call it…a beat down." She laughed again.

Mr. Sorrentino crossed his legs in the director's chair and yelled for the cameras to be turned on and tested for lighting and focus. The boom operators went among the cast so the sound mixer could get his levels right. The terrorist actors started walking toward the grove of trees to get ready for the 'attack'. A Reserve guard went with them carrying his ancient, but real, 303 British Enfield rifle. The guard needed to sweep the trees to make sure there were no dangerous animals in hiding.

When the actors and guard disappeared, shots from an automatic weapon rang out. Mr. Sorrentino looked at Laurie and said, "They must have found a lion in there."

Laurie got off her director's chair and stood with her hands on her hips watching Joshua while everyone else was looking at the trees. Joshua was trying to get everyone to hide behind the vehicles. The group was not cooperating. Laurie knew something was wrong by Joshua's actions. Laurie ran forward to be with Joshua. "What's wrong?" she yelled at him as he was trying to corral the actors and crew behind the safari vehicles.

"That wasn't the guard's weapon going off. Their weapons only shoot one bullet at a time because they're bolt actions. The shots fired came from a fully automatic weapon." Laurie didn't really comprehend but trusted Joshua. He could tell she didn't understand. "There's someone else in the bushes with guns. It's not us!" Now she understood completely.

The other two Reserve guards walked out in front of the vehicles facing the copse. More shots rang out and the two guards fell dead both being shot several times. Everybody in the rear near Mr. Sorrentino looked to him for guidance. Mr. Sorrentino had none to give except, "Keep the cameras rolling!" He then ran off in the opposite direction as fast as his Santoni loafers would carry him. Most of the crew followed his lead, leaving the actors and a few camera and sound men behind at the vehicles.

Laurie looked at Joshua as Joshua was watching Mr. Sorrentino and his small herd run off. "What do you want to do?" she asked him.

"I've got to get my hands on one of those rifles now."

"Okay. I'll distract them," and she ran to the rear of the middle vehicle. Joshua was at the front. "Okay go!" she said and Joshua ran out to the closest dead guard and grabbed his rifle while Laurie stepped out from behind the vehicle and shot the finger towards the woods. Her action drew a response of a dozen bullets slamming into the back of the vehicle as she threw herself backwards on her butt trying to get away from them.

Joshua safely returned behind the engine block with the rifle in hand. He gave her a thumbs up and she replied by smiling at him. Joshua checked the rifle to make sure there was a bullet in the chamber. There was not. He worked the bolt and a round chambered with ease. This old gun only held 10 rounds and he wasn't sure about working the safety. After a few seconds of study, Joshua determined the safety was off and the weapon was ready to fire. He shouldered it to get the feel and look down the sights. For some reason, it made him feel strong. When he was comfortable with the weapon, he said to everybody in a command voice, "We'll wait them out. When they come to get us, I'll do my best to pick them off with this." He held up the rifle for them to see. To the three groups of people hiding behind the vehicles, his speech did not instill a lot of confidence.

Chiara spoke up, "That's your plan! Wait for them to come get us?" Joshua looked at Chiara, "I'm open to any suggestions." Anyone? No one spoke.

Chapter 79

After a few minutes with neither side making a move, Joshua slid past Chiara to be near Laurie. "What do you think the chances are of them getting into the lead vehicle," Joshua pointed to the four actors shivering in fear hiding behind the first safari vehicle, "keeping their heads down and just driving off? I'll try to keep them busy with this rifle."

Laurie let it soak in a minute, pleased with them being a team again. If it was even possible, she loved him more than ever at this very moment. She reached up and took his face in her hands and kissed him deeply. Chiara took great offense to this and spoke her mind, "What are you doing?" She looked at Laurie, "You're not even a member of the cast or crew and shouldn't be here on location. You're not even afraid!"

Laurie looked at Joshua and back at Chiara, "It's not our first rodeo,sweetheart."

Chiara was about to make some snappy retort but a crashing noise could be heard from the bushes. Seconds later, two large warthogs ran for their lives out of the bushes and stopped immediately to graze because they forgot why they were running. Laurie laughed at them. Chiara's eyes widened as they were one more thing to be afraid of in this God forsaken Africa.

Joshua spoke to the four people hiding behind the lead vehicle and explained they should try to slowly and silently crawl into the vehicle, keeping their heads down and get ready to drive off. "As soon as you start the vehicle, I'll shoot a few rounds in their direction to keep them busy while you drive away. Drive away in same direction Mr. Sorrentino shagged ass."

"Shagged ass, Joshua! I'll swear you are from a different century." Laurie laughed at his use of words. Joshua smiled at her laughing and they noshed on each other again. Chiara was so mad at them and so scared she lost her breakfast near the rear tire. None of them knew they were still being filmed by the stationary cameras.

The four people at the front vehicle reached up and slowly opened both doors. A middle-aged woman actor crawled in the back seat; two male actors slithered into the middle section. All three of them hugging the floor. Another man awkwardly pulled himself into the driver's seat. He was leaned over hoping the terrorists couldn't see him.

Joshua went to the rear of their vehicle, carefully avoiding the gift Chiara left them and got ready to wheel around the back bumper and discharge the weapon. Joshua had a very serious look on his face and told Laurie to tell the driver he could go at any time. Laurie spoke calmly to the driver and said Joshua was set up and would start firing when the driver cranked the engine.

There was a pregnant pause. Then the engine cranked and the driver pressed the gas pedal to the floor. The vehicle lurched forward in a cloud of dust and turned left away from the terrorists, headed in the direction Mr. Sorrentino was last seen 'shagging ass'.

The terrorists blasted at the vehicle with a hail of automatic weapons fire. Two terrorists ran out from cover to get a better angle at the escapees. Joshua spun around the bumper, firing from a kneeling position. Joshua's first shot hit one exposed terrorist in the left upper quadrant and the man died before he hit the ground. Laurie watched Joshua work the bolt on the rifle like he'd done it all his life. He fired again at the other exposed terrorist, but that man turned to seek cover when his buddy fell to the ground. Joshua's bullet hit the terrorist in his right hamstring as he was fleeing. The man fell, dropping his weapon and quickly crawled off into the cover of the bushes.

The remaining terrorists concentrated fire on Joshua's position. Joshua sought safety behind the rear tire as hundreds of bullets crashed into the back of the Land Rover. When the terrorists ceased fire, Laurie moved to Joshua to see if he was okay. Of course, he was okay, he was always okay. However, Laurie had to inform him he was now sitting in Chiara's vomit. Joshua rolled his eyes and they laughed. Chiara was vomiting again near the front tire. Joshua said, "It's not safe anywhere back here. We may have to surrender."

He and Laurie laughed like hyenas which were probably circling the group waiting to clean up anything left over from the battle. "Now what?" Laurie asked.

"We wait."

"What for?" Laurie said as she sat next to Joshua making sure she didn't share his misery of Chiara's gift.

"Several things," Joshua said as he was thinking. "Maybe the vehicle can bring back help before we're all killed. Maybe I can get lucky and eliminate a few more of them and they'll give up after a while."

"I like the part about getting lucky," Laurie said with a grin.

"There'll be time enough for that later. A man's got to do some work now."

Laurie leaned on his shoulder and Joshua put his arm around her. They were lost in each other for a minute before a guy from the back vehicle hollered, "Is it our turn to drive off now?"

Joshua thought for a moment wondering if they could pull it off again. "I don't think we ought to try it again. You don't have a clear path to drive forward. You'll have to back up first."

"I think we ought to try it. I don't like just sitting here," the man said. The other three people with him agreed. Joshua refused.

Just as Joshua was about to get angry and say something he regretted; the two warthogs ambled between the vehicles. The pig-like things looked really big up close. Joshua estimated the big one to be nearly 250 pounds. They big hog flopped down on his knees and his huge gnarly head went to the ground to eat whatever was there. Joshua and Laurie were fascinated. Chiara would have vomited again had she any breakfast left.

They waited and watched the wildlife, an up close and personal view.

Chapter 80

After a few minutes, Joshua reached into the seat of the vehicle and pulled out three bottles of water. He pitched one gently to Chiara who didn't even try to catch it. It was her policy to do nothing that might break a nail. The bottle landed at her feet, "Thanks for nothing," she said.

"I'm going to have a little talk with that girl when this is over," responded Laurie as she downed half a bottle of water and wiped her mouth with her sleeve. Joshua let that go and told the other group to drink water.

Every few minutes, Joshua leaned over looked under the bumper into the trees to see if he could spy any activity. All was quiet but he feared it would not remain so. He got up into a position where he could easily fire around the back of the vehicle and continued to intently observe. Laurie could tell Joshua's demeanor had changed. That usually meant he was operating on instincts and his instincts were most often correct.

Laurie asked, "What can I do?"

Joshua looked behind him, away from the trees and glanced at the warthogs. He really didn't want one of them to gore him in the butt while he was kneeling, fighting for his life. As he was watching, the warthogs started meandering back towards them. "Well, you can keep those things off of us when the shooting starts."

"They're ugly," was Chiara's only comment. As much as Laurie and Joshua disliked Chiara, they had to agree. They were ugly.

Joshua heard movement in the trees. He readied himself. Laurie tried to figure out how she was going to redirect a couple of warthogs that were twice her size.

The croton bushes were rustling again. Joshua thought the bad guys were lining up for an assault. His thoughts were correct, six men broke free from the bushes. Five of them blasting away with their AK-47's. The sixth man was limping badly and had no weapon. He veered off to retrieve the rifle he dropped when Joshua shot him in the back of the leg the first time. The man was barely able to walk. Joshua sized him up as 'no threat'. Joshua was correct, the man fell near his rifle but never got up. He bled out lying on the African plains.

Joshua watched from cover as the five attackers riddled the vehicles with bullets. Joshua couldn't raise his head any further than to barely peep around the corner. The warthogs raised their heads too and Laurie pelted the biggest one with a half a bottle of water. The plastic bottle bounced off the hogs armor plated head. He grunted and both ran away. Mission accomplished.

As Joshua hoped, all five assailants ran out of ammunition at relatively the same time. The few seconds it took to switch out magazines gave Joshua ample time to shoulder the rifle and put a bullet through the lead man's kidney and liver. The bullet passed completely through his body. He died in seconds.

Laurie watched Joshua work the bolt and chamber another round, never taking the rifle from his shoulder. He was the picture of concentration and form. Joshua fired again, striking another attacker through the stomach. The bullet nearly disemboweled him because he turned slightly to the side allowing the bullet to pass from hip bone to hip bone instead of front to back. The man fell, not yet dead but out of the fight. He died within a minute.

As Laurie watched Joshua working the bolt again, she heard a thump and blood splatter covered Joshua's cheek and ear. He'd been shot in the shoulder, but he never flinched. Joshua fired again, hitting a third man in the neck. His head flopped forward although he fell backwards. This man was dead before he hit the ground. Joshua operated the bolt quickly, ready for another shot but the last two terrorists had enough and fled back into the bushes.

Joshua looked to his right and saw one of the actors, a Mr. Ralph Damian, had been shot in the calf and was screaming like a baby. A bullet must have gone under the vehicle because Mr. Damian never showed his face to the enemy. Joshua ran to him with Laurie right on his heels. Chiara remained behind to squat by the front tire with her pants around her ankles, purging away the fear. Little did she know, her act of defecation was captured on no less than three cameras.

Joshua kneeled by Mr. Damian and said, between the screeches, "You're an actor, right?" Mr. Damian managed a nod in between sobs. "Then act like a man!" Joshua cut away Mr. Damian's trouser leg to find the bullet had passed completely through the calf muscle. Painful, more painful to some than others evidently, but not a serious injury. "Clean it up and your as good as new."

Mr. Damian continued to act infantile. Joshua was about to slap him across his face for his own good but Laurie caught Joshua's eyes and they said don't do it! Joshua refrained and took another approach. "You're a famous actor, correct?" Mr. Damian was British and had been in eleven movies as minor character actors

"Yes, I am," uttered Mr. Damian, stretching the truth more than a little. "Why?"

Joshua looked like he was thinking. "By the time this gets out on Twitter, TikTok, Facebook and all the other social medias, you'll be invited to go on every talk show in the nation. What's that guy's name?"

Joshua snapped his fingers a couple of times. "Graham Norton?" he finally remembered. "You'll be on his show."

Mr. Damian shut up blubbering and began to think of ways this would propel himself into the spotlight. Joshua worked his magic once again, impressing the hell out of Laurie who didn't need to be impressed.

Laurie finally got Joshua sat down on the ground and leaned up against the vehicle so she could look at his wound. Joshua self diagnosed. "I think the bullet went through my trapezius muscle."

Laurie cocked her head and looked at him, "How do you know such things?" She was trying to put pressure on it causing Joshua excruciating pain. "Sorry," she said.

Joshua replied, "I don't know." He looked a little light headed to Laurie. She got him some water out of the vehicle. Once in control of his faculties, Joshua wanted to discuss their situation with the rest of the group.

Joshua convinced them since the terrorists had run off to regroup, the best thing they could do would be to get in the vehicles and drive very far away in the same direction Mr. Sorrentino was last seen. They all agreed and sneaked into their Land Rovers, fired up the ignition and drove away in a mini-convoy, leaving the dead bodies behind for the scavengers.

Several miles away, Joshua's convoy caught up with Mr. Sorrentino who had been picked up by the first escaping vehicle. Everybody was alright except Mr. Sorrentino had lost a shoe. After a short, excited conversation amongst themselves, Mr. Sorrentino wanted to go back and check on the actors who went into the woods and to retrieve the camera equipment. Joshua voted him down and insisted they go to the lodge, call the authorities and get the wounds treated properly.

The group convoyed off in the direction of the lodge. Halfway back, one of the more shot up vehicles pooped out and they had to double up in the others. Once back at the lodge, Laurie took Joshua to the room and began to scrub the ever loving out of his shoulder wound with bottled water and gauze from a first aid kit. The wound probably needed stitches but she wasn't sure she could make Joshua sit still long enough to sew him up with a needle and regular thread from the travel sewing kit.

Instead, he wanted to lie down with her in the bed. For the first time he didn't get aroused when she was lying next to him. She may have been worried on any other occasion but Joshua had just saved their lives in a gun battle and was wounded. She threw a leg over his and asked, "How many more times are you going to save my life?"

"As many as it takes, I suppose," was his reply before he dozed off. Laurie covered him up and went down to the lobby to see what was going on. More Reserve Guards were on site as was someone who looked like an army officer. The uniformed men were having a discussion with Mr. Sorrentino. Laurie thought it was funny they were talking to him because all he showed them was his backside, elbows and the bottoms of his Santoni shoes as he was…what did Joshua call it? Shagging ass away from the danger. She laughed to herself.

Laurie scanned the lobby and saw Mr. Damian sitting on a couch with his leg propped up, waiting on an ambulance. She went and sat with him asking about the pain and his general wellbeing. Mr. Damian was anxious to talk to anybody about his wound. It was going to make him famous again and get his career back on track. Laurie wondered what a wound, on camera while saving everyone would do for Joshua's career. Not that he needed much help.

The ambulance came to get Mr. Damian and started to drive off until Laurie stopped them and said there was another wounded individual. The ambulance crew got a stretcher and went to get Joshua who refused to be carted out but did agree to go get treatment. He walked to the ambulance.

Shortly after the ambulance left, a Reuters reporter showed up with a camera crew of his own. Mr. Damian would have been in hog heaven if he could have stayed and gotten his story on the evening news. Joshua didn't care anything about that but was angry because the ambulance was full and wouldn't let Laurie ride with him to the hospital in Nairobi. It was a long and miserable drive and Joshua was sick of Mr. Damian's complaints by the time they arrived.

Laurie spoke with the reporter briefly and they took some footage of her but she was mostly worried about getting a ride to Nairobi. Eventually, she rode back to Nairobi with the reporters and they got the real story from her on the way. At the hospital they got pictures of Laurie hugging the daylights out of Joshua who was clothed in a hospital gown that revealed a lot more than Joshua would have liked. The reporters ate it up. Ralph Damian was interviewed also but his middled aged flabby dad bod paled in comparison to Joshua's rock-hard features. Ralph couldn't wait to get out of the same room with Joshua plus he got tired of watching Laurie lay up on the single bed next to Joshua. Laurie was wearing Ralph out and didn't even know it.

Joshua only stayed in the hospital one night. He received three stitches on the entry wound and six stitches on the exit wound. Mr. Damian spent a week in the hospital because the pain was too great plus he needed a week to allow his publicist time to get to Nairobi to document his release from the hospital. Joshua went back to the lodge to finish the job for which he was being paid. Mr. Damian flew home to England.

At the lodge Mr. Sorrentino was busy with the writers trying to fit the actual footage of the gun battle into the script. It was going marvelously. The only catch was Laurie was in every scene of the battle. She had to be written into the movie some how because they wanted to keep all her footage. They also wanted to keep all of Chiara's puke and poop scenes.

They shot a few extra scenes of Laurie around the lodge to make it fit into the movie. She didn't have any lines at the lodge and none later because she was killed in the battle. Bless her heart. Mr. Sorrentino had pulled it off. Mr. Damian also died in the battle because he ran home to England and couldn't finish the shoot. Good riddance to Ralph. Even as chopped up as the script and filming were, Mr. Sorrentino thought he had a hit, a blockbuster.

When the movie wrapped, Joshua and Laurie skipped the party and went to Tanzania to the Serengeti. There they stayed in a lodge in the shadow of Mount Kilimanjaro, made love morning, noon and night, and went on game drives until their teeth were rattled loose from the rough roads. Laurie loved Africa and she loved Joshua more than a heart could possibly love but it was time to go home.

Chapter 81

Joshua was away nearly two months and could hardly recognize the place when they returned. All the old cabinets were new cabinets, the old fixtures were replaced, the flooring was different and the furniture made Joshua feel a little ashamed because it was so nice. However, it all came together perfectly and felt like Laurie. The estate, farm, ranch or whatever they were going to call it really felt like home. Joshua was pleased. Laurie was pleased and for two days and nights they expressed that pleasure to each other many times.

Laurie gave the staff three days off so Joshua could get accustomed to being home without the added distractions. Laurie absolutely didn't want Joshua distracted. On the third day the staff returned to their duties. Joshua met the cook who introduced herself with an outrageous meal of chicken fried steak, mashed potatoes, grilled corn on the cob, green beans, home made dinner rolls and peach cobbler. Joshua ate so much he almost didn't want to have sex later that afternoon and again that night.

Joshua met the estate manager and his helper who was mostly a groundskeeper. Laurie hired a maid/housekeeper who came in three times a week. That lady cleaned house, made beds, changed sheets and washed clothes.

Joshua met their financial adviser and their lawyer who Joshua looked at sideways comparing him to the smarmy little Italian avvocatto who worked for Cinecittia. There was no comparison, Laurie chose well.

Joshua liked all the staff and of course they liked him. Everybody loved Joshua but none more than Laurie. For the first three months, they adjusted to the roll of gentleman farmer and his wife. They had to purchase lawnmowers, blowers, small tractors, pick up trucks and assorted other devices needed to keep two thousand acres running.

Joshua spent the next three months exploring the acreage. He would hike out and sometimes camp among the cedars and sage. He fished a few times in their spring fed pond that swelled to the size of a small lake during snow melt. Laurie went with him into their wilderness a few times and he ravaged her just out of sight of the house. That's the only reason she went with him. He liked the land; she liked the house but a short hike was little sacrifice for the results.

After three months, the question arose, "Now what are we going to do?"

Joshua decided to continue to try to act and would get an agent here in the United States. If he got a gig, the money would keep flowing in. Laurie agreed. He also wanted to start his Arlington Arts and Sciences Academy. Laurie agreed once again.

She decided to operate a charity so she could give away most of Joshua's hard-earned money. He agreed but laughed and shook his head at her. She also said she wanted to open a 'branch' of Once Again Antique Shop in the Santa Fe area. That way she would have an excuse to work with Margerie. Joshua agreed.

They went to work on their projects. One afternoon while Joshua was working hard waiting for the phone to ring from his new agent, he read in the paper a new film called Fire in Africa would be playing at the KIMO Theater in Albuquerque. Fire in Africa was his movie. He asked Laurie if she wanted to go. Of course, she did and because of his success, he got a special trip upstairs to the bedroom where she put a little fire in his Africa.

They dressed nicely for the movie and took the Rail Runner down to Albuquerque. It was much easier to drive but they so loved a train ride. After Ubering to the theater, they bought their tickets and watched the movie. Mr. Sorrentino and the editing staff did an excellent job at patching the real footage together with the acting and made a decent movie out of it. Laurie even got credit for her part. She only had about thirty seconds of actual screen time. Joshua and Laurie were both pleased with the work.

There were twenty-five or so people in the theater. A mostly dubbed Italian film about international visitors to Africa was not what the teenagers of Albuquerque were going for these days. But when Joshua's and Laurie's faces appeared on screen, there was a buzz through the audience.

As the couple exited the theater, there was a small crowd of a dozen people waiting for them. A dozen was not a very big crowd but it was half the people in the theater. Relatively speaking they were mobbed. The fans wanted autographs and selfies. Joshua and Laurie gave them plenty of each.

They Ubered back to the train station and ate a pizza at a nearby joint. The rail trip home consisted of Laurie sleeping on Joshua's shoulder and her hand laying a little too snugly in his lap. After being teased all the way home. Joshua couldn't wait and had his way with her in the SUV parked in the lot of the Railyard District. That was Laurie's plan all along. Joshua was so easy.

Their love grew and their philanthropy expanded with their wealth. Joshua won the Best Supporting Actor David Di Donatello award (Italian equivalent to an Oscar) for his role in Fire in Africa. He was nominated for an American Academy Award for the same role but didn't win. Joshua and Laurie walked the red carpet like pros. Joshua wore Armani because the GIF from Cannes played a thousand times over every station. Laurie looked like a billion bucks in a Gucci dress slit all the way up to the waist exposing her thigh and hip. Joshua was ready to take it off her before they even left the hotel room.

Joshua's stock did go up and he was paid twenty-million dollars for his first American movie. He played a wildfire fighter in California. He wasn't going to be nominated for another award but the movie grossed four times what it cost to make placing it in the blockbuster category. As predicted, Joshua's name would be known in every household.

Laurie's antique business, which invested fifty percent of the profits into the community, was doing well. The other fifty percent was divided between Margerie and shop expansion. Margerie even came over for one of the larger auctions and was treated like royalty. For two weeks after that, Joshua, Laurie and Margerie traveled the country to anywhere Margerie ever wanted to go in America. They ended up going to San Francisco. Las Vegas, the Grand Canyon, Chicago, New York and Florida. They ended the trip in Florida because Margerie said she wanted to finish with somewhere warm before she went home. Laurie cried like a baby when Margerie got on the plane to go. Joshua, standing with his arm around Laurie, tried to wipe a tear out of his eye without Laurie seeing him.

They were at Miami International Airport and Joshua asked Laurie what she wanted to do now. She fell into his arms and cried another five minutes before she responded. "I want to go home."

La Fine